Prospero's Staff

Prospero's Staff

David Ackley

Rain and Breeze Books

MOSCOW, IDAHO

David Ackley/Rain and Breeze Books, LLC
P.O. Box 9874
Moscow, ID 83843
www.rainandbreeze.com

Publisher's Note: This is a work of fiction. Any references to historical events, real people, or real places are used fictitiously. Other names, characters, places, and incidents are a product of the author's imagination and any resemblance of these to actual people, living or dead, businesses, companies, events, institutions or locales is purely coincidental. Locales and public names are sometimes used for atmospheric purposes.

Book Layout © 2014 BookDesignTemplates.com
Cover photo: istockphoto.com/mike_drosos
Frontisepiece: Drawn by the author

Prospero's Staff/ David Ackley. -- 1st ed.
Library of Congress Control Number: 2020902865
ISBN 978-1-950631-08-7 (Paperback)
ISBN 978-1-950631-09-4 (Ebook)

This book is dedicated to Brien,
for his essential part in the play.

...I have bedimm'd

The noontide sun, call'd forth the mutinous winds,

And 'twixt the green sea and azured vault

Set roaring war...

— *The Tempest*, William Shakespeare

Chapter 1.

But this rough magic I here abjure;
And, when I have required some heavenly music,
—which even now I do,—
To work mine end upon their senses,
That this airy charm is for,
I'll break my staff,
Bury it certain fathoms in the earth,
And deeper than did ever plummet sound
I'll drown my book.

Prospero, Act V, Scene I,
The Tempest by William Shakespeare[1]

I'M GOING *to miss my flight,* thought Martin with a frustrated sigh, sinking back in his seat and drumming lightly on the steering wheel in time with Fleetwood Mac's *Gypsy* playing softly in the background. A pilot truck, with flashing yellow lights mounted above the cab, appeared from the thick smoke ahead, leading a long, slow line of cars and pickups past him in the opposite

---

1 A synopsis of *The Tempest* is provided at the end of the novel.

direction. The traffic moving in his lane had been halted for a full half-hour previously as emergency vehicles made their way to the blaze, and now he was stopped again. He'd just crossed the border into Idaho near Lookout Pass, and the forest fire was being battled on the steep slopes somewhere below the highway up ahead. *Lightning strikes, maybe once, maybe twice,* sang Stevie Nicks, and Martin became mesmerized as vehicles emerged from the dense bluish smoke about three or four car-lengths ahead, the motion and music taking his mind off his pounding headache.

He began dreaming of warm Mediterranean beaches and foreign food, and calculated that he was getting out of Montana at just the right time of year. They were entering the cold, wet autumn which should make this eruption one of the last major forest fires of the season. From now on, only rain, snow, and soggy ground lay ahead for those who chose to weather it out—and for once he didn't want to be among them. He needed a fresh start and was looking forward to this trip as a welcome break from the coming winter gloom.

Suddenly the car ahead of him was moving forward and disappeared into the dusky curtain before them, so he put his car in gear, finding and then following the dim brake-lights down the road. They moved over into the single, open passing lane, past a row of personnel and tanker trucks parked on the right side, and Martin could make out the orange glow of a fire below him. After five minutes, the once-trapped cars were free to gain speed through refreshingly clear air in the descent to Wallace at the base of the Coeur d'Alene Mountains and to race on to the west.

The delays had cost him at least an hour, and a six-hour drive at the minimum still lay before him. Martin now realized that if he was going to catch his flight to Greece, his best remaining option was to abandon the idea of driving all the way to the SeaTac airport, and instead to catch one of the hourly flights from Spokane to Seattle. Feeling woefully technologically challenged to book a flight from his car, he speed-dialed his daughter with a single tap on his cell phone but there was no answer. He next fumbled at the menu and tried his friend Frank.

"Martin, what's up?" asked Frank. "You can't be there already, can you?"

"Not hardly, Frank." said Martin. "This trip isn't getting off to the best start. Thanks to your send-off, I have a massive hangover, and to make matters worse, I've been held up by a forest fire that flared up just west of Lookout Pass. Now I don't think I can make Seattle in time for my flight out of there."

"Why don't you just fly from Spokane, since it's on the way?" asked Frank sagely.

"Well, that's why I called," said Martin. "I was thinking the same thing, but I don't know how to make a reservation or look up the number on this phone—especially while I'm driving. Can you do me a favor and make a reservation for me? I should make it to Spokane in an hour and a half, so how about the next available flight in two and a half hours or so?"

"Wellll," said Frank drawing out his answer as long as possible. "I suppose so, but it'll cost you a beer."

Martin could imagine him grinning on the other end of the connection. "OK," said Martin with feigned reluctance, "put it on my tab."

"Will do!" said Frank. "I'll ring you back if there's a problem, but have a good trip if I don't."

"Thanks a lot, Frank, I owe you one. See you when I get back."

Feeling much more relaxed, Martin settled into the remainder of his drive as he hit the flat expanse between the mountains and Spokane with an increased speed limit to look forward to.

Chapter 2.

WHEN HE'D first been in Athens in the '70s, the city had seemed exotic and ancient, and he'd loved exploring its narrow streets lined with whitewashed walls, colorful shutters, and wrought-iron balconies. On his visit yesterday, however, his impression had been of a typically swollen, congested metropolis—the same as any other modern city, but this one surrounding the Acropolis and sprinkled with historic ruins. Somehow the quaint environs had lost their unique character with glass buildings, air-conditioning ducts, and tourists seemingly everywhere. *Or is it just the same and this is my now-jaded view of them?* he wondered.

And now, on the ferry-ride to the Greek island of Kos, Martin had the feeling that he was just part of a tour on a cruise ship rather than riding a routine local transport. *Ah, the clothing is one thing,* he realized suddenly. *Back then Europeans dressed much differently from Americans, and the people from the country even dressed differently than those from the city. You could tell everyone apart. Now, we all look the same.* In his travels forty years before, the country had been more distinctly Greek, and he had been on what had seemed more of an adventure. This trip felt rather mundane in comparison, which was a shame in a way because he was searching again for the exotic. He sat in the shade while passengers from who-knew-where milled around on the deck, and his thoughts drifted back to a chapter from a book he'd written about his first trip; another Greek ferry ride taken, what now seemed like, ages ago.

"What?" I asked again, cupping my hands to my mouth to be heard above the roar.

Katrina repeated "Die Meere werden rauh," loudly with gesturing arms.

Seeing me shake my head she yelled, "The sea is becoming rough," and I nodded back as another blast of salty spray blew in from the side of the ferry and left some of her hair plastered to her cheek.

Dietrich pulled hard on the door handle against the now bracing wind, and the three of us squeezed inside and headed down the enclosed metal stairway to the crowded passenger compartment below. We were at the bottom steps when Katrina suddenly threw her hand up over her mouth and appeared about to retch. Dietrich and I mirrored her reaction when we reached her. The stench was not even as bad as the images: old Greek women in oversize black dresses clutching benches or their stomachs and mopping damp white foreheads with rags; a man jumping up and running unsteadily to the shallow gutters along the sides of the metal hull, suddenly bending over and releasing a stream of bile into the now sloshing vomit from what was likely the stomach contents of every person in the hold.

All three of us exchanged panicked glances and bolted back up the steps and out into the intensifying storm, gasping in fresh air and fixing our eyes on what we could make out of the dark and constantly moving horizon. We dashed across the open, wet car deck and rode out the rest of the trip tucked behind one of the tightly packed cars as the bow of the ferry crashed down into each cresting wave and sprayed seawater over the vehicles and us. We felt the car shift subtly behind us whenever the prow plowed into an oncoming surge. By now we were completely soaked, the water streaming down my long hair, under my collar and down the middle of my back. But I hardly noticed. We felt alive, and the pair of normally staid Germans were more energized than I had seen them since we'd met in Athens. At some level there must have been an element of fear in each of us, because our conversation in broken German and English was all about existence, purpose, and reincarnation.

Landing in Heraklion, Crete was like a sigh. We were the first off the ramp as sullen shadows emerged from the reeking hold onto the deck to find their cars or wobble their way ashore. The rain had abated here long before, and the sides of the narrow streets that greeted us still radiated the heat of the day. The youth hostel that we eventually found was a warm hive of untroubled activity. After showering and stowing our wet gear, the three of us discovered a nearby taverna and following servings of octopus soup, souvlaki, and bottles of retsina, I remembered little else.

David Ackley

How strange to be sitting in the bright sunlight the next morning sipping Greek coffee and finding I'd written this in my journal sometime during the previous night:

> *I'm pleading—don't disgorge us*
> *Don't dive to the depths and spit us out*
> *You need the air, so linger here*
> *Where the elements foam in meeting*
> *I feel your deep shudders at the heights*
> *And your urgent plunges toward the calm home below*
> *But please remember this*
> *We're not the putrid bile you feel in your throat*
> *We're not the gagging black cloaks*
> *We're not the bones of dead fish*
> *We are your sweet-scented ambergris*
> *I'm begging now—don't disown me*

I can recall that chapter almost word for word, but my being there, the actual experience, and he heaved a tremendous sigh, *not so much now,* as he stood and gazed out from the railing. The long-ago written words from his first novel were seemingly solid and tangible, but the actual images of the past he craved were much more ephemeral. In vivid contrast to his initial storm-battered trip, today was calm and clear while sailing over nearly the same Aegean waters. Martin could now make out the island of Kos in the distance and most of the other passengers on deck were taking in the placid Mediterranean vista and shouting when they spied the dolphins reappearing to play in the bow wake. He wasn't so easily impressed—and that bothered him. Had he seen his lifetime allotment of dolphins and porpoises, was that it? Did it now take an extra something, an additional special effect to make him take notice? A raging storm, perhaps? *Hell no*, he thought as he leaned over the railing with the rest of the oglers and tried to concentrate on the animals at this exact moment. Those beautiful playful creatures frolicking before a lumbering leviathan of a vessel.

But after a moment he felt queasy. The gentle sway of the ferry combined with the vision of the moving water below was enough to make him back slowly away from the rails and stare straight up at the sky, taking in deep breaths until the ill ease passed. *How I've changed*, he thought and looked around the crowded deck. *Storm waves didn't bother me in the least, and now I feel sick just turning my head too quickly. If those tempestuous surges were here today, I'd be among those poor souls puking their guts out down below.* Back then, riding out the voyage in the squalls and spray had somehow made him feel cleansed, superior to the poor slobs sentenced to suffer in the fetid dungeon below decks. However now, much older than he had been at the time, he sympathized with them—the people of the land: farmers or shopkeepers—probably at sea for the first time. Little wonder they had retched and wept.

The horn blasting above him announced their arrival at the harbor and brought him back to the present as he made his way towards the exit doors. The ferry pulled into the port town of Kos on the eastern end of the long, narrow Greek island with the same name, and he joined the stream of foot-passengers stepping onto the quay once the ramp had leveled with it. There was no need to hurry. The suitcase and carryon he dragged were a far cry from the small, light backpack he'd used when he'd been here forty years before, and he felt vaguely self-conscious as he clattered the noisy things behind him. He'd decided to spend the night here in Kos proper and see if the local sights jogged any latent memories. He could mentally picture the town of Kefalos on the western end of the island vividly, but he was not so sure about this town. Martin checked into his hotel and then began to wander the streets to see if anything seemed familiar. In the end, he had vague recollections of the Roman *odeon*, the large castle along one side of the harbor, and some of the waterfront scene, but beyond that, it was as if he had never been here before. However, that didn't matter. He was on a journey to build new memories and form them into something different. Something fresh. So far, he'd tried without success to work up the excitement he had expected to come more naturally, and he had high hopes that rural Greece and some time on the island would rekindle that enthusiasm.

He happened upon an elegant seafood restaurant situated along the waterfront that he'd never dreamed of affording when he was young and sat under the retro bare-bulb patio lights as the sun set, enjoying the cool breeze on his face in the gathering dusk. He sipped an up-scale wine and ordered the fish kebabs with an octopus salad on the side. Women tourists in Greek blouses and men in white deck shoes and cotton pants began to fill the empty tables. As he stared out over the harbor lights, he was suddenly struck by the subtlety of the wispy Greek-tinged mood music drifting in from unseen speakers. This was nothing like the blaring bouzouki and unintelligible vocals that had been ubiquitously emanating from metal trumpet speakers in every *taverna* on the islands so long ago. Things were rougher then, but he'd reveled in the foreign atmosphere.

He'd returned to Greece to create and document an entirely new memoir, but was already struggling to keep the past from getting in the way. It was occurring to him that this return to Kos was not the best way to start anew. In the early '70s, he and a high-school friend from Walla Walla had set out to travel to the East with the goal of roaming perhaps as far as Australia, but his friend's journey had been cut short by illness. Martin had explored the Mediterranean by himself for a few months and was eventually joined by another friend, Ryan, in Istanbul where together they'd set their sights on India. Traveling overland they'd traversed Turkey, Iran, Afghanistan, Pakistan, India, Nepal, and Sri Lanka. The trip had taken two years, and in the end the decision of whether or not to continue had come down to either embracing the life on the road as an end in itself, like many of the travelers they'd run into along the way, or returning home. They'd travelled for so long that it was ultimately not an easy choice to make.

Finally, they'd chosen home over travel, and it was during the two subsequent years while living in Montana that Martin had written his poetry-laced travelogue which had surprisingly become a national best seller. One critic had embarrassingly termed him 'the Jack Kerouac of the Seventies', and he'd spent the rest of his life, most would say unsuccessfully, trying to live up to the hype.

The thought of his long descent from that lofty height was too much—he took a sip of wine and then drained the glass. *I wish I'd never written that damned book!* he thought for the thousandth time, catching the waiter's attention and ordering a bottle of ouzo. *No,* he amended his previous thought, *I love writing. I wish I'd never published that damned book!*

Chapter 3.

MARTIN SETTLED into his cushioned seat in the sleek air-conditioned bus and stared out the window as they wove their way out of Kos Town and onto the main road for the hour-long trip to Kefalos. He'd tried a brief conversation with the elder Greek-islander sitting next to him, but the language barrier was too great, and his seatmate had donned his thick glasses and pulled out a local newspaper as a refuge from the interaction. The white and brown boulders amid arid vegetation flew hypnotically by the window, and Martin fell into his own thoughts.

The trip he and Ryan had undertaken forty years previously had ended up being more than a sight-seeing excursion; the experience had, in the end, defined them in truly unique ways. He realized that had he remained in Walla Walla at the community college, his future self would have been increasingly influenced by his hometown and his childhood friends, or had he enrolled in a different college, he would have been further rooted into the culture of whatever place that might have been, most likely in a larger city somewhere. Instead, he felt the journey they'd made had transformed them down to their cores in ways that were far different from the changes they may have undergone had they remained at home.

The first weeks and months of the trip had seemed like a normal vacation with the usual expired-by date, but after a time they'd somehow dropped the idea of returning to school or jobs, and broken free of the need to be from 'somewhere.' They'd then entered the miniature mobile culture of 'life on the road.' They never knew where they'd stay the next night—there were no reservations, cell phones with Google or Google Maps—and they had only the bulky, battered, general tourist guides which were in most cases of little practical use. They had to dine out for every meal, never sure what would be available when, or where the next one might be found. They walked wherever they needed in most towns and cities and never felt constrained to a schedule or agenda. The next destination for them was always mercurial and could shift by the chance mention of an interesting place by a fellow traveler. Mail was collected according to their best guess at the appropriate American Express available in the shifting route ahead. There was air-conditioning in few buildings except for the high-class, unaffordable hotels, and the rooms that they could afford were neither heated nor cooled even if they wanted them to be, making the both of them attuned to the local climate. By necessity they had to travel light, and eventually they possessed not a single article of clothing that they'd started with. In the same way, they'd slowly replaced every cell in their bodies with elements of the lands they traveled through.

They'd tried to absorb the cultures they encountered, but they'd never been able to become a real part of any of them. Instead, they'd become connected to the physical, to the environment, to the place. They'd soaked in the sights, the sounds, the smells, the country and become a part of that. Then during the first years after returning home, they'd felt like they were still traveling—houses, clothes, friends, seemed like they could disappear in a moment, and seemed to be part of a larger, mutable map. In time, these impressions had faded, but had never really disappeared for either of them.

In his bus-ride reflections, Martin suddenly realized that the substantive changes he'd undergone were what had been the true inspiration behind his first novel. None of the other later pieces he'd written had the same fundamental muse, and none had done nearly as well. *Not only that,* he thought, *but I'm always subconsciously comparing any new experiences to that trip, and any new writings to that first novel. Nothing so far has been as inspired. Probably because I can't allow it to be—I can't seem to discard the past.*

Almost reflexively, he thought back to part of the last chapter of that first novel as the Greek island scenery rolled by, and he pictured the well-dated scenes as freshly as if they happened yesterday.

This final chapter is my archive of memorable pictures. Since I had no camera to record my travels, the only collection of images I have left are those stored in my head; mental snippets filed in my memory to be recollected whenever I choose. However, like all media, they'll start to curl, wear, fade, or become misplaced. I'm recording some of them here so that I'll remember them in my old age.

* *The air erupting with thousands of beautiful butterflies on the isle of Rhodes—black and white outer wings, red and black inner wings—settling down onto the trees and my arms, hands and head.*

* *From the rooftop of the white-washed building in Isfahan raveled miles of dyed yarn looped around crossbeams below—brilliant colors drying in the sun on this street; the next; the next.*

* *A young man near the harmonium player swaying in rhythm with the music and the train, then rolling, thrashing, and gesticulating as if in a rapturous trance for minutes on end.*

* *Yellow lamplight on a frosty night up the Kali Gandaki River in a close room with beams blackened from the years of open fire cooking, the weathered Nepali inn owner huddled across a worn table.*

* *A distraught beggar woman with her baby bumping into us, a pleading look in her eyes, her hand out, cradling her dead baby.*

* *Dense fog at night along a New Delhi street, revealing a thin man on an old black bicycle carrying a bed across his head and back, cycling silently past us and then disappearing again into the fog.*

* *Setting sun from the top of Meenakshi Temple, and just as darkness wraps the temple with a deep aqua sky, flights of fruit bats, huge and silent, passing the temple heading for the palm groves outside the city.*

* *A huge water buffalo—nostrils flared, breathing heavily, eyes intense, ears dropping back—stepping forward, with the entire small herd similarly poised and us backing swiftly away up the dirt path.*

* *Doves flying against the rosy sunset sky above a red sandstone turret of the ancient, deserted palace at Fatipur Sikri.*

* *A laborer dressed all in white leading a cow pulling a lawn mower, cutting the irrigated grass in front of the Taj Mahal.*

* *A brilliantly flowered sari looped over a tree limb in the cool shade in the middle of a rice field with a tiny baby cradled quietly within it, napping.*

* *Colorful new to faded pastel Tibetan prayer flags, wind-whipped in long lines reaching to the top of a tall pole.*

* *Two thin men shoveling chipped stones for a road—a duet of one pushing the handle the other pulling a rope tied just above the blade.*

* *A naked, wild-haired* sadhu *covered in ash, standing stiffly in the middle of a South Indian street—a religious spear piercing his tongue, bright blood dripping down his chest.*

This is what I need to do again, thought Martin. *I need to create a new album and be free from this one.* He opened his eyes to the present and paid closer attention as the mountain on the left descended to the flatter portion of the island that led to the town of Kefalos.

Chapter 4.

HE'D CHOSEN the single-story Regal Inn in Kefalos based upon pictures he'd discovered on the internet—it was the one that most closely resembled the shell of a structure under construction that was lodged in his memory. It turned out that this was probably the right hotel, but there were many similar buildings laid out along the beach now, and after all this time it was hard to be certain. He left the cool lobby and headed into the sunshine and towards the beach. *Well, it was forty years ago, and the town is so much more built up now—the hotel wasn't even completed back then, so why should I care if it isn't the right one?* thought Martin, and then he shook his head. *I just seem to remember what's easiest to recall now, anyway—more and more details just seem to slip away.* As he got older, he could feel his personal historical library becoming lighter in the shelves by the year. He and Ryan still kept in touch, and they were both sometimes amazed at how different their recollections of events and locations could be. Ryan seemed to be able to remember people and conversations, whereas he was usually better with places. In 1973, Martin had come to Kefalos alone, before Ryan could join him, and so had no one to augment his memories of this Greek island that lay just a few miles off the coast of Turkey.

He yelped now with quick steps as he moved across the hot white sand of Agios Stephanos beach to the darker section at shoreside, lapped by the gentle waves. *Why is it that all of the beaches here are named after saints—but they burn like hell?* he wondered idly as he reached the refreshingly cool water's edge. Wiggling his toes in relief and gazing out at the calm Aegean, he was glad to once again see the little Agios Nicolaos chapel with the small rock mesa rising behind it on the tiny islet that lay one hundred and fifty yards offshore. He could make out the tourists who had dared the swim and were exploring the chapel and its surroundings. Turning to his left he could make out the ancient ruins of a familiar basilica wedged among the rocks near where he was currently cooling his heels.

Standing ankle-deep in water, he turned inland and gazed back at the hotel, the beach, and the rounded hill to the southwest rising over the main town of Kefalos: white beach chairs and umbrellas laid out in perfect symmetry along the flat expanse, with red, fleshy legs protruding from some; white sand leading up to the outspread arms of the low whitewashed resort, protectively surrounding a pool, restaurant, bar, and meager brown grass lawn. The bungalow he'd been given at check-in was the second from the end nearest the islet with the Agios Nicolaos chapel, and to his surprise it was an air-conditioned luxury suite with all conveniences at his fingertips which was a far cry from the empty shell it had been.

He'd stood in roughly this same spot on his first visit here, and his filmy memories slowly cleared a layer at a time until he was seeing things as they had been back then, and as he had recorded them in a chapter from his book.

> *Pale light filtering, ivory limbs*
> *Dangling in the softest pose*
> *Billowing hair tracing shoulders, neck, face*
> *Gooseflesh finally soothed*
> *Body suspended yet slowly rising.*
> *Languid legs stir, cross and now kick*
> *Longing to stay yet urgent to leave*
> *Sudden gasps, eyes now open*
> *At the cold lens of life*

My foot was shocked to leave the warm evening air, and I immediately jerked it back from the water, wondering if a night swim was such a good idea after all. Occasional jangles of tinny bouzouki music, distant town lights, the small fire lit in front of my neighbor's bungalow, and the gigantic sea of stars overhead, otherwise I was alone in the quiet dark. I'd dumped my clothes on the dry sand, so decided to take the plunge after all. So much colder than my daytime swim, the water was bracing, and I waded 'til it reached my waist, diving in, unable to see the depths below or the surface above. Gasping at first, I was still breathing quickly and stroking for the islet. Faint phosphorescence glowed about my fingers ahead of me and as I turned for a backstroke, I could see the wake of greenish glow flowing behind. The hint of reflection off the little white chapel on the islet was my only cue, and about halfway in swimming to it I paused to rest, needing to tread water. The unexpected chill was penetrating now, and I thought it best to swim on or head back. My body turned to vertical when incredible warmth hit my feet—what's this? I dove down into the most unexpectedly luxurious heated spa. Staying down as long as possible I warmed and then surfaced again into the chilly top layer. Time disappeared as I treaded water at the surface, gazing at the starry gauze, until cold, diving into the black yet balming waters below. How weird—the dangerous depths beaconed, and the safe surface repelled.

Abandoning my goal of the islet, I was soon back at shore and sat on the beach to dry before joining my neighbors around their fire for some wine and lively discussion. The few of us here each had our own suite, and it was free. Somehow the owners of the unfinished resort were OK with us camping out in the empty shells after construction had stalled. Or at least that's what we'd heard. We built fires outside or inside, had cement quarters including a bathtub, and were in heaven. A taverna with food and wine was just down the road. When we wanted a bath, we'd tote fresh water and fill the tub in the morning so that by the evening the water would have warmed from a day in the sun. We'd scrounged candles to read by at night and lived in quiet.

No suntan oil, so under the relentless sun I swam daily in my tattered T-shirt with a cheap diving mask, snorkel, and fins, occasionally visiting the tiny chapel of Agios Nicolaos and exploring the semi-submerged caves around the back of the islet. This spot and Vai beach on Crete—diving and turn-

ing to watch Katrina, hair streaming, floating naked with the sky above, I hoped, would be my memories of Greece when I got old.

"Well, those are the memories that have stayed," Martin sighed aloud, "and those days are long gone," as he waded out into the water that was exactly the same temperature as the air and submerged his sun-screened body to swim out to the islet. There was no discernible temperature inversion to the water today, so it was chilly when he dove more than a meter below the surface. He puffed as he found his footing on the slippery rocks at his destination and half-crawled onto the hot hard ground. Agony came with every step as he tried to hop and leap his now much bulkier shape up the rough path to the chapel. Once in the shadows he shifted from foot to foot until his soles cooled. *Well, thank goodness there's no graffiti—this is exactly how I'd remembered it with white walls and blue door.* He wanted to scramble over the rocks of the island and explore it as he had before, but sat on the stoop of the chapel instead, letting his young, lean, tanned, hard-soled spirit loose in his memories. *And what exactly am I doing here?* he wondered, still sitting on the porch sometime later. *I'm definitely not going to write about reminiscences, and an old guy limping his soft, white body up to a chapel he'd visited years before.*

In the afternoon, back on the main island of Kos and wearing sneakers and sporting a newly purchased sunhat, he strolled the beach and investigated the small Greek ruins now much better kept-up and with some new signage explaining the history of the basilica. He could make out the mosaic design on the remains of the old flooring that had been preserved and wondered if the curators had brought in or newly excavated a few of the columns since he didn't recall nearly as many standing forty years in the past. That the site now looked like something made for tourists rather than the original ruins of his memory vaguely pissed him off. Feeling the weight of nostalgia, he made his way back to his hotel room to take a rest before dinner. Instead of napping, however, he opened his computer and began to type out a piece that was the exact opposite of the kind he was hoping to write. Rather than capturing exciting new thoughts and observations, he found himself writing about the lamentable changes that time and age brought about.

Chapter 5.

HE'D JUST ordered the calamari stew for dinner and was gazing out over the twilight sea from the outdoor patio when he startled suddenly as his cellphone belted out Santana's *Black Magic Woman* ringtone, matching the restaurant's background music in volume. "Hello?" he asked, looking at the name of the caller on the phone display as he answered. "Leira?"

"Hi, Martin!" she answered. "I just wanted to check in with you. I thought you were going to drop by on Wednesday so we could talk before your trip."

"Well, I was," replied Martin, "but my plans hit a snag."

"Oh, no. What happened?"

"Well, I was headed to Seattle, but traffic got delayed because of a late forest fire near Lookout Pass—you know, the one on the Idaho border. They had us necked down to a single lane and held us up until a pilot car could guide us through. The smoke was that bad. Anyway, I ended up stopping at Spokane instead of driving all the way to SeaTac and caught a flight out from there. I don't think I'd have been able to make the plane out of Seattle otherwise, let alone our meeting. In hindsight, I should have just flown from Kalispell instead of trying to drive in the first place, but who knew?"

"Where are you now? What's that noise?"

"Greek music in Greece, of course."

"What? You're there already?"

"Yep," said Martin. "Athens the day before yesterday, and the island of Kos today."

"And how's it going?" asked Leira.

"Just getting started, but all I seem to be doing so far is reminiscing about the past. I was telling you that I want this story to be based on new experiences, and so far, that hasn't happened. Maybe it would help if I didn't visit old locations. I'm going to give myself time to settle into travelling though and not push things. I'll find my stride."

"Well, good luck with that, Martin," she said with an unexpected tenderness. "I hope you find your inspiration around the next corner." There was a pause and then Leira continued, "Say, the reason I wanted to see you before you flew to Greece was to discuss something." Another pause. "And give you time to think about it."

"What's that?" asked Martin.

"Well, I'm finding out that several of my newer clients are much needier than I ever expected, and one author in particular requires more hand-holding than normal. He's really taken off and is starting to tour—book signings and the whole shebang."

Shit! She's dumping me! thought Martin with a sinking feeling in his stomach.

"I just wanted you to think about whether you really need me to represent you anymore," Leira continued, "or if you want to find someone who can be more responsive to your situation."

"You've been responsive," he ventured.

"Yes, but that's going to change since my schedule is so crammed lately. In fact, the whole agency is so busy that I can't pass anything off at the moment."

She wants me to find another agent since I haven't written anything worth a damn in years, thought Martin. Instead he said, "Well, I've always been happy having you as my agent, and I really think that I'll have something new and exciting fairly soon. Do you mind if we wait and see how that goes? At least to the draft stage of my new book?"

"Oh, of course!" said Leira a little too lightly. "I just wanted to plant the seed that my time is getting more constrained lately, and I wanted you to know that I wouldn't be hurt if you wanted to sign on with someone in a different agency if it came to that. I feel that I might not be able to keep giving you the level of representation that you deserve if things continue as they are. Just think about it anyway."

Damn it! She wants me to set her free of the contract, thought Martin. "OK, I'll keep that in mind, Leira. Sorry I couldn't make it into your office as we'd planned."

"That's fine," she replied. "Have a great trip, and I look forward to seeing a draft of the new book when you write it!"

"OK, thanks," said Martin. "I'll check in from Istanbul."

"OK, talk to you then," said Leira and rang off.

Martin slumped in his chair and suddenly wasn't very hungry. He was thirsty. He nabbed the next waiter and ordered a large carafe of red wine. *Now the pressure is on,* he thought, and knew his own pattern. The more it mattered that he produced something, the more his writing became blocked and stilted, and the more he tended to drink. It had happened before. Riding the success of his first book which he'd written with no thoughts of publication, his subsequent collection of poetry had received a tepid review at best; his second novel written in the throes of new love had been panned; another book of poetry had only been printed by a boutique press that Leira had miraculously unearthed; and his next published novel, written only during sessions when alcohol had been his muse, had received mostly bad reviews. His one smidgeon of success in the last few years had been a book capturing a slice of Montana history. The new book idea that was the purpose of his present journey felt like his last gasp of effort, but he could already feel the warm depths of a drunk coming on.

Leira was an angel, and he was losing her. His first agent had dumped him in frustration after the failed book of poetry. Leira had been fresh out of college from Spain and newly hired by a minor literary agency—The Pinewood House based in San Francisco. She'd read his first novel and swooned over the prospect of being able to represent him. *The thrill is gone,* he thought as he took another gulp of wine, leaned back in his chair, and watched his mood slowly sinking over the Mediterranean and his cold bowl of seafood stew.

Chapter 6.

HE WASN'T sure how much later, he found himself sitting in the dark on one of the sunchairs that were spread out along the now-black beach in front of his hotel. The moon hadn't yet risen, so it was difficult to make out the ghostly chairs, let alone the water's edge; but there was plenty of night-life in this darkness—rap music poured out of the Mystic Lounge several hundred yards away, enveloping him in its unwelcome waves.

Maybe a beach like this, he thought. Leira's phone call had thrown him into a deep funk. The latest book she'd tried to promote for him had died a miserable death. "Of course, I'm against banning books, but then again there are some novels that should just be banished—or perhaps their authors should be exiled to a desert island and left to their own devices. *On Whom These Airs Attend* is decidedly painful to read in every literary aspect. It..." Martin still flushed at the memory of this review with a mixture of embarrassment and anger. He'd published his latest novel before the divorce, but the reviews had only started coming in, coincidentally, during the months following, and there wasn't one that ended on a positive note. There was no describing the feelings of desolation and betray-al that had built up within him during the past year, although he'd tried unsuccessfully to capture the personal agony on paper—many times—which only made matters worse to him as an author.

A failure both at home and in his chosen vocation, he'd impulsively decided to take the unkind reviewer's advice and sell his house and move to the remotest location he could find. There was a deserted property on Curacao that had caught his eye, and he planned on snapping it up as soon as he had the capital raised from his home's sale.

The evening of the day his house was listed on the market there had been a knock on the door. He'd opened it, thinking that a realtor had forgotten to schedule an appointment, when in walked Frank—a bottle of tequila in hand. "We need to talk about this, Martin. Seriously. Sit down," Frank said, his normally jovial manner abandoned for the moment.

"Frank," began Martin, "Hi, I didn't expect to see you tonight. What are you…"

Frank held his palm towards Martin's face as he headed to the kitchen glassware. "Not another word until you're anchored," he said. He speared two shot glasses with his forefingers, brought them to the table, opened the bottle, filled each glass to the brim, and said simply, "Drink."

Martin stared at him, but Frank lifted and tilted his own glass towards Martin until his friend shrugged, clicked glasses with him, and they both downed the contents.

Frank peered intently into Martin's eyes and then shook his head. He filled the glasses again and then repeated the process. After another assessment, he finally nodded. "I'd have chosen another drug, personally, but knowing you as I do, I figured that it had to be alcohol and fairly potent to get you to your proper place."

Martin was beginning to feel the warm glow from the tequila and sank down into his favorite chair. He sighed and began to visibly relax.

"So, what the hell?" asked Frank. "You're selling this place? One of the best spots on this whole freaking planet?"

Martin shook his head. "You don't get it, Frank," he said. "It's over. This place. This life. It's not working. I'm old enough that I figure that I've got one more chance to break all of my ties and start over. I'm going to find some nice, remote spot and just disappear."

Frank suddenly burst out laughing. And he didn't stop politely after a few seconds—he started in and for half a minute was doubled over into a paroxysmal fit. Martin was at first offended, but when Frank howled, "Nice remote spot! He said here in..." was all he could manage, and Martin was soon irresistibly drawn in until they were both helplessly wiping their eyes and stomping their feet. When they both subsided, he intuited where Frank was going with this and leaned over and poured them each another shot.

"Sorry, Martin," said Frank. "Couldn't help that outburst." Then after a moment, "Disappear!" And then they were both lost in laughter again. Finally, taking deep breaths, they toasted each other and Frank continued. "Dude, you have to take your house off the market."

Martin looked at him and shook his head, suddenly serious again. "Look. I'm a pariah here, my latest book has been trashed by the reviewers, and Mandy has headed off for college. There's honestly nothing left for me here anymore. Besides, the weather sucks in winter—as you're well aware. What I need is to be alone on a tropical island where I can live out my old age in peace."

Frank visibly held back another fit of laughter, reaching for the bottle. "You're out of your mind. You know that, right?" After an uncomprehending stare from his friend, he continued. "This place is almost as isolated as you can get, Martin. It *is* a deserted island. How many visitors have you had here, even though they can drive right to this spot from anywhere in the entire country?"

"Well, no one—unless they're totally lost."

"Exactly!" cried Frank. "You have it all here, Martin. Great view, solitude, nature. You don't need to move from here to get more isolated—you need to leave here for a while and get your bearings, get some inspiration, get laid, for god's sakes—but this is your home, your roots. You can't leave here because then you'd never get anywhere."

Martin's sudden realization that Frank was right had convinced him to keep the house and take off to seek adventure, but not without huge residual consequences the next morning. Martin vowed to never touch tequila again after that night.

A blast of ska music from the Mystic Lounge snapped him from his recollection. *A beach somewhere far from everyone you know where you can walk out into the water and then swim 'til you're too tired to swim anymore.* He nodded to himself as his dark mood resumed. He was half-considering taking off his shoes and testing how cold the water was when his cell phone buzzed. Hey Dad, did you make it? Bet you're in the hot sun. Freezing here. Let me know, or I'll worry. LYF, Mandy.

Martin stared at the bright screen and exhaled in a strange but welcome relief. He texted his daughter as he followed the light toward the waiting hotel.

Chapter 7.

*"**KNOCK IT** off, Toni!"* Martin mumbled and reached out to push her away. She kept shaking the bed. "Toni!" shouted Martin as he opened his eyes and could make out the light fixture swaying in the semi-dark room. Turning in confusion, he saw that he was alone in his bed and realized there was no probability that his ex-wife would be standing in this room in Greece. He threw off the sheets and swayed as he got to his feet, reaching out for support. *Definitely too much wine,* he said to himself when an unnatural jolt jerked his feet to the side. Martin was now fully awake and realized that he was in the middle of an earthquake. *The doorway, you're supposed to stand under the nearest doorway,* as he pitched and staggered to the patio door and threw it open. A few shouts at first, and then the once-quiet night was filled with screams and wails, especially from the nearby town center. A low rumbling was fading when another stronger jolt elicited snaps and pops from the plaster and stucco around him as he held fast to the door frame. *What am I doing?* he asked himself as he looked at the white of his gripping fingers and then bolted onto the open patio in front of him. A gathering of guests in all states of dress began milling in the hotel grounds, moving safely away from the building itself. The commotion from town continued undiminished, and there were a few sobs from some in his

immediate group. A lady in a thin shimmering green robe was shivering uncontrollably. The electricity had gone out at some point, Martin hadn't noticed exactly when, although he felt that he could see perfectly fine regardless. About five minutes after the event, the hotel staff began checking on the guests and bringing out lit candles, blankets, pillows, and roll-out beds. It was recommended that everyone remain outside for the night until they could assess possible damage to the building structure and learn the status of the town from the police. Martin stood at the edge of the small crowd; the effects of the wine now completely dissipated.

After a time, the distant howls and shouts from town subsided, only to be replaced by a string of sirens from emergency vehicles running between Kefalos and Kos town. Many of the resort guests began to lie down for a fitful night, but Martin knew he would now be unable to sleep. Against orders, he'd gone back into his hotel room and retrieved his phone, passport, and shoes. He checked his cellphone with the intention of calling his daughter, Mandy, but cell reception had disappeared. He was unexpectedly chilled on this warm evening and wrapped a blanket around his shoulders like a shawl. The action of throwing the end of the blanket up and over his left shoulder suddenly brought back the feelings of well-being he'd been trying to capture when he'd written a chapter in his first book.

Horse, snow, statement, wool, security, fog, silence—those nouns all went with 'blanket', the word heavily on my mind.

Autumn had arrived and although warm under the sun during the day, it was freezing at night in Mashhad, Iran. After a long summer in Greece and Turkey, and being dressed in thin cotton clothes, we seemed to feel the chill even more bitterly—especially once the sun set and we could see the clouds of our breath in the frigid air. Layering on the clothes we carried in our packs was useless, so when we got down from the crowded bus in the next town, Herat, Afghanistan, I bought a brown woolen shawl similar to those worn by almost everyone else we saw. And suddenly everything was all right. As long as my neck and shoulders were warm, I didn't notice the cold elsewhere, and the shawl could be bunched along my neck to make the climate bearable. It soon became my favorite article of clothing and I wondered how I'd made it this far without ever wearing one. Practical, multi-purpose, adaptable, it was my covering, bag, pillow—whatever it needed to be.

As it turned out, the shawl made things even better than all right. We became invisible. The further east we'd come, the more we stood out, the brighter our skin shone, the rarer we seemed to be to the eyes of the curious locals. And, although we were becoming increasingly habituated to the stares, we never felt completely comfortable, no matter where we were. A cup of tea in a stall could draw a crowd. However, during the day, we could wrap up in a shawl, fling it up over the left shoulder and be much less conspicuous, especially if we wore one of the commonly-donned wool hats as well. But at night it was a new world, and we never drew a second look—the shawl brought up over our heads before wrapping over the shoulder enveloped us. When we walked at a slow pace, not a soul noticed. We were free.

It was the right cure at the right time. Being different was good when we were offered tea, cigarettes, conversation, friendship. It was tolerable when kids begged for candy; shop keepers wanted to show their silver, rugs, spices, hash; or runners wanted to show us the best hotel in town from the bus stand. But being different was dangerous at times: standing at a bus stop on the Caspian Sea when a few people gathered, then a few more, then everyone starting to get close, elbowing, and the kids starting to kick and poke—with the bus showing up just in the nick of time and still having to wrestle ourselves inside; or mud coming in through the window of the double-decker bus when we were on the top level in Teheran; or hands running up toward our pockets; or Ryan and I staying out near curfew on a foggy Kabul night when a single, armed soldier tried to take us in, but we somehow manage to talk our way out of it—for the second time during our stay.

A Canadian, Audie, had joined Ryan and me as we left Turkey by bus, and her newly purchased shawl/hijab saved her as well, hiding her long golden hair that shown like a beacon. Although still noticeable, her effect on the populace was dulled and made more manageable. Being a western woman, she was often an object of derision and drew spits, pinches, pokes, and jabs, so Ryan and I learned to run interference— one ahead and one behind, or each to a side, deflecting would-be strikes. However, defense was difficult in heavy crowds, and Audie had the bruises to show for it. So, the shawls weren't perfect, but they helped immensely.

Tugging the blanket tighter around his neck, but still feeling the tension of the evening, Martin wandered away from the now-crowded resort plaza and toward the beach. Gazing at the town in the distance, he could make out faint points and flashes of light from candles, oil lamps, and flashlights. *Oh,* he thought, *and cell phone flashlight apps, of course.* Bright blue flashing lights showed the areas where the police and ambulance crews were focused. *This may have been much worse than I thought,* worried Martin. *Maybe I should go up into town and see if I can help.* He took a few steps in the direction of the frenzied activity, but then realized that with the distance involved and his lack of language ability, he really could do little more than get in the way. Instead, he headed in the opposite direction with the vague curiosity of discovering whether the ancient ruins had made it through the quake unscathed. Taking another glance back at Kefalos, he wondered how long transportation to the island of Kos would be disrupted. *I may be here longer than I'd planned,* he thought.

A newly-risen quarter-moon and starlight made finding his way easy, and he left the shoreline as he approached the basilica site, climbing the short distance on a path through the rocks to be among the ruins. One column had indeed fallen and cracked against a stone bench, but otherwise he could make out little else that had been disturbed. He sat on a nearby marble plinth, making sure he was out of reach of any of the standing columns should there be a second quake or aftershocks. With buildings presumably crumbled in the town and the column fallen here, he wondered how different tonight would be from a similar night two-thousand years before when the temple would have been in use. Other than the flashing blue lights and sirens, he was bathed in what was probably the same fearful nighttime aftermath as would have enveloped the inhabitants back then. *However, I know about earthquakes,* thought Martin. *And don't have the added trouble of wondering if the gods were angry and out to punish me.* He looked out over the glistening white-stone ruins and the toppled column. *They're not, are they?* as he remembered Leira's call earlier that evening and the intense feeling of gloom that had accompanied it.

Still incredibly chilled despite the warm climate, he needed to move and so made his way to the other side of the ancient basilica. He was about to step down from the uneven marble foundation and make his way back to the beach when he noticed a wide crack that had newly formed at the base of the final column in the row. He immediately stepped back and surveyed the column to be sure that it wasn't about to topple, but as far as he could discern it appeared to be sound. Moving hesitantly, and constantly glancing up at the solid-looking marble pillar, he edged toward the crack and peered down at it. Of course, it was completely dark within. There was a sudden shake to the ground, and Martin immediately tensed to dash in whatever direction the column was not falling, made easier by his being right at the base—all he would need to do was to jump to the side if he could make out any movement in his direction. Distant cries arose, but the tremor was minor and nothing around him was disturbed. Still curious about the fissure, he brought out his cell phone and activated the flashlight. The ground was suddenly brilliantly illuminated, and the long crack was shown to be a foot wide at one point, jagged along its length. He trained the light down into the dark space. It wasn't empty. At the bottom, what first appeared to be a root was protruding from the dirt, but it was strangely fashioned and straight. He lay down on the adjacent cool pavement stones and reaching into the fissure was just able to grasp the stick with his fingers. He pulled it up and trained his flashlight on the brown, smooth wood. His initial impression had been correct—this wood had been crafted by someone. A gentle spiral had been carved into it, along with occasional figures too faint to be recognized. *What is this? Am I raiding an archeological site?* he wondered as he turned the stick over in his hand. *If it's anything valuable, I'll gladly hand it over to the authorities.* The length was a dark oak color and well-worn, with one end a polished nub. However, the other end was splintered and exposed the paler wood at the center. *This has been broken—probably in the quake,* thought Martin. He laid the stick aside and shown his flashlight into the crevice again. There, near where his first discovery had lain, was a patch of white jutting from the dirt. He again laid down and reached in as far as he could stretch, just catching hold of the jagged end. It took some time, but he worked the other piece out of the oddly loose, sandy soil around it. This part was thicker at the end away from the break and had a carved and well-worn knob. *A staff of some kind,* he thought. *This is the end for gripping, and the other was the tip. It has to be.* Martin took the two pieces and held them side-by-side. They were roughly the same length, and as he rotated them in his hands, he could see that the snapped ends matched at one point and could be joined. He twisted one in his hand and holding both pieces horizontally moved the splintered ends together. There was an immediate brilliant flash of light accompanied by a searing pain in his skull, making Martin idly wonder if someone had hit him on the head with a hammer as his face made contact with the hard stones he'd been standing over the moment before, and he blacked out.

Chapter 8.

HE HAD the odd feeling that he'd been somewhere else, but couldn't conceive of where that previous place might have been. And then a thought came, *How long have I been standing in this same spot anyway?* It seemed that the one memory he'd ever had was of staring out from this windblown bit of beach with scrubby dark plants poking out of the nearby rocks and sand. Gentle, quiet waves lapped at the nearby shore. *And why is it never sunny?* It had forever been this single murky scene and he felt rooted to the wasteland, just as were the juniper-like bushes near him. He'd become one with them. He found himself scanning the empty horizon as though this was his post and his purpose.

Wait, what's that sound? he vaguely wondered. *This is something new.* And he had a hard time processing what the noise meant. It finally registered as the rhythmic cheeping of a bird. Gradually, the scene seemed to be brightening as well. A breeze touched his arm and then what seemed to be fingers were gently gripping him near his elbow. His eyes jerked open and then immediately squeezed shut recoiling from the sudden light. But the nurse noticed this reaction. "Keerios—Meester Ropers?" she asked in a low tone, and then there was another, further off voice, "Dad? Dad, can you hear me?" He knew that voice—he was pretty sure it wasn't from the island and it took several minutes for the identity of the owner to sink in.

"Mandy," cracked Martin's voice as if he hadn't spoken in months. Peering through eyes squeezed nearly shut he said, "What are you doing here?" and after a pause, "Where am I?"

"Oh, Dad!" cried Mandy. "We've been worried sick about you. You've been in a coma since the earthquake, and no one knew how long it would last—thank god, you're finally awake!" The nurse checked his pulse, consulted the beeping monitors, and then said in English, "I go and fetch Doctor." Martin was in a continuing struggle to open his eyes, and yet was oddly still staring out at the same barren shoreline. "How long have I been out?" He was struggling to understand how he could be standing and viewing a beach scene and yet simultaneously see the bright lights of the room as he lay in bed. *Am I really out of a coma?* Martin asked himself with a growing concern.

"You've been out for five days now," said Mandy. "It took them half a day to get word to us and two days for me to make it here, so I've only been at the hospital for a little more than two days."

"What happened?" asked Martin now aware that his cheekbone and eyebrow ached terribly. He tried to reach his left hand up to touch them, but it didn't move at his command, so he lifted his right hand and felt the intravenous drip lines move with his arm as he touched the bandages on his face. "Did I get in a bar fight or something?" His head was throbbing.

"I don't think so," said Mandy. "They found you the morning after the quake lying next to an old Greek column. You apparently weren't hit by anything, but you have a cracked cheekbone and some bumps from where you fell onto the hard-stone slabs. Oh, and a bad concussion, too. Maybe you tripped in the dark?"

"Did I?" asked Martin. He could recall nothing of the specific event and was just now remembering details from the night of the quake.

Slowly opening his eyes, he looked up at Mandy, shut them hard and reopened them, his eyes quickly darting about the room. "What is it, Dad?" asked Mandy in a worried tone. Martin shook his head only to produce a low moan. "Should I fetch the nurse?"

Martin opened just his left eye and could see only a ruffled sea lapping at the edge of a dark landscape. He opened his right to see Mandy in a bright room anxiously peering into his good eye. "Yes, please get her," muttered Martin in a rising state of panic. "Something's wrong," he whispered, as the world spun, and he passed out.

Chapter 9.

AGAIN, HE was part of the dusky landscape on what he somehow knew to be a small island, and he found himself staring out at the placid surface of what now seemed to be a sickly green sea. He was at the water's edge and found that he was holding a crudely carved staff which he tapped several times on the compacted sand. Within moments, half a dozen small specs of light seemed to fly up and hover about at arm's length, as if at attention. He pointed the staff towards the horizon and the points began skimming the water's surface and heading out to sea, slowly gathering speed and pushing up increasingly bigger wavelets, and then waves, as they went.

This scene passed as a dream might and later he became aware that a stiff breeze was blowing in off the water and he was leaning against something to steady himself against the sudden gusts. He looked down at the sturdy staff beside him and then out again over the seascape. Nearer at hand, little flashes of faint light raced here and there amongst the sparse vegetation, seemingly eager to stay close at hand.

Who the hell am I? he thought. And then, just on the heels of that question, *Why would I ask that? Why not 'Where the hell am I?'* However, his brooding thoughts of Toni somehow invaded even this remote island, almost as if they had caused the worsening weather, and he knew exactly who he was—the former husband of Toni Lonzo. Thankfully, he rarely dreamt about his ex anymore, but often thought about her when he was awake, even after two years since the divorce. So why would she be brought to mind now? Was he awake?

His stomach churned just like the waves now hitting the beach. He'd loved her, reviled her, cursed her, reviled himself, cursed himself. And here he was at it again. After twenty-five years together, she'd shattered their marriage in an almost breezy manner, yet at the same time striking coldly to try and grab everything he owned. Almost everything, that is. He'd fought valiantly during the divorce trial, but every blow he'd struck was weaker than the previous one as her accusations piled up into an unassailable wall. By a stroke of luck, he'd escaped with their daughter, Miranda, since Toni's soon-to-be new husband already had two children by a previous marriage and poor Mandy was an outcast to that brood from the start. In a way, this rejection of their daughter had been no surprise to him since Toni had been shocked to be suddenly pregnant in her late thirties and had inwardly resented the girl since the moment she was born anyway.

There's something else I should be worrying about besides this old history... thought Martin. *Ah! I've been lying in a hospital bed...* when he was suddenly awake again, blinking at the bright lights in a white room in need of a repaint. Miraculously, a metal bowl was available right at his side, into which he heaved what little remained in his stomach.

The window near him was open and took away the stink of his sick as a nurse helped clean his face and get him into a more upright position in the squeaky hospital bed. She walked away carrying the bowl, and he was left facing the other window at the end of the corner room crowded with three other beds. Hill in the distance, murky beach scene, hill in the distance, murky beach scene, as he alternately closed first one eye and then the other. Now his battle wasn't panic but more a sense of ill-ease and nausea. The nurse had placed a cool towel on his forehead and another empty bowl beside him just in case his stomach revolted again. The anti-nausea pills he'd swallowed were beginning to take effect, and he lay now with both eyes open—two scenes before him simultaneously.

"Hi, Dad," whispered Mandy as she came quietly into the room with a bunch of white flowers gripped in her hand. "Are you feeling any better this morning?"

"I think so," said Martin, finding himself answering in a hushed tone. "Worried, but not frantic."

"They still don't know what's wrong, and you're scheduled for a doctor's appointment tomorrow. Is your vision getting any better?"

Define better, Martin was about to say in a sarcastic tone. Instead he said, "I'm not sure; my eyes are screwy, but my head is starting to get used to it."

"Well, that's something," said Mandy optimistically. "I talked to the doctor this morning, and he said that after an eye examination, you should be fine to head home."

"Home?" asked Martin, and then with a dawning awareness, "Oh yeah, I guess it would be silly for me to try and keep travelling until I find out what's going on with my vision. Say,

I never had the chance to ask—why did you come to help me out instead of, say, Toni or Frank?"

"Well, Dad, did you really think that Mom would come? Even in an emergency? Frank volunteered, but it was easier for me to come from Missoula than for him to leave Whitefish on a moment's notice. I'd just started my fall semester and my professors said that I could easily make up a week or two of missed classes—all except French—that's a class I can just drop if I can't catch up."

Martin was suddenly overwhelmed by the realization that the only people he currently had in his life on whom he could really rely in a situation like this were his daughter and his best friend, Frank. Somehow, by saying the wrong thing at the wrong time, forgetting to reply to emails, or just by losing interest, getting older for him meant jettisoning more old friends with each passing year. And the divorce hadn't helped on that front in the slightest. As he fought back tears, Mandy said, "Oh, are your eyes acting up again? Should I fetch the nurse?"

"No, honey, they're OK. Just getting used to the light," he lied. "But thank you for leaving everything at the drop of a hat and making the trip over here."

"Who could say 'no' to a trip to Greece?" asked Mandy with a chuckle. And then, "no, really—I had to come." more seriously. She found a glass vase and filled it with water, arranging the flowers into a spray for him and the other three patients to enjoy. "So, can you tell me again what's happening with your vision? What you see?"

Focusing on his eyesight brought a sudden resurgence of panic, but Martin fought it down. "Looking out of my right eye, everything looks normal. I see you, the flowers, the window. When I close my right eye though, all I see is this dreary shoreline with scrub bushes, beach grasses, some dunes, and rocks. I know it's on an island, but I don't know how I know that since I haven't walked around much and have no recollection of what else is nearby. I just saw the waves on the water pick up when I was thinking about your mom." *Or did I do that, because I seem to recall making it happen somehow?* he thought briefly. "Pretty much it's the same monotonous scene."

"You mean it's not just a static image like a painting? It moves?

"Yeah," said Martin. "Now, isn't that odd?" He had a sudden memory, "Say, did you hear if they found a staff or walking stick lying next me when I was discovered that morning? It was old and could be quite valuable. I found it down in a wide, deep crack made by the earthquake."

"I'll go ask," said Mandy, "just a sec." and left the room to find the doctor and attendants who might have been present on the scene. Sometime later she returned. "Nope, I talked to several people from the ER unit, and they all said that they found you with a blanket wrapped around your shoulders, a cell phone and passport, your clothes as expected, and blood on the paving stones next to your head. No one remembered a crack in the rocks, and they were certain that there was nothing else found anywhere close to you."

Martin nodded, but thought to himself, *Although, didn't I just see one in my hand at that gloomy beach? Didn't I use it?*

"I wonder what happened to it, if it was there?" asked his daughter.

"Oh, it was there all right..." answered Martin hesitantly. "At least, I think it was."

"Well, maybe someone smacked you on the head and stole it?" asked Mandy in what was meant as a joke.

Martin shook his head which brought up a mild feeling of nausea. "No, somehow that doesn't seem right. Even though it was dark, I know I was alone at the basilica after the earthquake."

Mandy stared at him for a long moment. "I know, Dad, but think about it. You hit your head enough to concuss you, and when you were found there was no opening in the ground? No staff?"

"Yeah," said Martin as he closed his eyes. "Maybe my concussion was worse than I thought."

Chapter 10.

"*I SEE* a coastline. Rocks, sand, some dunes, some bushes, and the ocean," replied Martin with his right eye closed.

"You don't see what I'm holding in my hand?" asked Dr. Mytro.

"What hand?" asked Martin.

Dr. Mytro was silent and then said. "Now, close the left eye, and tell me what you see."

The doctor was holding a white and red Greek-English dictionary which Martin proceeded to describe in detail.

"Well, it's odd that your left eye is physically responding to stimuli—I flash a light on it, and the pupil contracts. I act like I'm going to touch it and the lids close. I don't think that your retina has become wholly or partially detached, but it's more than likely that the optic nerve was damaged in your fall. It could also be that some undetected swelling is impinging on the nerve, but we don't have the resources here to investigate. I recommend that you have extensive testing done as soon as you get home."

"Will flying be dangerous?" asked Martin.

"No, with modern pressurized cabins, I can't see that any further damage could be done," replied Dr. Mytro.

"And what about this scene of a barren beach that I keep seeing?" asked Martin.

"Well, admittedly, that has me puzzled as well, but I suspect that the brain is retaining an image that has been "burned" onto the back of your retina or is being sustained where the optic nerve joins the brain. To tell you the truth, I don't know." He shifted his chair over to his computer and after typing and scanning some pages he said, "There is palinopsia, or cases of a persistent hallucination that can result in an image like that, and it is possible that a head trauma could be the cause. A diagnosis by an eye or brain specialist would definitely be in order for you. I'll give you copies of all of my notes to take back to the U.S. with you, and they may help in reaching an informed opinion."

Mandy assisted Martin in the check-out procedure at the crowded hospital front desk near the waiting area that was still packed with those injured in the earthquake. As they stepped outside, Martin was surprised to find that the hospital was in Kos town. *Of course, Kefalos would be too small for a hospital,* he said to himself. A white taxi took them to the terminal where they were to catch the ferry to the mainland. A flight out would have been quicker, but the small airport was closed due to runway damage. As they waited for the vessel, now visible in the distance, Martin turned to his daughter and said, "I thought we were in Kefalos this whole time and I wanted to go down to the beach before we left."

"No, Dad, this is Kos town," said Mandy. "Why did you want to go to the beach? Just for old-time's sake?"

"I wanted to look for that staff," said Martin. "I found it just before I cracked my head."

"I didn't see it," said Mandy.

"What?" asked Martin. "You were there?"

"Yeah, Dad," answered Mandy. "After you mentioned finding it, I was curious and took the bus to Kefalos when the ER folks said that they hadn't seen anything. You were conked out from the drugs all of that afternoon, anyway. The police weren't allowing traffic into the center of town, but luckily the bus let people down near the basilica. I walked all around the ruins, and it was obvious where your accident happened. The stones were pretty clean from where they'd tried to scrub away the blood, except you could see where it seeped into the soil. At the base of the last column, right?" Martin nodded, and she continued. "There was no sign of a staff anywhere nearby, and, to tell you the truth, I couldn't find a crack either. However, there was a column that had toppled during the quake and was broken over a stone bench."

Martin shook his head, staring at the ground. "But I could have sworn…"

"On the bright side, I had a great swim at the beach, and I can totally see what drew you to that town," said Mandy with a smile.

A short time later, Martin sat on a bench in the shady side of the boat while Mandy went to the front of the ferry to watch them cast off and begin the ten-hour trip to the mainland. *I'm heading home now, which is in the opposite direction I'd intended,* he thought as memories flooded back to the start of their trip all those years ago in Istanbul which he'd recorded in his first book. *That journey hadn't begun well ei-*

ther, but had endured, this trip has had a lousy start, too, but it's over now, he lamented.

Ryan had finally arrived in Istanbul earlier that day and stood next to me in shock—as white as Jack who lay on the bed across from us. Without a word we made our way downstairs, into the remaining daylight and started toward the hostel where I was staying. Without a word he gave me a look that said, "What the fuck was that?" and which also contained an element of "You idiot!" This was not a good introduction to the Gateway to the East for Ryan.

We'd made our separate ways to Istanbul where we'd agreed to meet before we headed to India. I'd started out with another friend from Walla Walla, Mark, but he'd contracted hepatitis—probably in Morocco—and sadly, too ill and jaundiced to continue, had flown home from Switzerland. Corresponding with Ryan, we'd agreed that I'd hang out in Turkey and await his arrival, giving me time to explore the beautiful beaches of Izmir, the Roman ruins of Ephesus, the passages and rooms carved into the natural spires of Goreme, and the cascading azure pools held by white limestone in Pamukkale. I'd also been welcomed into the homes of families for tea, a meal presented on a gorgeous carpet, or for a hooka smoke which I usually declined. Awaiting exploration in crowded Istanbul were the teeming covered markets, the musty bookstores of the old sections of the city, and the quiet cool calm interior of Hagia Sophia with its Weeping Column. Then to escape the city clamor, there was the occasional warm *evening trip on the Bosphorus, taking a water-taxi ride to stop at a shore-side restaurant for dinner.*

I'd finally met Ryan at a café near the central square where the Magic Bus he'd taken from Amsterdam let down its long-haired passengers. Backpack still on Ryan's shoulders and him wiped out from the journey, we'd run into Jack on one of the busy nearby market streets as we headed to the hostel. "Hey, Martin," he'd said in his strong somewhere-in-London accent, "why don't you guys pop up to my room for a taste?" I'd looked at Ryan and knowing that both of us would accept a hit of pot if we were asked had said "Sure, why not?" I'd first run into Jack at a hotel in Athens and we'd crossed paths a few times in Istanbul. Amiable, wiry, and hyper he always kept up an entertaining monologue of tales.

A few blocks along and following Jack's banter, we turned into a hotel with a frontage on the square across from the domed Hagia Sophia. We climbed the narrow stairs to the just-as-narrow hallway and entered Jack's small room. We then learned what a taste meant to Jack. In seconds, he had a spoon held over a lighter and soon had bubbling liquid heroin dancing before him. Both Ryan and I immediately declined, and with an unfazed shrug of his shoulders, Jack wrapped a belt around his bicep and tugged hard. The liquid was into a syringe and then into his arm in what was probably an eter-nity to him and a matter of moments to us as we stepped back, wide-eyed and as far away as possible in the cramped room. Releasing the belt, Jack was gone after quickly puking in the corner of the room. We, too, were gone in a flash.

Gone, gone, gone to the long gone
Gone to the far-away sea oh
Gone in a rush
Gone with a push
Gone to the long away me oh
Into the land of the far-off sand
Into the temple of peace

Out within reach of the Hagia Sophia
Out of touch with the beach oh
Out with a sigh
Out with a lie
Out with it all within reach oh
Into the land of the far-off sand
Into the temple of peace

A piercing pang in Martin's head brought him back from his reminiscences, and he tried to focus on the deck of the ferry with one eye in his oddly separated visions. His life at one time had been all about surprises, detours, meeting the unexpected, and those were what made him feel alive, even if they weren't all pleasant. *I'm not so sure I like this unexpected surprise, though,* he thought, hoping it was just temporary but harboring a deep-seated fear that it wasn't.

Chapter 11.

MARTIN BLINKED a few times and sat back. He'd just realized that he'd spent an entire half-hour without consciously noticing the beach scene that played continuously to his left eye. He'd been watching an in-flight action movie and had been so absorbed during part of it that he'd paid no attention to anything but the film. He paused the movie and peered out the window at the clouds slowly passing far below. Now that he thought about it, he hadn't noticed his impairment during the hubbub at the airport, passing through security, and searching for their departure gate either. Maybe it was the wine service, but he was relaxing some. *Perhaps this will be something like tinnitus where you eventually don't notice the constant ringing in your ears unless you pay specific attention to it,* he hoped.

Turning to his left—far to his left so that his right eye could see in that direction—he found Mandy napping next to him in an obviously uncomfortable position. There were two odd things he'd noticed in his vision lately. The first was that his depth perception seemed unaffected by a blinded left eye. He knew that normally when one eye is closed, it's difficult for the remaining single eye to judge distances, and so picking up a dime on the first try, for instance, can be a challenge. He'd experienced no problems in this regard and was relieved at how well he'd adapted to his new monovision.

The second thing he'd noticed was stranger. He was convinced he was beginning to see Mandy with his left eye as well. Whenever she was in his normal field of vision, he saw a faintly glowing shape among the juniper bushes. At first, he hadn't made the connection and thought that a white bird or something was fuzzily stalking in the background dunes. Now he noticed that the shape corresponded to Mandy's physical location and that it was a dim, roughly human form he was perceiving. No other person elicited this response in his affected eye. Facing forward again, he noticed a faint glow coming from the left as if the sun were just beginning to lighten the sky, and so he knew Mandy was there. He'd tried the same thing when she'd gotten up to visit the bathroom and there was only the monotonous shadowy landscape when she was away.

Mandy stirred and then stretched. "How are you doing?" she asked, lightly touching his arm.

"Fine, hon. In fact, I just noticed that I had a long spell watching this movie when I was completely unaware of my screwy eye."

"Hey, that's good—maybe we'll make a TV watcher out of you yet," Mandy said, grinning and giving him a poke. Martin smiled knowing that Mandy knew he would never turn to the TV if his life depended on it. And then his face fell. He was watching this movie because he found reading was difficult and tiring with a single eye. "Oh, god, what if it does make me watch TV?"

Seeing his sudden concern, Mandy said, "No need to worry about that just yet."

"So, tell me how your college semester is going," said Martin to change the subject.

"Great, so far," said Mandy. "I like all of my courses, especially ecology. We've already made two trips to the Lolo National Forest to study different ecosystems there, and my professor wants to fit in some trips to Glacier National Park before the snow starts to fly. Then it'll be only book work in the classroom. I really like Missoula and I've made some friends there. Of course, Evelyn, Jason, and Brook from high school are all there, but we're all so busy that I rarely see them."

"Any special friends yet?" asked Martin. "Cute guys?"

"Seriously?" asked Mandy in exasperation. "No need to rush things," and she gave him another poke, "or pry!"

Martin was glad that some of the 'gentlemen' who'd sought Mandy's attentions in high school were rebuffed, although there had been some that he'd really liked who'd met the same fate. *Probably just like any single father,* thought Martin. *Worried if any boy gets too close, but also wanting your daughter to find a real connection with someone special.*

The conversation ended with the arrival of lunch, which he ate with no problems.

Once the trays were collected, he'd pulled out his laptop to try and record some of his new experiences with his transformed vision, but found the exercise too frustrating. His fingers knew where the keys were, however, looking at and reading the display was wearing on his good eye. Reaching up to close the blank screen after shutting down, he caught his re-flection staring back at him. *God, what a sight,* he thought—deepening wrinkles, bristly eyebrows and whiskers, hair thin to the point of baldness, and now a couple of steri-strips and some impressive bruising. Focusing for some reason on the hair in his image, another page from the past came back to him. *Hair used to be such a big deal in those days!* he reflected.

We were part of the small but constant stream of travelers hop-scotching our way overland from Europe to India, and in Afghanistan we'd run into several of the guys who'd been through the Iran/Afghan border—heads shaved before they were allowed in. There were also those with cuts and nicks where they'd been grabbed off the street and forcibly shorn once in the country. Ryan had trimmed his hair before we went through customs, just to be safe, and I'd tied my thinner hair into a ponytail and stuffed it down the back of my shirt. On top of the expressed concern for our personal hygiene, there were rumors of stolen money and confiscated passports by the military police, too. Patrols were all over Kabul, and it was the first city we'd been in that had such a strong military presence.

Early one evening, Ryan and I were walking across a wide bridge crossing the Kabul River to watch the water at sun-set when a military truck full of soldiers slowed as it passed us and then stopped up ahead. Uh oh, *I thought, and Ryan looked at me as we decided at once to turn around and head in the opposite direction. A jeep with two officers that had been following the transport stopped just past us and both men started shouting to us in Pashto as they climbed out of the vehicle. We turned to face them, but kept moving backwards slowly as the two approached, one unslinging his rifle. We were about to turn and walk quickly away, but both of us somehow sensed that putting our backs to them would be absolutely the wrong thing to do.*

When they reached us, the message in pantomime was clear—one hand pulling upwards and the other making snipping motions with finger scissors. We feigned ignorance and acted like we had no clue what they were talking about, all the while pointing in the direction of our hotel and backing in that direction. "No, no, no, no," *was all that was screaming in my head, but we kept our voices low and tried to keep smiling as if it was all a simple misunderstanding. At one point the officer with the gun made a grab for Ryan's elbow, but luckily missed the mark. Somehow, dancing backwards and avoiding attempted grabs, we had backed 50 yards from their jeep and were nearing the end of the bridge with its cross streets. The one in charge pointed down a little side street at the junction and they began to try and herd us in that direction. By now we were backing, bowing, and scraping in a not-so-subtle retreat away from the bridge and that alley. In some manner that is still a mystery to me, we'd become as elusive as smoke and vapors and seeing how far they were now from their jeep, the two officers abandoned the effort and headed back up the bridge. We went to the nearest side-street and broke into a run as soon as we were out of sight, all the while looking over our shoulders to make sure that they didn't follow. Luckily for us, they didn't.*

Martin ran one hand over his head as he folded the computer closed with the other. *Wouldn't bother me a bit now if my head was shaved,* he thought, *but it sure mattered then.* After a pause, he continued, *But now everything's flipped, isn't it? The Taliban and Muslim fundamentalists seem to require beards and long hair, don't they? What a funny world.*

Chapter 12.

THEY'D JUST collected their luggage at the SeaTac airport
and were making their way to the arriving passenger pick-up
area when Martin stopped and bent over to adjust his carryon. Painfully aware of his left eye, he saw the subtle glow of
Mandy, again to his left when suddenly there was a strange
object at the top of his vision. Startled he stood up as a shout
of "Hi, Martin and Mandy!" rang out from the exit doors.
Leira was coming towards them, and an indistinct iridescent
form resembling a dragonfly hovered in the corresponding
spot in his left eye. He stood there blinking at her dumbly,
mouth open.

"Hi, Leira!" said Mandy, and then throwing an amazed
look at her father, "Dad, what's wrong with you? Aren't you
going to say hi?" And then after a pause, "Dad, are you all
right?"

It was as if his brain circuits had momentarily been shut
down. He just couldn't reconcile the new image he was seeing
with the physical body coming toward him across the lobby.
The fluttering shape was getting closer—a subtly glowing being of indistinct form. He closed both eyes and slowly shook
his head, but the scene in his left eye didn't alter.

"Martin?" asked Leira with concern as she neared them.
"Should we find a place to sit down?"

Opening his eyes again and concentrating on his right one, he saw the worried expressions of the two women standing before him. "No, no!" he said in a dismissive tone. "It must just be jet lag. Or the flu," he joked lightly. "Hi Leira," giving her a quick hug. "Thanks so much for picking us up on such short notice."

"Definitely, Martin," said Leira, the look of concern not leaving her face. She took control of his carryon bag. "That's a nasty bump on your head—I had no idea you'd knocked it so badly. I've been so worried about you since Mandy called from Athens saying that you were heading home. She told me all that she knew about your vision problems, and I've made an appointment with an eye specialist at Virginia Mason for tomorrow, if that's OK, but I haven't managed to line any-thing else up yet."

"Wow—that's a surprise—thank you so much for arrang-ing an appointment," said Martin.

"And before you even try to wiggle out of it, I absolute-ly insist that you both stay with me in my townhouse while you're here. There's no need to waste money on a hotel when I have plenty of space in my place. I've already arranged the extra room for you, so you can't say no."

It was dark and rainy as Leira drove them toward the townhouse she was renting near Madison Park in downtown Seattle. Leira and Mandy kept up a lively conversation in the front seats, while Martin feigned dozing in the back. Eyes closed, he was mesmerized by the two images before him, floating above the scrub bushes on the desolate beach. Mandy was now a subtle yet distinct person of impeccable beauty, and Leira resembled a glowing nymph that he could swear had gossamer wings gently flapping in the background. *No, it must be the motion of the car,* he thought drowsily. The lilt of their voices and the buzz of the tires on the wet pavement really did have him soon asleep.

Chapter 13.

H_E **AWOKE** the next morning to the smell of coffee and the sound of laughter coming from the kitchen and dining room area. Martin threw on his clothes from the day before and stumbled out to a rare sunny autumn morning in Seattle. Mandy and Leira were seated at the built-in dining table chatting and joking like old friends even though they had only met a few times previously when Leira had visited their house in Whitefish, Montana to discuss Martin's writing projects and Mandy had been much younger.

"Hello, sleepyhead," said Mandy. "I was going to give you fifteen more minutes before I roused you. You have an appointment we need to get you to in one hour."

"Did you sleep well? Do you want some coffee?" asked Leira.

"Love some," replied Martin as he accepted the cup and stood in the path of sunlight streaming in through the window. "The bed was comfortable, and I slept like the dead." He blew across the surface and then took a sip of the steaming brew, closing his eyes into the sunshine. His right eye saw bright red from the intense light, but in his left remained the semi-dark scene. Keeping his eyes closed and turning toward the dining table he smiled as he saw the two beings, emanating warm light, subtly brighten the gloomy vista. His smile faded as he faced the window again. *I might be getting used to this, but I don't know what I'll do if the doctors can't find out what's wrong and fix it,* he lamented.

As if intuiting his thoughts, Mandy said, "It's OK, Dad, they'll find out what's going on."

He turned to her and joined them at the table for some breakfast. "Thanks, honey, I sure hope so."

"Oh, by the way," said Mandy, "I talked with Mom this morning and let her know how you were doing."

Did she care? he wanted to ask, but instead said, "I'd be surprised if she showed much concern."

"Well, she did ask some questions, but you know Mom. Not exactly into what's happening in our lives." Martin nodded and took a bite of bagel and another sip of coffee. "She also said to tell you two things. First, she said she's heard through the grapevine that Caleb and some of his friends have taken over your old writing studio as a hangout and they might be doing drugs up there. She also said that her lawyers are going to get in touch with you and for you to expect a call from them."

"Fantastic," said Martin. "Caleb had better not destroy the place." Without finishing his bagel, Martin excused himself and went into the bathroom to take a shower before his appointment.

He let the water flow over his head and then positioned himself so that the stream hit him just at the base of the neck and top of his shoulders. He relaxed into the spray and rotated his head, consciously trying to ease his tenseness. His relationship with Caleb was just like a torn muscle—it would be near healing and then re-injure from use. His neighbor Al's son and now his ex-wife Toni's stepson, Caleb had never hit it off with Martin, even when he was young. The kid hated him and eventually the feeling had become mutual. Caleb had lately entered a punk, or gang, or goth phase, or whatever being tough, brooding, and aggressive was called now, and hung out with what seemed like some pretty shady friends, especially over the past year. He'd slipped out of most charges of robbery and assault, all based on the status of his father, and as far as Martin knew he might even have skipped out on his last year of high school. Caleb and Mandy were the same age and, even though neighbors, they had grown up worlds apart.

Martin had built his studio by himself down on a corner of his sloping property where a small rock outcrop jutted out of the steep hillside overlooking Whitefish Lake. At first, when he was married, it had become his sanctuary and a calming place into which he could retreat and write. As his marriage and writing had both begun to falter, he'd used it as a retreat to go and drink quietly alone. Now, he rarely ventured down there, although he still cherished the spot. *If that kid destroys it, I'll destroy that kid,* he thought—or at least in his fantasies he would. Caleb had no respect for property and would take things from the neighbors, ride off on one of their ATV's, and one time had taken a joyride in Martin's car. Luckily the only damage done had been a pile of beer cans in the back seat. He hated the possibility of confronting the young man and kicking him out of the studio, but also wanted to ensure that his shack survived the onslaught that was Caleb.

Turning his thoughts to relaxation again, he suddenly remembered that Toni had told Mandy that her lawyers would call. *What now?* he wondered as he turned off the shower, his neck having suddenly seized-up.

Chapter 14.

"I CAN'T believe that there's absolutely nothing wrong with my eyes," a bewildered Martin was telling Leira, "especially since I can't see anything out of one of them." He then deftly dabbed a piece of artisan bread in the balsamic vinegar/olive oil mixture set out on the table between them and took a bite. "Did you see that? I didn't miss the oil and didn't miss my mouth. It's like I have two useful eyes, only I've apparently lost awareness of one of them—that's exactly what Dr. Springer said anyway."

"Can you describe what you're seeing out of that left eye again?" asked Leira. She'd driven them to a nice Italian restaurant on Eastlake Ave. and they were enjoying an early dinner. Mandy had several friends in town and had zipped off to join them for the evening, mentioning a friend who was DJing at a local club.

"I'm actually getting kind of sick of it," admitted Martin. "For some reason, the landscape's not very well lit, like there's a building storm with gathering clouds in the distance, but it's located on what I can only assume is a Mediterranean island with rocks, sand, and some scrubby bushes because it looks exactly like parts of Rhodes or Kos. The spot I stand on is near the shore, and I can see small waves rolling in and hitting the beach. I find myself constantly surveying the horizon for god knows what reason. One time I changed to a position nearer the water, and the waves and wind kicked up." He was looking at her and saw the softly shimmering glow of her form in front of him as well, but for some reason, was reluctant to reveal that. "Otherwise, nothing much else to tell."

"So, the scene does change, and things are moving?" asked Leira. "Isn't that weird? Is there anything else?"

"Well, there are some sparks of light that seem to flit about now and then, like fireflies, or scintillas from a fire. Come to think of it, they're almost more than that—more like little fairies, I'd say."

"Even stranger. So, can you see yourself when you look around, or is it only facing forward like a movie camera or one of those video games?" asked Leira.

"I hadn't thought about it in that way before," said Martin. He closed his eyes and tried with some effort to break away from staring out to sea and to look down at his own body, but for some reason couldn't manage it. He gave up and looked again at Leira, shaking his head. "But, now that I think about it, I do remember seeing myself once, while that storm was blowing in. As I recall, I had to steady myself, and I could see my arm—holding on to a stout stick for support..." His eyes opened wider with a sudden realization. Hesitating for a moment, he blurted out, "Leira, I think it was the walking-stick from the ruins!"

"What walking-stick from the ruins?" asked a perplexed Leira. Martin told her what he could recall about the night of the earthquake, the discovery of the broken halves at the bottom of the fissure, uniting them, the blinding light, and his blacking out afterwards. "And now I'm positive that the staff that I was holding during the storm is somehow the same one I found that night in Kefalos. I think it's an old walking staff that somehow ended up in the vision I keep seeing."

"But where is the real one now?" asked Leira. "Did you bring it back home with you?"

"No one has seen it," replied Martin. "Mandy even went back to the spot and there was no sign of it."

"That's the oddest thing I've heard in a long time," said Leira with a questioning look. "In fact, it sounds exactly like the type of story I have submitted to me on a daily basis by aspiring fantasy writers." She took a bite of antipasto and fiddled with her wine glass. "But doesn't the whole scene sound familiar to you?"

Martin stared at her blankly.

"Come on, Martin—deserted island, guy with a staff staring out to sea? Elizabethan play?"

"You mean *The Tempest*?" asked Martin. "You're saying I'm not just having any old hallucination; I'm having a Shakespearean one? Why would that be, for heaven's sakes?"

Leira shook her head while Martin took a sip of wine, and then stared into his glass lost in thought for several minutes. She let him have his space and took the opportunity to check her phone for messages. He then leaned back in his chair and said, "But you know, the psychology of the thing actually makes some sense, doesn't it? It happened when I was on a Greek island, I coincidentally have a daughter named

Miranda, and I've been feeling sort of at-sea and isolated for the past year or so... But if that's the case, and this is from *The Tempest*, where the hell is everybody? Where's Miranda? Where are the shipwreck survivors? Where's that sprite—that—what's his name?"

"Ariel?" she asked. "Don't ask me—it's your hallucination," she continued with a smile. She took up an olive and then asked curiously. "So maybe it's not psychological after all, and just physical? What exactly did the ophthalmologist say?"

"He said that both of my eyes are perfectly fine. They both react to stimulation identically and both optic nerves are healthy and completely intact. He said that Dr. Mytro was correct in suspecting the optic nerve, but that the connections at the eye and at the brain are both normal. He now suspects that it's possibly an issue with my brain, and that perhaps the fall and concussion affected how it's perceiving what the eyes are actually seeing. You know, I have a headache just thinking about it," and he rubbed his temple as the low-level pain lingering constantly in the background became increasingly apparent. "He was concerned enough that he's made me an appointment with a neurologist and has me scheduled for an MRI tomorrow morning on top of that." He picked up the glass of Chianti and clicked it against Leira's once she had lifted hers. "Here's to tomorrow."

"To tomorrow," said Leira in a worried tone and with concern knitting her eyebrows.

Was it a trick of my vision? thought Martin, *or did her glow just get a bit brighter?* then shaking his head wearily—it was too much input, and he was tired of concentrating on his eyes.

The waiter brought a polenta and pesto appetizer they'd ordered, and they spent some time in silence as they tasted this recommended dish. "Martin," Leira said cautiously. "I don't want to be insensitive to the trauma you've been through, so tell me if this isn't the right time. But, do you mind if we talk about what we discussed on the phone when you were in Greece?"

And now his eyes, or his left eye anyway, reacted again and her glow suddenly seemed diminished. He looked at her with a slight smile and said, "No, this is as good a time as any, Leira."

"Are you sure?" she asked. "I just want to be square with you and not drop any sudden bombshells." He nodded and so she continued. "It's not you, and you know I love your work," she said.

But you need to keep moving, he thought, *I'm holding you back.*

"In fact, I've also explained my situation to two of my other long-term clients. It's a combination of my getting stretched too thin and feeling the need to move in a different direction at the same time." He nodded as a sign for her to continue. "I've been concentrating on a certain genre with the authors I represent, and I suddenly realized that this is limiting the types of publishers that I'm able to pitch to. A once-open field has become a small intimate group of interested companies, and because of the market, they're getting very, very picky about who they'll put into print."

The dinner arrived, and Leira was able to maintain the flow of her explanation through the service. "My clients are also my friends," and she looked at him with a smile. "You know that! But I feel like I'm letting some of you down on the 'work and results' side of the equation."

"Now wait, Leira, I don't feel like you've let me down—in fact, you've always managed to find at least some kind of outlet for my works. At least most of them." *And please don't do this,* Martin added to himself.

"But, see? You make a perfect example, Martin. They have you locked into a specific genre, and we ended up having to go with a small boutique press to publish your poems because we tried our already established pool of publishers in literary fiction—and their interest could hardly be called rousingly enthusiastic. And then we had to go with the Montana Historical Society to get your piece about Bill published."

"At least we got them both out there," said Martin with a sigh. "But I think I see where you're going with this." *Leaving,* thought Martin.

"Yes," she replied. "I think if I break out of the mold I'm in, I could be a better literary agent for my clients. Say I find someone who writes a how-to book, and then a thriller, and then a historical novel. I need to be able to follow them through their careers and have the access points established to plug them in wherever they best fit. It's the authors who can change in their interests over time, and I need to be able to keep up with them. I need to give them the freedom of expression that they deserve. Instead of 'Go to Leira, she represents Literary Fiction,' period."

"You may be right, Leira." said Martin. "Who knows what any one author is going to come up with?" He took a big gulp of his wine and immediately realized that he didn't want to let his drinking get out of hand tonight. But he also knew that his lack of success was what was driving her decision, and that made him want a drink. "You said that you'd wait and see how my next project comes out before you, um, let me go, though?"

"Yes, of course, Martin, I was just trying to give you a heads-up about where things might be going for me in the future." She gave him a smile. "And we'll always be friends."

"To staying friends then," said Martin raising his glass.

"Agreed," she said as they toasted again.

Chapter 15.

DR. POWELL greeted Martin in his office after the expedited MRI scan results came back late that afternoon. He sat facing Martin and had two computer screens arranged on his desk—one oriented so that Martin could see it and the other screen facing himself, the one which he was currently examining.

"Mr. Ropers, we've just met this morning, but I already have to say that yours is one of the more intriguing cases in which I've been involved for quite some time," turning to Martin as he spoke. "It's obvious to me that you've had normal right-brain functioning prior to the concussion and that these recent hallucinations have come as a surprise. The MRI has revealed some significant abnormalities that must have coincided with the accident, otherwise, if you've had this severing since birth, for instance, your physical brain would have adapted to the circumstances and created new connections."

"Abnormalities?" asked Martin, grasping for comprehension. "Severing?"

"Yes," said Dr. Powell. "A section of your brain appears to have been damaged at some point—in effect severing some of the connections."

A stupefied Martin stared at Dr. Powell.

"OK," said the doctor. "It may seem strange that I'm not overly concerned about this, but to put it very crudely, and I can't guess at the mechanics of the damage, but it looks like something has fried part of your brain."

Martin immediately thought of the flash of light he'd seen when he'd been knocked out in Kefalos. He gaped in alarm as Dr. Powell raised two hands in a calming gesture.

"No need to worry," he said immediately. "The damage was in an area that you may not necessarily need."

"Not necessarily need?" asked Martin in a high-pitched voice. "I need all of my brain!" After a pause, "Don't I?"

"Let me explain, and I'm sorry if my little joke and choice of words has caused you concern," said Dr. Powell. "Here, we can look at the results of your MRI scan together on the displays." And he activated the screen in front of Martin. "These are 'slices' of your brain taken by magnetic resonance imaging. Here, you can see that these big circles I'm highlighting are the left and right lobes of the brain and they sit right next to each other. These are all healthy images on both sides, and so there is absolutely no problem with either hemisphere of your brain. Quite good in fact." Martin stared at the screen as the images flashed by and to him it looked like other images of brains he had seen in magazine articles. "But the problem is here," continued Dr. Powell as he pointed to the scan images, "as we reach the lower sections of the brain."

Martin saw the area Dr. Powell was now highlighting. In the center of the picture was a darkened, and to him unnatural-looking area. Dr. Powell opened a book in front of Martin and pointed. "This is a picture of a normal corpus callosum. It's like a fibrous tuber, sort of like a sweet potato that is nestled in the low center of the brain. It's actually a dense collection of nerves that connect the left brain to the right brain. The left brain controls the right side of the body and is considered to be the center of language and logic. The right brain then controls the left side of the body, and it is where much of the intuition and creativity come from—or at least that's the current thinking. In humans, the corpus callosum unites the two so that the right hand knows what the left hand is doing, so to speak."

"Now look again at the computer screen," he said leaning over to Martin's monitor and pointing. "This is your MRI from this morning, and I have to say that the corpus callosum is missing. Or rather, it has collapsed into this dense area that looks sort of like a dried-up stick."

Martin looked up at him with a stunned expression, and Dr. Powell again made a calming gesture. "We wouldn't know for certain unless I cut into it and took a look." At Martin's wider eyes, he said immediately, "Of which, of course, there is no need."

"Sooo, what?" asked an alarmed Martin. "I'm becoming an idiot? An invalid? Is something eating my brain from the inside out?"

"Hmm, hadn't thought of that," said Dr. Powell with a grin. "No, in all seriousness, there appears to be no pathogen, nor risk of further damage. I've consulted with several colleagues and I must say that you've been the subject of some very animated discussions. You might even end up in print at some point." Martin was about to say that he already was in print, but let the doctor continue. "We're all in agreement that if you did have a normal brain before the episode in Greece, something we've never seen previously has happened during or after your fall."

"Well, I'm pretty sure I had at least an adequate brain before," said Martin. "But what do I have now? How worried should I be?" He raised both hands, and one by one touched his opposing fingertips together. "And my hands still work together, just like before. My right hand knows what my left hand is doing."

"As I said, I'm certain that you were normal before the accident, otherwise your pathology would have shown symptoms throughout your life. And, no—you won't need to worry, although you'll need to adapt. You see, there are people who go through what you've gone through nearly every day."

"Are you kidding?" asked Martin in amazement.

"No, not at all," was the reply. "As it happens, a treatment for individuals with severe epilepsy is to undergo this exact same procedure—dividing the corpus callosum so that the left brain can't communicate with the right. This is the area where all the turmoil for them occurs, and for most patients there are no differences or symptoms after the corpus callosum has been severed, other than a cessation of seizures, that is. How your separation happened is an absolute mystery—it's almost as if it melted, like Styrofoam in a fire, but the results are the same. And, I have to say that I really can't understand how a simple concussion could have caused this. Your brain is functioning normally, but we'll need to see how it adapts to the inability of the two hemispheres to communicate with each other."

Martin sat back in alarm. "This must be what's made my left eye wonky? I can't see a thing out of it." He paused as the enormity of all that he'd heard sank in. "What, exactly, does that mean for me? Will I still be able to function? Lead a normal life?"

"Let me show you something," said Dr. Powell, grabbing a firm foam ball from his desk. "Let's play catch," and he tossed the ball to Martin. They exchanged the ball across the desk a few times and then he said, "Close your left eye, and try it—catching with your right hand." This was more difficult for Martin even though this was his good eye, since his depth perception was off. He missed once but managed otherwise. "Now try it with your right eye closed and catch with your left hand."

"Are you joking?" asked Martin. "As I said—I can't see a thing out of my left eye."

"Just close your right eye and give it a shot," said Dr. Powell. "Come on, it's just a foam ball." Martin hesitated and then closed his right eye and waited. "Open both eyes," said the doctor.

Martin looked at his outstretched left hand and was amazed to see the ball in it. "You see?" asked Dr. Powell. "Everything is working perfectly, only the logical part of yourself isn't able to tell you about it."

"I don't get it," replied Martin.

"I'll show you," said Dr. Powell. "Close your left eye again." He looked around his desk and held up a pen. "What do you see with your right eye?"

"A blue pen," said Martin.

"Now close your right eye and tell me what I'm holding."

"I can't see anything but the dunes and beach I told you about before," said Martin.

"Well, I'm going to put this thing in your left hand and have you use it as it is intended to be used, but I'm not going to tell you what it is."

"OK," said Martin. After a moment a baseball cap was on his head. He took it off with his right hand and stared at it with both eyes open.

"You see, your left eye knows what things are and how to use them. It saw the cap and the left hand put it on your head. It can see them, but you aren't consciously aware that it can. In the very few cases that are even remotely similar to this, the patients can see out of both eyes, but when viewing an object, say a pear, with the left eye alone, the subject might say 'I'm holding nothing in my left hand' and yet at a deeper level he knows what it is. The reason is the connection with the part of the brain that can name things is cut off. So, the person is holding a pear, and knows what it is, but can't put a name to it, so in a way for him it doesn't exist. Your condition is very similar except for the fact that you have a consistent hallucination occurring on the left side. If you'd had damage to the optic nerve, or to the actual right lobe of the brain, I might have some theories about this, but since you don't, to tell you the truth, I'm stumped. And so are the others I've consulted. You, Mr. Ropers, are currently a mystery to modern medicine."

"An honor," sighed Martin. "So, where does this leave me?" he asked.

"Well, I'd love to run some more tests without being too invasive, if you'd be amenable to that, but otherwise I would have to advise counseling and possibly some therapy to help you adapt."

"And what about the headaches?" asked Martin.

"Ah, yes, I would think that would be expected—not really from that damage itself, but from the changes in pressure in the brain that would be caused by the sudden shrinking of the corpus collosum. I can prescribe medications to help with the pain, and I would think that the pressure will normalize over time, and the pain should subside. Those tests I'm recommending might tell us more, too."

"I guess I could stand a few more tests," said Martin, "and I'll need to think about where to go from here. This will take a while to process."

"For all of us, I'm sure," said Dr. Powell. "With your permission, I'd like to image your brain using a functioning MRI, or fMRI, that can see your neural activity in real time to start off with and see what parts of your brain are lit up by the hallucinations."

"As long as it's fairly quick and non-invasive," said Martin. "I don't want to stay overly long in Seattle."

Martin was about to get up, but felt compelled to say, "I didn't want to mention this before because it's so weird, but since it's part of my 'hallucination,' I feel I ought to tell you about it. I know it's strange, but I think I can see some people with my left eye."

"Really?" asked Dr. Powell suddenly very interested. "Are you saying that you can see some things out of that eye? And you're aware of it—you can recognize who it is? Put a name to them?"

"Well, no, I can't really see them as people. At first, they were like indistinct glows, but now I actually see both my daughter and my literary agent as sort of luminous bodies."

"What about me, or anyone else? Can you see me now if you close your right eye?"

Martin tried and shook his head. "Nope, so far no one else registers. What do you think is going on?"

"I have absolutely no idea," the doctor replied, "but this is certainly a twist." Then mainly to himself he said, "So, it's not a full-blown hallucination." He considered this for a moment. "We don't know the true extent of damage to your corpus callosum, but I suppose there could still be vestigial connections that remain intact. That said, consistently seeing only two people out of all of those you've encountered seems very strange to me." He paused, typing some notes into the computer. "Oh, I forgot to ask if you can see yourself with your left eye."

Martin shook his head, "No, only one time when a storm blew in, and then it was only my left arm," and he proceeded to tell the doctor about that episode, without mentioning the physical staff he had found and joined together in Kefalos.

"My guess is that we have some mix of a psychological effect—how you're interpreting what you see, and the impacts of the physical damage you've suffered, going on here," said Dr. Powell finally. "And I'd love to study the heck out of you, but realize that you have a life to live as well. Any chance we can we set up some tests besides the imaging tomorrow?"

"I suppose so, but I'm keener on getting some rest and trying to normalize at this point," said Martin.

Dr. Powell nodded. "I don't see any chances of this advancing, so I suppose there is no need to rush. How about if we make an appointment for you to come back to Seattle in say a month or so if the symptoms still persist, or especially if they get worse?"

"Yes, maybe I could plan on a trip before Christmas," and they left it at that.

Chapter 16.

A **FEW** days later, Martin and Mandy landed in Spokane and Mandy drove them out of the airport's uncovered long-term parking lot in Martin's now dust-covered car.

"I wonder if I'll ever be able to drive again?" asked Martin as he settled into the passenger's seat.

"The doctor seemed to think that you could do anything you wanted to, didn't he?" asked Mandy.

"Yeah, I guess he did," said Martin. "But I still don't believe it."

The further tests had perplexed everyone. His corpus callosum was shriveled in a manner that had never been previously observed. In the active imaging scans, his right brain revealed a glowing hemisphere that was much more active than scans of a normally engaged brain, even though his was supposedly in a resting state. Following up on Martin's suddenly growing concerns, they'd examined him for possible arterial blockages, signs of stroke, signs of Alzheimer's plaque or dementia, indications of atrophy, and all appeared to be well and within normal ranges. It was just as if he had spontaneously had a corpus callosotomy without the need of a knife. The doctors had all reassured him that in most surgical cases, the patient went through life with little or no discernible effects. But to them the mystifying element was that the right hemisphere of his brain was acting as if it was continuously occupied, although no stimulus for this activity could be detected. In searching for possible explanations, the experts had been unable to come to any agreement.

Well, I guess I will be published after all, Martin thought to himself with a small laugh as they listened to the music that Mandy had selected from her playlist. They'd left the flat plain the airport was situated on, dipped down to the cut made by the Spokane Falls and Spokane River which the older part of the city hugged, and as the newer Spokane Valley sprawl of industry and malls passed by the window, Martin thought wistfully about Leira. The day before they'd parted, she'd again made overtures about wanting to see the draft of the next book he'd set out to write, and he'd been hopeful that he could still come up with some inspiration that would grab the publisher's and her attention, even though the trip he'd made for that purpose had been preempted. However, in the next breath she'd mentioned the need for them both to reconsider their contract, and hearing this had instantly deflated him. She was such an amazing woman, and he enjoyed her company immensely—he hated the thought of being out of her life altogether. *Maybe our friendship will be able to survive if she isn't also my agent,* thought Martin as they sped out of the greater Spokane area and approached nearby Coeur d'Alene and the rising hills beyond. However, picturing himself—an older man with brain problems, withering away in Whitefish, Montana—he doubted the relationship would last.

"Is the music OK?" asked Mandy.

"Just fine," said Martin although he had not a clue as to what group was playing. He closed his eyes seeing a lonely landscape luckily brightened by a friendly glow from the left.

They drove past Wallace in Idaho near the Montana border and up the winding road to Lookout Pass in a drizzle that changed to light snow near the top. Except for some isolated pockets of smoke, all signs of the wildfires had vanished; extinguished with the arrival of the moisture autumn had delivered. "This is sure a lot different from a few weeks ago when we were down to one lane and could hardly see twenty feet," said Martin.

"I know," said Mandy. "Even when I flew over the blazes after leaving Missoula, it looked horrible down here—billowing smoke everywhere. I'm glad that fire season is finally over."

Martin nodded and sank back in his seat. Gazing out on the suddenly wintry landscape he thought, *Comfortable seat, warm car, nice music, racing through wilderness on paved roads...* and memories of a slow, bone-jarring truck trip in stark contrast to this pleasant drive welled up from another chapter written years back.

I reached into the hole in the burlap bag and pulled out a chunk of jaggery, breaking it into bits and handing some to Ryan, Audie, and Donnie. We each sucked and chewed on the sugar lumps as the truck jostled us about in the high-sided but open-backed bed, and we lay or sat on the cargo of fifty or so bags of the sweet stuff. The driver didn't mind our indulgence, and it filled in the gaps between meals. We'd left Gilgit in the morning, following the Hunza River up into the Pakistani portion of the Hindu Kush, the broad plains slowly shrinking as the banks along the river became steeper and the river moved ever further below us. It was getting near dark and the truck pulled over at a small collection of stone huts with flat rock fences built to confine the sheep.

I didn't sleep much that night. The ground was hard and frozen, but there were cots placed outside that we could use—frames with thick rope in a crisscross pattern to hold us a foot up off the ground. Our weathered and smiling host had provided a meal of curried potatoes and some kind of meat that we ate around a fire, and then each of us curled up to try and get some sleep. I wrapped up in my shawl and thin sleeping bag, but was enthralled: the smell of wood smoke and sheep; the lights of small fires dotted here and there across the narrow valley; the sound of the river churning down below us and the occasional calls of humans and bleats of sheep; the crystal-clear night air hosting thousands of twinkling lights in the black sky above. I must have slept some, because I started awake and roused myself with the others in the morning. It took several minutes of walking and stomping to get feeling and motion back into our cramped, cold limbs, our breath visible in the frosty morning air. Delicious hot tea from heaven for breakfast.

The next two days became grueling, only we never realized it at the time. Ryan would break out into a Joni Mitchell song, Donnie told us about the job he'd left teaching in

Scotland, Audie had Canadian tales to tell. All the while the road grew narrower, the valley sides steeper, the vegetation sparser, the turns sharper, and the grades more ominous. We sat in the truck bed on the jaggery, or on the flat, short box built out over the cab—our favorite perch. We watched the cliffs above, and the silty, gray-green river now three hundred, now six hundred, now eight hundred feet below us in spots. Increasingly remote, still it was populated: passing shepherds who struggled to keep their goats along the wall as we squeaked by; round skin boats attempting crossings in the calmer sections of the river far below; workers chipping away at rocks above the road or clearing fallen rocks on the road ahead; other trucks—god help us when one or the other would need to back for five or ten minutes along the narrow, precipitous path looking for a spot where two could pass side-by-side—and once in a while—the tangled remains of a vehicle smashed on the rocks at the bottom.

And we discovered the limitations of the truck. The load was too heavy for the steeper grades, and it soon became a rhythm of stopping, blocking, roaring, repeating. The truck would drive up an incline as far as the engine would allow and the driver would set the brakes—sheer wall to the right, drop-off to the left. The assistants, one young and one grizzled, would jump out and put chocks behind the two rear wheels. The driver would ease up on the brakes and rock the truck back up against the chocks—the only thing holding the truck. The driver, who insisted that we get off for the worst bits and us so glad that he did, would roar the engine, let out the clutch, and climb the hill as far as the struggling gears would allow, and then he'd set the brakes to start the whole process over again—finally waiting for the assistants and chocks at the top of the grade. Not so bad unless the incline ended in a sharp turn we'd just come around. Those were the times we preferred walking to riding. And the road was custom-made for the truck—spots where we just squeezed beneath an overhang (jumping down from our perch), just made it around a bend, or were just able to allow another, rare, truck to pass.

Toward evening on the second day, we stopped for a group of men. Reflection shows we had no choice: weathered skin with long beards and hair; well-worn long wool coats tied with a sash or wearing shawls; pantaloon ballooning pants tight at the ankle; wool hats that were a tube closed at one end, rolled up until the roll met the top; sandals or thin leather shoes with pointed toes that curled up; bandoliers with copper rifle shells; and a slung short or long rifle across the back. What they saw of us: long hair and some beards; local shawls, but wearing clothes too thin for the climate; fair hair on some, blue eyes on some; a woman whom they seem to cluster around protectively; worn sandals; backpacks made not from canvas but some of those newer synthetics; no weapons. The driver was respectful, and they were respectful in return. They were also dark, intense, and wild. We exchanged some sign language, but not much. They all climbed on the back of the truck and shared jaggery as the truck rolled into the darkness. When it stopped, they got off as if the trip was owed them.

The last day we eventually drove into the mild, gentle paradise of the Hunza valley and our final stop less than 100 miles from the Chinese border, Haider Abad, under the shadow of the Karakoram Mountains and the low snowline stopping just above the valley.

What luxury this is by comparison, thought Martin, leaning back and watching the miles rip by on smooth asphalt. They pulled in at a gas station in St. Regis to pee, gas up, and to leave I-90 behind, then headed east and north on smaller roads further into Montana towards Kalispell and Whitefish. As Mandy settled into this next segment of their drive, Martin thought about his youthful adventure, and his recently failed attempt to create a new one. *Damn it, what the hell am I going to write now?* he asked himself. The ideas that had been germinating were pitiful dead sprouts now, and he felt empty. *Damn it,* he saw the scrubs move in a breeze, some small lights flit from bush to bush, the gentle waves hit the sand. *Damn it!* he thought of losing his agent who he was now realizing was one of his few friends. *Damn it!!* as they rolled through some absolutely gorgeous terrain with music for a younger generation pounding away in the background.

Chapter 17.

FRANK HAD intended to order a second beer for them at the counter, but had run into a friend to talk to on the way, so Martin shifted to a more comfortable position in his chair, finishing his first beer and staring out the large picture window at the yard beyond. During the summer, the lawn of Bonsai Brewing on the northern end of Whitefish was crowded with groups, couples, dogs, and kids, but now it lay empty with fallen leaves and snow in the forecast. Martin relaxed and stretched. It was good to be home, even though it had been barely a month since he'd left on his trip to Greece. Mandy had stayed for two nights at their house on the outskirts of Whitefish, and they'd spent the first day on rural Whitefish roads making sure that Martin was comfortable driving. Then, on the next day, she'd driven them to nearby Kalispell so that she could catch the bus back to Missoula, and he'd driven home by himself, feeling fairly capable by the time he pulled into his garage. That was the previous day, and his friend Frank had insisted that they go out for beer and a bite of dinner late the next afternoon.

This is nice, Martin thought staring at his now empty pint glass of IPA. *I don't know anyone in this place, and no one here knows me,* although, the gentleman Frank was talking to seemed to be giving him the eye from time to time. It wasn't often that Martin had a completely enjoyable experience when dining out or having a beer in downtown Whitefish. Too many people believed Toni's side of the story, which seemed to be the only version available. It was not uncommon for him to need to leave after rude remarks, sneers, shuns, or, once, a glass of wine tossed in his face. He was used to it, and it had come to be expected, but this afternoon was a pleasant change.

Frank was back at the table with two pints of an Irish Red that looked intriguing and had ordered burgers for them both as well. "So, you were about to describe the problem with your eyes," said Frank as he slid Martin's beer over to him.

"Come to find out, it's difficult to explain what's going on with them," said Martin, deciding on the spot not to mention his apparent brain injury so as not to worry his friend. "The doctors said they have no idea what happened or what's causing it, but I seem to be stuck with a persistent hallucination in my left eye, even though they say that I can see just fine out of it. All I know is that my left eye keeps seeing this desolate beach on what reminds me of a Greek island, and it's always overcast, like there's never a sunny day there." As he spoke, he closed his right eye and tried to see Frank with his left. Since he knew both Mandy and Leira well, he thought that it was people he was close to and cared for that might show themselves as a glow. He was wrong. As much as he liked Frank, there was no sign of him being at the beach. He did, however, notice a small, gnarled tree in the background that he hadn't registered before.

Martin had inevitably grown closer to Frank after his friend had helped Mandy when she needed it the most. Frank was a free-spirit and preferred to live alone, although a string of lady-friends had tried to convince him to do otherwise. His ponytail was now thinning, but Frank Gonzalo remained true to an internal flag that transcended state, ideals, and probably time, as well. He'd been a school bus driver when Martin and Toni had first met him and was still at it even though he could retire at any time. "They keep me young," was all he said when anyone asked him why he still drove a bus. He was also a respected nature photographer, and his pictures graced many of the galleries in the Pacific Northwest. Known to his oldest friends as 'Gonzo', he'd decided that 'Frank' was better for his photography business and now preferred the latter.

The rural hillside the Ropers lived on was part of Frank's bus route, and so he'd driven Mandy daily during the school years from when she was in kindergarten 'til she graduated from high school. As Frank told Martin later, he thought that Mandy had seemed a little 'off' when she'd gotten on the bus after school one day at the beginning of her freshman year. He'd dropped her at the entrance to the short road leading up to her house near the end of his route, and she'd ignored him when getting down. "You OK, Mandy?" he'd asked. She'd turned back without her usual bright smile and said "Fine," but Frank hadn't been convinced. When he'd finished his route, he'd driven the bus along the road constituting the long driveway to Martin's house, just to check on her. Halfway up the road he'd found her sitting on a log above the uphill ditch with her face buried in her hands sobbing uncontrollably. A bottle of prescription pills had been perched on the log next to her. Frank had parked the bus, sat beside her, and they'd begun talking. He'd immediately established that she hadn't taken any of the pills and had found that Mandy was desperately lonely but ultimately not suicidal. When Mandy had settled down, Frank had walked her to her house, and with her permission he'd told Martin and Toni about the pills, the four of them then talking late into the night.

The incident had brought Martin even closer to his daughter, not realizing at the time the impact his deteriorating relationship with Toni was having on the girl, since she'd always been something of a loner and was by nature optimistic regardless of circumstances. Toni, for her part, had done the best she could with the news, but had found less and less common ground with Mandy as time passed. Frank, on the other hand, had taken on Mandy as a personal mission. He'd begun to take her out on weekend hikes laden down with cameras, and Mandy had soon become an avid birder, capturing beautiful shots of wildlife with one of Frank's borrowed cameras. Over that winter, Frank had dragged Mandy up on the ski slopes with the vow that they'd both give up their skis and learn to snowboard. Frank had never really taken to snowboarding, with a sprained knee to prove it, but had seen and admired the community the local kids had developed around the sport and soon had Mandy becoming one of them. His taking Mandy under his wing had created a lasting bond between the two and cemented his friendship with Martin.

Glasses clattered in the background and a waitress gathered their empties as Martin finished telling Frank about his altered vision and took a long sip of beer. True to form, Frank said, "Maybe a psychic or hypnotist could help you find out what's going on. Perhaps your fall knocked you partially into another reality, and you just aren't aware of it yet."

"Hmm," said Martin. "At least that's something to think about if it doesn't improve soon."

"Well, let me know if I can help in any way," said Frank. "Do you need a hand around the house? Getting it ready for winter? If so, just give me a call." Martin nodded his thanks as the burgers arrived, and they both started in on the fries.

"I should be able to manage, but thanks," said Martin. "I think my bigger problem is going to be Toni. She left a message with Mandy that her lawyers were going to be in touch. Again."

"What?" asked Frank. "What more could she possibly want—or get? What's that old saying about squeezing blood from a stone?"

"Who knows?" replied Martin. "And Caleb's been hanging out on the property." Frank raised his eyebrows as he took a bite of burger. "Mandy and I walked down to the studio before she left and there was no sign of Caleb, but the place was trashed—beer and liquor bottles, joints, pizza boxes thrown around the place. I guess I'll have to shovel it out either this fall or in the spring."

Frank shook his head. "Whatever happened to that kid?"

"I think he was always like that and is just growing into himself," said Martin.

Chapter 18.

THE NEXT morning, Martin gave up and pushed himself
away from his computer desk, rose, and carried his mug of
coffee over to his favorite chair in the living room. He'd stared
at the white page display for a few minutes, surfed the news,
come back to the blank document waiting for inspiration to
strike, but nothing had come. His normal strategy was to just
start typing and see what flowed out, but he couldn't seem to
get started with even the first word. The sun was streaming
in through the window, and he nestled into the warm stuffed
chair, clasping the mug in both hands, and gazing out at the
clear day from his lofty perch. He realized he was noticing
the vision in his left eye a little less lately. Whitefish Lake was
beautiful, as always, and had trailing fingers of mist playing along the opposite shore below the yellow tamarack and
birch-covered lower slopes of newly snow-mantled Big Mountain and the Whitefish Mountain Resort with the white ski
trails now clearly visible and outlined by the dusted pines. He
did love this spot.

When he'd returned from his travels to India in the '70s,
he'd visited a friend in Kalispell, and they'd backpacked together in nearby Glacier National Park, wrapping up the trip
in Whitefish, the nearest town which served as a gateway to
the park. Preparing to leave Montana for Washington that

morning, he'd met a hippie waitress and fallen in love as she served him a stack of pancakes at the Grizzly Den, a local Whitefish café. Toni's casually braided hair, flouncy step, and that smile under the deepest brown eyes had him hooked the moment he'd seen her. He'd left that day for Washington, but they'd traded addresses and kept in friendly touch as he'd worked the summer surveying for new logging roads on the Olympic Peninsula.

That autumn, he'd returned to Toni and Whitefish, and then followed her to Missoula for the fall semester at the University of Montana. She'd studied while he'd snagged a job at the local newspaper and had begun writing his book on the side. It was when they'd returned to Whitefish for her summer job that they'd first visited the property he now owned. Martin's daily routine had been to have breakfast at the Grizzly Den before going off to his newly-landed construction job for a local carpenter. Crotchety old Bill Sims was at the cafe every morning as well, and he, Martin, and Toni had become fast friends. Bill lived up on the hills to the west overlooking Whitefish Lake, and Martin and Toni would go visit him there occasionally, chopping wood, carrying water, and cleaning up to help old Bill out. He'd let them camp on his land, and their favorite spot was the site where Martin had later built his studio above the small rock outcrop.

The following winter had not been kind to old Bill, and when they returned from Missoula the next summer, his visits to the Grizzly Den were rarer, and his trips to the clinic were, unfortunately, more frequent. In need of money, he'd asked if they'd be interested in buying part of his land, and they'd readily agreed. Near the end of the summer, Bill Sims' pickup had given out, and so had Bill. An unknown relative revealed himself soon afterward and immediately sold the remainder of Bill's property to another interested party through an aggressive young local realtor.

With the help of the carpenter for whom Martin worked, Martin and Toni built a cabin on the steep property the next summer and moved in for good, Toni giving school a rest. There were very few other houses in the area, and they reveled in the forested seclusion the site provided. Martin was now sitting in that original part of the house that had eventually seen the addition of a two-story section for an upstairs master bedroom and bigger kitchen, a solarium, a study and loft, a potting shed and a garage. It was ramshackle, but he loved it. Toni, unfortunately, had grown to hate it.

It was in the cabin during the first winter that Martin had finished his book. He'd struggled at the end for a title. "I love *Lost Horizons*, but that's already been taken," he'd lamented to Toni. "I want it to be about travelling, but *On the Road* is gone too—and I really do need to read that Kerouac book sometime. I think the best I have right now is *Over Land*. What do you think?"

"*Overland* sounds too much like it could be a Science Fiction book," said Toni. She'd just finished reading one of the poems from his novel and after a moment had said, "Hey, how about *Faint Trails*? That's in the poem I just read, and it sort of shows that you had no idea where you were really going? I like it." And so that had become the title of his first novel and was Toni's main contribution to the project.

Untouched morning snow on an unfamiliar ridge
Wide windswept braided valley all glacial stone
We pick our way by guesses
A possible marker, a smell of smoke, a broken twig
The next step that sudden cliff
Or the next turn the warmest smile
We follow subtle signs, faint trails
Glancing back to fading tracks.

Chapter 19.

NOW HIS attention was on the dreary shoreline in his left eye and something was odd. That gnarled tree he'd noticed at the brewpub was gone. *Had that been Frank?* he wondered idly. *A plant?* Unsure whether the disappearance of the tree was the cause, it seemed to him that the scene felt emptier than usual. *But maybe emptier is good. Maybe this thing is finally going away—except for this damn headache,* he thought absently, and gave it little more notice.

Looking up later from his computer, he became aware of two things nearly simultaneously—smoke in the trees below the house and a sub-sonic thumping like far-off rhythmic hunters. *Caleb's back,* he thought immediately with a sinking feeling in his stomach. Opening a window, he could smell the wood-smoke, and the beat of some gangsta rap made its way into the house. He wondered if he should call anyone for help, but realized that he really had no one to contact other than the police, and decided he could take care of the situation by himself. *No, I'll call Toni,* he thought as an alternative. *Keep it in the family,* he added with a touch of sarcasm.

After a few rings, Toni answered. "What is it, Martin? I'm with a client right now and sort of busy," and then a little more loudly, "we're viewing this beautiful designer home."

Then, obviously turning away from the client, "Are you back in town?"

"Hi, Toni," he replied. "Yeah, I'm back and up at the house." He didn't ask how she was doing but got right to the point. "The problem is it sounds like Caleb's up here on the hill too, down in the studio."

"Well, that's hardly my problem now, is it?" asked Toni in a hushed yet harsh tone. "He barely visits us anymore, let alone talks to us, and he's old enough to be on his own anyway. Even legally. Just a sec," and he heard a muffled conversation in the background. "Look, I gotta go. Why not just let him hang out there? You never use that old shack anymore anyway."

"It's not a shack, it's my studio! Mandy and I went down there a few days ago, and he's absolutely trashed the place. Call him right now and tell him that he's not welcome. In fact, tell him he's trespassing. Or, better yet—have Al do it. Caleb's his son after all. I don't care who, but one of you tell Caleb to take his partying somewhere else."

"He doesn't listen to me much anymore, let alone Al, and I'm sure he's doing no real harm," said Toni quickly.

"But he's your stepson..." began Martin.

"And he's your problem, Martin, not mine," came the immediate reply. "Look, I gotta go—some of us have real work to do," as she rang off.

Great, thought Martin, noticing the extra dig she'd just given him. He went to the closet, grabbed his coat, donned his boots, then picked his way down the well-worn dirt and rock path. The music increased in volume with every step, and he could soon feel the bassline pounding into his chest, making him vaguely wonder if this kind of thing could trigger a heart attack. He skirted the wide branches on the tall evergreen near the small, weathered studio and noticed Caleb's Jeep further down the slope, with an unfamiliar truck parked next to it. The interlopers had used the remains of an old logging road to access the bottom of the property. *Definitely a party*, thought Martin. *I hope they're in a good mood.*

He climbed the few steps onto the narrow wooden porch and hesitated. His run-ins with Caleb were usually unpleasant, but they also included a measure of tolerance between the two of them. When Caleb was younger, he'd tested out his increasing size on Martin by getting into playful shoving matches that evolved into physically using his bulky body to knock Martin aside, step into his path, or press him into a wall or a kitchen counter. Eventually Martin had called him on it and Caleb had backed off, but then resorted to verbal retorts and slights common among most teenagers. From what he could tell, Toni and Al received the same treatment, so he knew such behavior wasn't reserved for him alone.

Martin took a deep breath and knocked on the faded blue door, the only painted feature on the entire cedar-sided shack. There was no reply or reaction from within. He pounded a few times with his fist, but this was no match for the music that now seemed thunderously loud. He kicked at the door with his boot, leaving a black scuff mark. The music suddenly stopped. He heard some footsteps and then Caleb threw the door open wide.

"What'd ya want, Marty?" asked Caleb with the normal sneer he reserved for adults, even though he was becoming one himself.

Martin stood frozen. In his left eye vision, a dark shadow had immediately spread across the sand when the door opened. This quickly coalesced into a squirming black mass on the nearest dune, and as Caleb moved, it followed, becoming larger as he neared. Martin was confused and speechless as he stared at the ominously dark hulk.

"Wanna join our little party?" asked Caleb with a slur, and there was laughter from the two lanky young men dressed all in black lounging on the bedraggled sofa behind him. Caleb reeked of alcohol, and there were a nearly empty bottle of Jack Daniels, several beer bottles, and a small mirror sitting on the card table they'd positioned in front of the sofa.

Martin shook his head to try and clear the vision and to focus more with his right eye, and briefly held his head in his hands to try and reconcile the dueling images. His mild headache was now beginning to pound in his skull.

"Why not?" asked Caleb. "Too drunk already, Marty?" More laughter.

"No," Martin found his voice. "No, I don't want to party, and I don't want you to party either—especially here in my studio. I've come to ask you to leave, Caleb."

"Why should we?" asked Caleb and the black blob in his vision seemed to dance up and down. "You're not using it, and besides it should be half Mom's anyway. No, come to think of it, this should all be hers."

"Toni got everything else in the divorce, but this property is mine, Caleb."

"Prove it," said Caleb in a most juvenile fashion.

Fantastic, thought Martin as he said, "I don't need to prove anything to you Caleb. You're trespassing on my land, and I want you and your friends out of here. Now."

"Who's gonna make me?" asked Caleb, stepping in at him. "You?" giving Martin a little shove that rocked him back a step onto the porch. One more shove and Martin would be down the steps on his back.

Suddenly on the lonely island, there was a staff in Martin's left hand that he lifted high and then jammed into the sand—and the blob seemed to recoil at this. At the same time, he was aware with his right eye that he'd raised his left hand with palm forward toward the young man as a sign of caution and calm. It was a simple motion and he'd made no contact, yet Caleb jumped back as if Martin had pulled a weapon. Caleb tripped on his next step backward and fell into the card table sending the bottles flying and cracking his head in the process. Both of his friends staggered up and took in first Caleb and then Martin with bleary, confused eyes. Martin held his hands up to show that he hadn't done anything to hurt Caleb, and the staff was again held aloft and clutched commandingly, tilted towards the quivering black mass on the desolate beach.

Their reaction was unexpected. The pair helped a thrashing Caleb up and then all three came towards Martin together.

His immediate thought as he stepped to the side of the doorway was, *Oh, wonderful. I'm in for the first real beating of my life.* He briefly considered turning and trying to outrun them when, amazingly, they pounded across the porch and down the steps past him.

Caleb pivoted in the dirt at the bottom and glared up at him. "You're gonna pay for this, Marty!" he shouted, stabbing a finger towards Martin.

"For what?" asked Martin genuinely curious. "I didn't do anything!"

"You sure as fuck did!" shouted Caleb, rubbing his head. "I could beat the shit out of you," as his friends were running to their truck. "And I'm gonna—just you wait!" The blob seemed to cower into the sand as Caleb backed away, turned, and then stalked down to his Jeep.

"Caleb, I..." began Martin.

"Fuck you, Martin!" yelled Caleb, throwing open the Jeep door and giving him the finger. "I'm gonna fuck you up some day!" slamming the door, starting the engine and tearing off down the hill.

Martin sat down shakily on the porch, listening to the sound of the engines fading around the side of the hill and into the distance. He closed his eyes and there was no sign of the staff or the black, hulking shape in his left eye at all. A gentle breeze blew, and the waves lapped the shore as always. *What in the hell was that?* wondered Martin staring at his hands with his good eye.

Chapter 20.

"**A**ND **THEN** he just fell over backwards," said Martin.

"Dad!" exclaimed Mandy, "you pushed Caleb over?"

"No!" exclaimed Martin in return. "Like I said, I didn't touch him. In my left eye I was suddenly holding up this staff…"

"But Caleb's a big guy," said Mandy, "how the heck did it happen that he ended up on his back then?"

"I have no idea, honey," said Martin, now feeling somewhat defensive. "He wasn't hurt. Much…" as he remembered Caleb rubbing his head after hitting the table.

"Well, I believe you, but I just don't want an angry punk like him coming after you," she said.

"Don't worry, I'm sure he was just drunk and will forget about the whole thing."

"Well, make sure you keep your cell phone with you when you're out on the property or downtown, just in case," urged Mandy, "and call the police if he comes to the house."

"I will, hon," said Martin. "So, you think you'll be able to make it home for Thanksgiving?"

"Of course," she said. "I need a break and it'll be good to spend a couple of days at home."

"Anyone you want to bring along?" asked Martin. "Any friends who don't have plans?"

"No, Dad," said Mandy wistfully. "Plenty of friends, but none I'd especially want to invite home for Thanksgiving. You know, you worry too much. I'm hardly a hermit."

"Just want you to be happy," said Martin. "See you in a few weeks."

"Bye, Dad," said Mandy.

Martin set down the phone and walked over to the picture window. The small lights of Whitefish twinkled below to the right, but high clouds were obscuring the stars. He thought of running into town to a brewpub to wind down, but the idea of encountering any of Toni's friends made him go to the fridge and open a beer in the kitchen instead. He hadn't seen Toni since he'd returned from his recent trip to Greece and was glad in a way that he hadn't. He sat down and watched the few red or white car lights moving slowly along the far side of the lake across the valley.

Troubles with their marriage had been brewing for several years, but had culminated in a simple misunderstanding—with huge ramifications for him. On Halloween two years before, he and Toni had argued as they'd dressed in their costumes: Martin went as a hobo, "A hobo??" Toni had asked incredulously. "That's so dated and lazy—no one will even know what you're supposed to be! Can't you be more creative?"; and she'd gone as Kim Kardashian, "A reality TV star? Are you kidding? Do you really watch that stuff? What happened to the soulful person I married?" Martin had asked. Their neighbor Al lived in a beautiful house further up the hill and had arrived later at the party which was hosted in a local downtown bar. Al came dressed as the current stud from *The Bachelor* and Martin thought later that he should have seen it coming.

They'd all had a lot to drink, but Toni was clearly over her limit. She and Martin left the party with him flopping in his oversized shoes as they walked down the graveled parking lot to the car. Another argument erupted when Toni laid into him as they reached it. "You fucking loser!" she screamed. "I'm the one who has to do all of the work in this family! I'm the only reason that we're still afloat!" stabbing dramatically at her own overinflated chest.

"Toni, you know that I'm bringing in some money as an editor of…"

"Of shit!" she said. "When I married you, you were going places! Now you can't write your way out of a fucking paper bag. What have you written in the last year? The last five years??" turning to open the car door, long false hair flying.

He was accustomed to her attacks about his being such a failure as an author. He'd learned to keep quiet at those insults in order to maintain the peace, but could see that she was really about to blow this time. Still screaming insults, she whirled back around to face him beside the car and stopped, staggering and swaying in front of him. He gave her a goofy smile as if to say, "Really, now what?" and she lost it. To his shock, she took a huge roundhouse swing at him, but missed. The momentum spun her around and her forehead collided violently with the car and then her face hit the sharp rocks in the driveway as she plowed into the gravel. Trying to stop her fall, he'd grabbed at mostly wig hair and gone down as well, landing on his knuckles in the jagged gravel. He'd lifted her up, used some of his costume to stop the bleeding on the both of them, and then opened the car door to help her in.

"What the hell are you doing in here?" he'd asked, staring into the rear seat of the Subaru. Caleb was slumped in the back, barely able to open his eyes which were framed by long stringy black hair, oddly similar to Toni's costume.

"Jes chillin', man," Caleb said in a slur. "It's Halloween!" Not sure what he was high on, Martin noticed an empty bottle of codeine cough syrup beside him on the seat.

Martin carefully arranged a softly moaning Toni into the front seat, shut her door, and then opened the rear passenger door to pull Caleb out. Caleb waved his hands and slunk into the far corner of the back seats, evading Martin's efforts at extraction. Martin sighed. Rather than hassle with Caleb, he went around to sit in the driver's seat, but paused for a moment before he turned the ignition, and he took a deep breath. He knew he'd had too much to drink, but decided he'd better take Toni to the ER to make sure that she was OK since the bleeding from her forehead was substantial. When they arrived at the entrance to the ER, he helped her in through the automatic doors and then returned to the car and parked it with Caleb nodding off in the back. He tried unsuccessfully to roust the boy one more time and then gave up and went in to help admit Toni to the hospital.

The doctors ended up picking gravel out of her bleeding nose and right cheek and used ten stitches to sew up a nasty gash over her left eyebrow caused by her run-in with the car. Martin's scraped hands required light bandaging, too. As the doctors were finishing up, Martin was surprised to be interviewed by a police officer, who took copious notes, but didn't seem to notice that Martin had been drinking as well as had Toni. Back at the car, Caleb had vanished, nowhere to be seen. Martin drove them home and helped Toni, who was now feeling no pain at all, into bed before they both collapsed into a ragged sleep.

The next day was pure hell for Martin. Toni was on the phone before he awoke, and by the time he was eating breakfast, the police had arrived. Toni had accused him of assault. They examined the car and the bedroom, and then put Martin into a patrol car and took him to the station. He spent all day under questioning, and they gave him a physical examination including blood and urine tests and paid special attention to the cuts on his hands.

A brief arrest, court appearances, and a trial ended in a suspended sentence for assault. Toni claimed that he'd attacked her for no reason and had hit her in the face with his fist. She said that he was drunk and probably high on something, and her attorneys alleged that he had consumed codeine from the bottle discovered on the rear seat as well as the alcohol he was seen drinking at the party, even though none of these were found in his bloodstream the following day. Martin had pleaded his innocence, but it was Caleb's testimony that had backed up Toni's story and sunk him. Caleb claimed that he'd been tired and asleep in the back of the car and then been awakened by a fight. He swore that Martin had swung on Toni with no provocation. And that was that. Except for the cuts on his hand, there was no firm evidence to aid either argument. The jury of local businessmen had come down hard on Martin, but the judge had been more lenient in the final sentencing.

The day after the verdict, Toni had fled to the open and waiting arms of their uphill-neighbor Albert Lonzo, a location she had probably been running to all along.

Coming out of his gray thoughts, Martin realized that his bottle of beer was now empty and that he'd been staring at the black scene outside his window. He rose, went to the kitchen and opened another beer and then took it out onto the deck. In spite of the cold, he gazed for a long time at the sporadic cars making their way north, out of Whitefish, and he was happy with the distance time was providing from all of the drama of the past—it made his head injury seem a mere trifle by comparison.

Chapter 21.

In THE dream, he was for the first time fully immersed in the environment of the windswept island. Calmly, he'd surveyed the entire 360 degrees of a small cove, gentle dunes, short hills, and far-off promontory. He'd walked inland for several yards to the bed of a seasonal creek and multiple firefly-like lights had come and flitted about in front of him and then zipped off as if on some errand. He'd climbed to a higher ground and paused to survey the entire watery horizon. Walking further inland, he'd glanced down at the once-elegant cloak he had draped about his shoulders and had pulled more tightly about him as the winds seemed to increase. He'd followed a faint path that merged with a more substantial track and was soon approaching a trio of low, crudely built structures. The center one appeared to have been built at the mouth to a natural cave with stones piled up in front to form a main shelter, and the two others seemed to have been constructed by the laborious stacking of flat stones until huts were erected on either side. Pavers had been laid in front of these rock structures to create a small square or courtyard. He'd entered the middle room by pulling aside a tattered tapestry that had been hung as a make-shift door. He'd been struck with amazement as he'd stepped inside. Myriad books were stacked along every wall, and two open volumes lay across a small desk cobbled together from flotsam. He'd approached the desk. The book on the left had included an engraving of a shipwreck, and the volume on the right was open to a language that looked to him like Greek. Apparently, he was familiar with this language because he'd began to read. And that's all he remembered.

He lay in his bed as the sun was just streaming in the window and thought about the dream. *Some of that fit so well with Leira's idea that my hallucination is taken from* The Tempest—*those cells seem just like the ones in the play. I know that Prospero was able to bring his books with him in his exile, and they were right there in the middle room.* He tried to recall details from Shakespeare and decided that he needed to reread the play to see if it brought anything else to mind. *But then if my left eye is somehow acting out the play, where are all of the characters? Where's the shipwreck? If Prospero is a sorcerer, how can he work his magic if there's no one to cast a spell on? Wait, was that black blob supposed to be Caliban and I used the staff to subdue him? Then where is the spirit Prospero summons—that…Ariel?* He decided that his questions couldn't be answered, so further pursuit was pointless. *Besides, just dreaming it doesn't make it so. I think my mind just took off from Leira's suggestion that what I see is like the play.* He got up and showered to wash away his confusion.

Later that morning, Martin made a trip into town to pick up some prescriptions. He was just at the bottom of the hill and entering a shaded section of the road down near the lake where the sides were overgrown with denser vegetation when his attention was diverted to his left eye. One of the specks of light flitted up to him and began to hover at arm's length in the middle of his field of vision. Standing on the island, he made no reaction, but in Whitefish he began to mentally swat at the thing—it wasn't an annoyance he needed when he was driving. Suddenly the point of light flew right up to his eye and commanded his full attention. He slammed on the brakes as he felt he could no longer see, and then suddenly he was aware with his right eye that a deer had stepped out into his path. They were common enough along this unpaved stretch of road, so he should have been more watchful. He was momentarily stunned because the instant he'd stopped, he was hit with a screaming headache that coincided with a blinding glare in his left eye, as if the fiery speck had entered it, burning as it did so. Then, as the deer slowly stepped off the road and into the brush, he was able to focus again, and the pain immediately subsided. There was no one ahead of or behind him, so he slumped his forehead against the steering wheel and thought, *What the hell is going on? When is this going to end?*

After picking up his eye drops and pain and ulcer medications from the pharmacy, he decided on a whim to stop by the Grizzly Den for a cup of coffee. He hadn't been in the café since the divorce, but he'd always liked the place and stubbornly decided not to let memories of Toni keep him away any longer. After all, the recollections weren't all bad.

Martin did a doubletake when he walked up to the entrance and there, staring at him through the glass door, was Toni. Just below her smiling visage were the words: *Toni Lonzo – the Whitefish Choice for Mayor.* This nearly made him decide to take a pass on the coffee, but he pushed through the door instead. He found a table and ordered a cup of coffee and a Danish from a young waitress—Kaitlin, as it said on her nametag. He was bothered that, as he sat, a friend of Toni's gave him an unfriendly frown and moved from where she was sitting to another table much further away.

"Say, you're Mr. Ropers, aren't you?" asked Kaitlin as she set a carafe of coffee in front of him.

"Yes, I am," said Martin, unsure if this was a good thing and whether he should smile.

"I just love *Faint Trails* and am reading it now for the second time!" she effused, appearing to want to shake his hand. "I especially love the parts about Nepal and Kathmandu. I plan to go there some time. What a journey you must have had!"

"Thanks," said Martin. "It was the same trip that so many others were making at the time, but I just happened to write about it."

"You did a great job!" she exclaimed. "I wish I had my copy for an autograph."

"Maybe some other time," said Martin, "I live here, after all."

"I know!" she said. "I'm going to keep a copy here for your next visit!"

"That would be wonderful, I'd love to sign it," said Martin. It seemed a little petty at this point to ask for his forgotten Danish.

He watched Kaitlin leave, and Toni arrive—in his memories. On their first meeting, Toni had chatted with him and his Kalispell friend as she waited other tables, stopping by often to see how they were doing, and pretty much ignoring his friend in the process. She said she had a break coming up, and so they waited for her near the front counter after they'd paid their bill. They all stepped outside into a gorgeous early summer day and walked around to the alley behind the cafe where they shared a joint.

"So, what are you doing this summer?" asked Toni.

"I'm heading to Washington to join a survey crew for logging roads. It's in the Olympics, so I'm looking forward to it," he said.

They touched. The fine art of gently passing and pushing the thinly rolled tube of smoldering herb into the waiting thumb and finger of another. Such long slender fingers.

She took a long hit and let the smoke slowly out through her nose. Such a cute nose. "Must be heavy," she said, "to work in paradise to ruin paradise."

They all nodded and stared up at the forming clouds. "I know," he said. "I've thought about it and thought about it. I need the money and I need to see the Olympics. But then there's that."

She'd stared at him and seen that he had thought about it.

"So, what about you?" he asked.

"Here for the summer and then off to Missoula to school."

"In what?"

"I love anthropology, but now I'm thinking about art," she said, looking at her watch. She took a final drag on the joint, lips pursed as if to whistle or kiss, and then said, without trying to exhale and so more whispered, "I gotta go, but I hate to leave."

Me, too, thought Martin.

"I love your glow," said Toni with a beautiful smile as she tipped up and gave him a kiss. "Come back."

"OK," he'd said as she walked down the alley and gave a languid wave and a flirty look. *OK,* he thought.

His memories were interrupted by, "Sorry, I forgot your Danish!" as Kaitlin set down the plate.

"No problem," he said with a smile and looked around the place. His favorite table was gone, and they'd remodeled since those days, but it remained a pleasant café. It still elicited fond memories of breakfasts, Toni, and old Bill.

Visions of the past came like frames in a slideshow. The day they'd finished the platform for the cabin, celebrating with a bottle of wine. The sun setting over the hill behind them with Big Mountain across the lake lit up in golds and reds. Him entering her gently from behind, their sways slowly building to a more urgent rhythm. Lying and watching the lights come on below in the warm darkening valley. Her reading something he'd just written in the fading light and saying, "You have the soul of a poet."

Toni never finished school. She'd loved to read what he'd written and was absolutely ecstatic when he'd found a publisher. She was in love with the tours, in love with the crowds, in love with the royalties, and for a time, she was in love with him.

She wasn't happy waiting tables, and once they could afford it, he'd built the pottery shed where she'd spent a few years perfecting her craft and selling some items at the shops in town. Then she wasn't happy with pottery, nor with much else, and having their daughter hadn't lifted her mood either. Something happened a few years later when she'd discovered the joys of selling real estate, of all things. Suddenly she was buoyant much of the time: not necessarily happy with him, less so with their sub-perfect house, but still, happy.

Martin finished his Danish thinking, *I haven't eaten one of these in years. They were a favorite of Bill's, and I can see why.* He pictured the old guy with crumbs on his mustache and beard, both stained from tobacco smoke, laughing with a missing tooth at some joke Toni had told, eyes twinkling.

He'd written about Bill, and a chapter from *My Wooded Acres* suddenly came to mind.

The snow was blue in the predawn light, and each step sunk up to mid-calf as he trudged his way up the mountain. Thank god for the railroad, thought Bill as he broke out into a sweat, dragging the sled behind him.

He'd worked on the railroad just before the war broke out and had fallen in love with Whitefish, Montana, a spot he never would have discovered without being assigned there. As soon as the war ended, he'd built a homestead on the hill to the west of town, and besides work in a mill and some carpentry, his job was to run the rope tow on the ski slope every weekend during the winter. He wasn't a skier himself, but loved being out of town and on the slopes, nonetheless.

He'd driven his truck up the road as far as he could and then, as every Saturday morning, climbed up to the tow-shack to be ready for the first skiers of the day. It was freezing in the shack, and he removed his gloves for the shortest possible time to light the fire in the small oil-drum woodstove in the corner. Once it was lit, he stepped outside to relieve himself and to gather his gear out of the sled. The shack never became really warm, because it was open on the down-hill face where the rope entered and exited the huge wheels driven by the big gas truck engine. If there was no wind, the cabin could become quite toasty, but if it was gusting, the fire at least took the edge off.

The sun was just rising above the ridge when he started the big motor to have it warmed and ready. Ten minutes later the phone buzzed. It was one of those old hand-crank military phones, and someone down at the bottom had spun the crank to call and let him know that the first skiers were arriving, and he could start running the tow anytime. Bill rolled and then lit a cigarette first, pulled back the lever to engage the rope in the spinning wheels, and then set to his routine of throttling the engine to keep a fairly constant speed to the rope given the weight of the skiers that clung to it for the ride to the top, one after the other throughout the day.

Bill was always the last one off the hill as the sun set. He sat near the front of the sled and guided and slowed his down-hill descent by sticking his feet out of each side. Grinning at the bottom, he was sure he enjoyed his run better than any of the skiers had that day.

Martin missed the morning coffees and bullshitting with Bill Sims. He drained his cup and left a generous tip as he rose from his seat, making sure to wipe the crumbs from his chin and shirt.

Chapter 22.

GRAVEL CRUNCHING on the driveway outside caught his ear, and he rose from his desk to see who had arrived. He flipped the drapes on the back window aside in time to see a police cruiser park and two troopers step out.

Oh god, thought Martin, *What now?* One was adjusting his belt and holster.

In a moment there were weighted steps on the porch and a knock at the back door. Martin turned the knob and opened it up, noticing that his heart rate was up as well. The beach lay sleepily in front of his left eye. For once, he wished he could go there.

"Mr. Ropers?" asked the first patrolman. "Yes, it is you." nodding in confirmation to himself, "I'm surprised to visit you again."

"Hello, deputy…" and he stared at the badge on the man's chest, "Thompson. How can I help?"

The other officer, staying behind and to the side, had moved his hand onto the handle of his pistol. Deputy Thompson, sensing the motion, waved him off. "It's OK, Jim, we know this guy." Looking at Martin he said, "He shouldn't be any trouble."

"What brings you gentlemen up here?" asked Martin.

"Can you believe it, Mr. Ropers?" asked Deputy Thompson. "We've had another complaint of assault against you."

"What?" asked Martin incredulously. "By whom?"

"Ah, 'whom', very literary," replied the officer. "The charges were brought by Caleb Lonzo. He claims that you acted violently and shoved him into a table. Mind if we look around?"

"No, I don't mind. I didn't touch Caleb, and nothing happened here."

"Still, we'd like to examine the premises," said the deputy.

"These aren't even the premises of what didn't happen," said Martin.

"Now, let's not get smart, Mr. Ropers," said the other deputy, who then paused. "Say, you're not Martin Ropers the author, are you?" Martin nodded, and he saw several gears click and levers settle in place as the policeman processed all that he'd heard and read about Martin. The policeman nodded as all this information seemed to reconcile itself.

"I'm not trying to be flippant, or smart," said Martin. "Caleb and his rowdy friends had taken over my studio further down the property, and I just went down and asked them nicely to please leave."

"It's how you said 'Please', that we're interested in," said Deputy Thompson. "Mind if we have a look?"

Martin described the situation and series of events from a right-eye perspective on the way down the rocky path. When they reached the studio, he let the deputies open the door and enter by themselves. "I haven't touched a thing since they left," he said as they went in. After five minutes and some flashes of a camera, the deputies emerged from the studio.

"Please tell me that you're not going to arrest me again," said Martin.

"No, to tell you the truth, the evidence matches your description of the incident much better than Caleb's, and it really comes down to one man's word against the other. Besides— three young punks against an old guy like you? Unless you were armed, you wouldn't stand a chance. And Caleb's size and temper? I don't think so."

Martin let out an audible sigh. "Thank you for believing me," and after a pause, "this time," he said.

"Not that I didn't believe you before, Mr. Ropers. It was the law that didn't believe you," said the deputy. "And this time, if Caleb wasn't already on our books for assault and robbery, I'd be a little more of a skeptic. I'm writing this up as a spurious complaint, and that should be the end of it."

"Thank you for being impartial," said Martin as they trudged up the hill.

"Oh, you don't need to worry about our impartiality," said Deputy Thompson. And then more lightly, "Caleb might need to worry about it, but not you." At the top of the hill he turned to Martin and looked him in the eye. "You need to worry about the impartiality of Caleb. Watch your back after this incident."

"Thanks, deputy, I will."

But how? he thought as the cruiser pulled away.

Chapter 23.

"HI MARTIN, this is Leira,"

"Hi Leira!" said Martin, "So good to hear a friendly voice."

"Yours, too—wait, they haven't all been friendly?" asked Leira with sudden hesitation.

"Oh, I didn't mean it like that—they're not all bad. I've just had a rough couple of days, that's all."

"Sorry to hear it," said Leira. "Everything OK?"

"Yeah, fine, it's all worked out," said Martin more lightly than he intended.

"How about your eyes? Have they cleared up? Still the same vision?"

"Yeah, everything's the same on that front. At least it hasn't gotten any worse."

"Well, that's good," said Leira. "Maybe I have some news that will help cheer you up."

"What's that?" asked Martin. "A publisher?"

"Well, almost as good," said Leira. "I was at a recent writer's conference and did find another literary agent who would be very excited—as excited as I am—to represent you."

Martin's breath caught in his throat. His stomach suddenly knotted. "Really?" he asked as cheerily as possible. "Who's that?"

"Cathy Mills. She works for Chatham-Grant out of San Diego, and she says that you're exactly the type of author they hope to represent. They're relatively new, but have been very successful in connecting authors with publishers. Do you know Jeremy March?"

Martin managed a forced "Yes," and she continued.

"He had those two blockbuster thrillers ten years ago and then disappeared off the map? Well, under their wing, he's suddenly back with two more hit novels. I've had a couple of very detailed conversations with Cathy and she and the others in Chatham-Grant are definitely interested in meeting with you and hearing about your latest project. They even think they can revive your poetry collections."

"Wow!" said Martin. "This is totally unexpected. I can't believe that you've found someone who's so interested."

"Well, they are, and I'm glad that I connected with them. So, when do you think a good time to meet with her might be? It would mean a trip to California."

"Soon might not be possible, since Mandy is coming for Thanksgiving," said Martin. Inside he was a storm of conflict—but still, to have an interested agency? "Say, I need to be back in Seattle before Christmas for some more tests. What if I piggy-backed a trip to San Diego onto that visit?" He noticed that the scene in his left eye remained placid and calm, and there was no sign of Leira.

"Fantastic," said his agent. "By the way, I hope you don't mind, but I'll need to get over to your area sometime soon for an unrelated meeting, and it would also be a great opportunity to revisit our contract—especially in light of the possible interest of this new agency. Would it be OK if I tried to drive up sometime around Thanksgiving? Just for a short meet?"

"That would be great," said Martin. "I'd love to see you again," and then a pause, "to go over the contract."

"Me, too, Martin," she said cheerily. "Now what is it you mentioned that happened recently? Are you doing OK? You said it wasn't your eyes?"

"No, not my eyes," he replied. "How about I'll tell you about my little adventure when you get here?"

"Are you sure? I have time now…"

"Nah, that's OK, it was nothing important," said Martin. "It can wait."

"OK, see you soon then, Martin," said Leira.

"See you soon, Leira," as he set down the phone. It was darker than dark outside. Martin went to the wine rack and uncorked a bottle of Syrah. *If this isn't enough, I think I can find some scotch,* thought Martin somewhat jokingly, and poured a healthy glass for himself.

Chapter 24.

THE MORNING was wearing on, and Martin alternated between sitting at the computer and pacing in front of the windows in the living room that had comprised the original cabin. The previous night had been below freezing, and even though he had a furnace, he'd built a fire in the woodstove on waking just to drive out the morning chill and to try and cheer up the house. It hadn't worked—the room was warm, but in his mind, things were hardly upbeat—and he was fighting a growing agitation. He knew the cause, but couldn't think of a solution. Leira's phone call had bothered him, and he was becoming increasingly desperate to latch onto a story concept that would allow him to move forward with his professional life.

Following the success of *Faint Trails*, his second novel had been an allegorical love story about Toni and what she'd inspired in him from the moment they'd first met. He'd had a storyline from the beginning and filling in the details had seemed an easy thing. The reviews, however, had complained of a cramped style, a meandering plot, and stilted language. Then the next book had been just the opposite stylistically, and admittedly overly grandiose—he'd been inspired to write a stream-of-consciousness saga of the rise and fall of nations, of life, and of love found and lost, all centered around the

Khyber Pass. Even Toni had hated it. Reviewers had surprisingly loved some sections and destroyed others. His latest and safest published prose effort had stuck to familiar ground and was loosely based on the life of their old friend Bill Sims and the gentrification of Whitefish. The reviews had been tepid, which to him had seemed like a rousing success. It was still a popular seller in the local bookshops when shelved in the History section.

Then most recently he'd set out to recreate the feel of *Faint Trails*, but now back in his cabin, he could see the fatal flaw in that idea—trying to get into modern Iran and Afghanistan, and then bypassing them and landing in Pakistan some forty some years later would have only been a tired rehash of the same story. And then trying to explore India with fresh eyes but an old body? *Well,* he admitted, *maybe not even fresh eyes,* staring at the barren island with his left eye and the right side of his brain. If he was going to write anything after his accident, *What the hell will it be?* he'd asked himself countless times over the last few weeks. He'd tried to compose without a plan in mind, but this was going nowhere quickly and was the cause of his growing vexation. He'd also attempted to write about the earthquake and the accident, but found this to be surprisingly elusive for some reason. He had no real idea what it was he wanted to create otherwise. He needed inspiration and found that he couldn't focus—couldn't even think clearly enough to begin an outline.

He sat down roughly in the stuffed chair and lamented, *I think there was some significant brain damage after all. I can remember the past just fine, I'm organized enough to get my prescriptions filled, I can drive, I can even confront an oaf like Caleb in a coherent manner. I have all these ideas—concepts I can usually string together—but I can't seem to congeal them into any kind of meaningful shape at all. I see wisps of inspirations floating by, but can't grab ahold of even one of them. What if I've lost some kind of cognitive ability from the concussion? God damn it!*

He squeezed his eyes tightly shut and thought back to the earthquake and finding the stick. There was something about that night in Kefalos that kept needling at him. *What was familiar about that night?* he wondered, and then he suddenly remembered the section in his first novel he'd written about Kopan in Nepal—sitting quietly with others in a cross-legged position when the earth had begun to shake beneath them.

We'd decided to take the month-long meditation course offered by Tibetan Gelugpa monks. We weren't going anywhere soon anyway—Ryan had had his passport stolen. It was taking months to get it replaced, and happily, they allowed me to remain in the country with him, although normally the stay limit was three months. Another reason we'd loved Nepal.

We'd explored the area surrounding Kathmandu and had been to the giant Buddhist stupa at Boudhanath, so finding the Kopan monastery at the top of a small hill north of Boudhanath had been relatively easy. Now we and the rest of the male students were staying in a mud and stone house with clay floors at the base of the hill, the women were situated in a similar house further up the road, and we were all walking up the switch-back path to the top of the hill each morning for our lessons. We lined up outside the long canvas canopy that had been erected for the teachings and had tea and porridge before beginning the day.

Lama Zopa and Lama Yeshe were our two teachers, and there were two western nuns who helped them and facilitated the gathering. Lama Zopa excelled in patience and began nearly every sentence with his long, contemplative "Hmmmm" that eventually resulted in surprisingly good English. He sparked hushed laughter when he made an error and chuckled at himself about it. The lamas sat cross-legged for hours, rocking back and forth to adjust their maroon robes, us copying in agony at first with some never being able to manage it.

We learned about The Four Noble Truths, and the myriad complexities of Mahayana Tibetan Buddhism which detailed the stages of rebirth—the hells, the suffering pretas, animals, *the perfect human rebirth, heavenly beings, bodhisattvas, and Buddha. They also taught us the technique of building Buddha bit by bit in our minds, absorbing his clear light, and then transmitting that light out to all sentient beings, and about the perfect human rebirth—as rare as the disappearance of a brass ball the size of the earth floating in space where a sparrow flies by once every thousand years and brushes it with the tip of its wing. We did our best, taking notes throughout the course.*

An earthquake shook us one morning and stopped the teachings. The Kathmandu valley stretching out below us showed pockets of mist interlaced with the horizontal streams of blue smoke from innumerable home fires. Up through the mist, rising from the valley, came wails of fear, cries and shouts, dog barks, and prayers welling up as we all rose as one to look out across the landscape. It was a beautiful morning, and we found later that no real damage had occurred. This became a natural segue into a lecture on impermanence and the illusory human existence.

Walking away from the course after four weeks was like leaving our parents for the first time. It was a shock to be back in the comparatively frantic and bustling pace of the large foreign city of Kathmandu. We felt raw—like we'd lost a layer of skin, and yet we worked hard to keep that layer thin so that we could remain as sensitive and in tune to ourselves as we had felt during the course.

And now I have the opposite of a tranquil, equanimous mind, thought Martin, *I should have kept up the practice.* He looked down at his hands laying palm up in his lap. *That earthquake in Kos has split my brain in two—and I saw the scanned pictures to prove it. Instead of seeing one thing clearly, I'm of literally of two separate minds.* He looked out the window seeing the conflicting dual images in front of his eyes. "Aaaaaaah!" he shouted, jumping up and letting out a long scream, immediately feeling like an idiot.

Chapter 25.

HE'D SET off on a walk down the yellow leaf-littered road towards town to take in some of the cool air and clear his head. He was coming out of his funk and starting to admire the fall palette when a car driving up the road slowed and then stopped next to him. He couldn't see who was driving because of the reflections from the dark-tinted windows, but he knew the big black Cadillac Escalade well. As the passenger window near him whirred down, Martin had a mind to keep walking, but felt compelled to be as polite as possible. It was Big Al, Toni's husband, dressed as usual in a suit and tie.

"Martin, what the fuck is going on?" shouted Al. "I heard you attacked my son, you son-of-a-bitch!"

Martin immediately took it as a good sign that Al hadn't gotten out of his car. He knew that Al and Caleb had their problems as well, and that Caleb was becoming impossible for him and Toni to control.

"No, Al," said Martin flatly. "I didn't attack Caleb—in fact neither of us laid a finger on the other." *Mostly true,* he thought.

"Toni said that he called the cops on you," said Al less loudly, "so it had to be something."

"He and his pals were partying in my studio. I asked them to leave and somehow Caleb, who was drunk, by the way, stumbled backwards and landed on a table. That was all."

"Yeah, well expect the cops anytime now," said Al, "and maybe my lawyer."

"The police were over yesterday and found nothing amiss," said Martin.

Al stared at Martin for a minute as if doubting him, but then said, "That damn Caleb! He could make trouble in a church service."

Unapologetically, he pressed the button to roll up the window, but Martin stopped him by saying, "Hey, Al. Speaking of lawyers, Mandy heard from Toni awhile back that I should expect a call from her lawyers. Do you know anything about that?"

Al gave an evil smile and said, "I think she's planning on giving you a nice little Christmas present. And just wait 'til she's Mayor. See you, Martin," and he was pulling away before the window was closed.

Walking back up the hill, Martin wondered what Toni had in mind. Al was the eager young realtor who had handled the sale of Bill Sims' land all those years ago, ending up with the best chunk for himself. Over the decades, he'd bought up adjoining lots until the top of the hill with the finest views for miles around were all his. He'd started off in real estate at just the perfect moment as Whitefish was becoming an 'in' place to live and property values soared. Lonzo Realty was now the biggest real estate company in both Whitefish and Kalispell combined, and Al had become a millionaire several times over. He'd financed and owned a huge condo project at the base of the Whitefish Mountain Ski Resort, some time-share condos on the lake, and was part owner of several golf courses in the area.

Martin now knew that the reason Toni had turned away from her artistic pursuits and become a realtor herself was because of Al. Al had married about the same time as Martin and Toni, and had two children, Caleb who was Mandy's age and a daughter Ferny who was two years older. Al had always been charming and attractive to the ladies, and rumors of affairs swirled as his marriage began to disintegrate. One of the ladies who'd fallen under his spell had been Toni.

Feeling that her life with Martin was going nowhere, and frustrated at her attempts at pottery, among other ventures, she'd decided that real estate would be a good career move—"for the family," she'd said. She attended classes, and Al's company had taken her on as a sales associate. It didn't take long for Toni to move up the company ladder. At about the same time that Martin was accused of assault, Al's wife was admitted to a rehab facility. Both divorces happened within weeks of each other, and Toni had moved in with Al as soon as the dust had settled.

It had been incredibly awkward at first to have his ex-wife living just up the hill from him, but the calm and quiet he'd discovered after she'd left made her leaving more of a relief than painful.

Chapter 26.

GIVEN THE mood he was in this evening, Martin knew that it would be better if he was alone, so he stayed at the house and built a fire. He ate little for dinner, had an extra glass or two of wine, and then fell into deep brooding while sitting in his favorite spot next to the woodstove. He thought of his failed marriage—*How is it that Toni hasn't only fallen out of love with me, but has come to hate me on top of it?* His failed career—remembering some of the harshest reviews he'd received, his struggles to find his voice and his passion. His unfair assault charge—*No, now that might turn into two charges if Caleb has his way!* His rejection by Leira—*She's been my agent for all these years—why is she choosing to leave me now?*

Since dinner, the image in his left eye had become dominant and intrusive. It seemed the more he dwelt on his failings, the clearer the beach scene became. Rather than fading into the background as his thoughts became more morose, he felt he was almost swept by a spell to that quiet island. In the living room, he could barely see out of his good, right eye and could only dimly make out the flames in the woodstove window. Seeing nothing but scraggly brush swaying in a dark Mediterranean wind, his attention on his troubles seemed to inexplicably diminish. He was intent on having another drink, but was suddenly overcome by exhaustion so he damped down the woodstove, dragged himself upstairs, and collapsed into bed.

Martin awoke the next morning clear-headed and with two dreams vividly etched in his mind.

In the first, he'd somehow never gone to bed, and his dark thoughts had taken over. He'd never been as negative as he was that night and had worked himself into a sullen despair. The final indignity on which he'd obsessed was the fall and the crack to his head that he'd suffered in Kefalos and the resulting sickening image presented constantly to his left eye. In his dream, which had quickly morphed into a nightmare, he'd had enough. The split-brain phenomenon was driving him mad, and he decided he needed to end it. He'd gotten drunkenly up from his chair and nearly fallen, reaching out to steady himself and burning his right hand on the woodstove in the process. In a blind fury, he'd stumbled over to the kitchen counter and grabbed a kitchen knife in his throbbing right hand, since he'd tried with his left hand, but it wouldn't cooperate. He was intent on stabbing out his left eye, even if it meant his own death in the process. He'd tried to raise the knife to make the plunge, but found he couldn't manage it. Looking down, he saw his left hand was holding his right hand tight against the counter, trapping the knife. Try as he might, he couldn't will his left hand to let go. He'd dropped the knife into the sink and then begun to storm away from the kitchen. Still intent on ending this, he'd suddenly whirled around and grabbed for the knife in the sink. Again, he found his right arm pinned by his left He'd begun a scream of frustration when the left hand unexpectedly released its grip and whirled up and struck him in the face. He'd staggered back, lunged forward for the knife one more time, and the left fist again swung up and caught him full in the jaw, snapping his head back. That was all he remembered of the nightmare.

In the second dream, he was standing in the middle of a paved square and could see the three stone huts in the background. There was a firepit before him and slabs of flat rock had been arranged to hold a large cooking pot filled with water above a stack of wood. He was holding a book in his right hand and the staff in his left. He looked down at the book and recognized it as the one with Greek lettering, turned to a page that showed orange and red flames springing up from a stone floor with no apparent source. He tapped his staff on the pavers and a dozen of the little specks of light came to his beckon and hovered almost anxiously for his bidding. In a moment they gathered at the tip of the staff he had raised and then followed it down as he knocked it against the paving stones. The points immediately turned into live sparks and flew into the awaiting wood placed beneath the pot. Within minutes a roaring blaze was lapping against the bottom of the vessel. He'd begun to walk back towards the huts when he woke up.

Yawning, he arose from bed and took a shower, wrapped himself in a robe, and then plodded downstairs to make some coffee and breakfast. *That's odd,* he thought at once. *I don't recall leaving a knife in the sink.* In a flash of remembrance, Martin ran to the nearest mirror and examined his face. There was no sign of any cut or bruise, and feeling about his jaw, he detected no portion that might have been struck. He looked down at his right palm and although it seemed much redder than the other hand, there was no sign of a burn. *What a dream that was,* he thought as he lit the gas stovetop to warm a skillet for his morning eggs.

While he was mopping the remains of egg on his plate with a piece of toast, Martin thought about the second dream, and this now elicited a strange feeling of disconnection as he concentrated on what his left eye could see. He was back at his sentinel spot looking out over the cove and the sea beyond. *I know there's more behind me. I know there are huts inland. I know I started a cooking fire. Can I turn around or walk?* He concentrated and tried to pivot the scene, tried to look down at the cloak he now knew he was wearing, tried to take a step. Nothing moved. He was just recalling the enchanting of the sparks when they seemed to fade from his memory as his mind tried to focus on them. Shaking his head, he got up and washed the morning dishes. He held up the knife as he dried it, turned it over, and brought it up to his face to examine it closely. His left hand functioned normally and didn't try and stop the knife from being held so close to his eyes. With a shrug of his shoulders, he set the knife in the drawer.

Chapter 27.

THE PHONE rang as he was catching up on his email. Caller-id showed that it was Leira. "Hi, Leira!" said Martin as he answered the phone.

"Hi, Martin," she said, "is this a good time to call?"

"Sure," he said, "I was just deleting some junk emails."

"Hey," she said, "I wanted to let you know that I'm planning on being there on the 23rd. Are you free that day? How about around 4:00 in the afternoon?"

Martin flipped open his calendar which was totally blank for the next week, except that Mandy was scheduled to arrive on the same day. "I should be free; the only thing is that Mandy is coming in sometime that afternoon from Missoula."

"Oh, will that be a problem? I can make it another day—I just wanted to try and be back home by Thanksgiving on the 25th."

"No, it should be fine, and if Mandy's here, I'm sure she'd like to see you again."

"Oh, I'd love to see her, too. This will work out well. A friend at the U of M in Missoula wants me to give a talk to her English department, at least to those who haven't left on break. She said that she's also inviting any local unpublished authors who are interested. I'm going to explain how to write an effective query letter and how to hook up with a literary agent. We've tentatively set that up for the 24th, so seeing you the day before would be perfect."

"Great," said Martin. "You're more than welcome to spend the night here if you want; I have plenty of room."

"Thanks, Martin," said Leira. "I'd love to spend some time with you and Mandy. A friend who owns the Cast A Spell bookstore in Kalispell has also asked me to spend some time with her, but to tell you the truth, I'd rather spend the evening up there with you two, since you've been so nice to offer. How about if I make it weather dependent—if it's crappy or snowy, I'll stay in Kalispell to make sure that I can make it to Missoula the next day. Otherwise, I'll plan on staying over."

"Perfect." said Martin. "I don't suppose there's any chance that you'd be able to spend Thanksgiving with us as well?"

There was a pause at the other end of the line. "Hmm," said Leira. "That was nowhere on my radar scope." And after another pause, "Do you mind if I think about it?"

"Not at all," said Martin. "We have nothing special planned, but you're more than welcome to join us. My friend Frank said he might be able to make it, too."

"Well, thanks," said Leira. "If I let you know what I decide when I get there on Tuesday, will that be too late?"

"Nope, that would be fine," said Martin. "Like I say, we're easy and have plenty of food."

"Oh, and I forgot," she added quickly, "do you think your lawyer should be there on the 23rd to look at the contract?"

Martin's heart sank for a moment, but he said "I'll give him a call and see if he thinks it's necessary. If so, he'll be here too."

"OK, great," said Leira before she hung up. "See you in a couple of days,"

"OK," said Martin and he hung up, too.

A couple of days? thought Martin, the timing of the holiday suddenly sinking in. He knew what his schedule was going to be like for the next two days—cleaning and shopping.

Martin began to pick up the living room in a much better mood. It was always a pleasure to talk to Leira. Although her English was perfect, she still had traces of a Castilian lisp and ever so slightly rolled her 'r's, and Martin loved to listen to her speak. Her accent had been so much stronger when they'd first met and when they'd toured to resurrect *Faint Trails* from the dust and to promote his new novel at the time, *On Whom These Airs Attend*—a book the entirety of which, unfortunately he saw now, was devoted to Toni. He and Leira, and for a portion of the tour, Toni, had had a blast. Martin had remained popular from his first novel published ten years before and was still able to draw crowds, Leira was excited by her first major book tour, and Toni loved the parties after the book signings and public readings. They'd avoided the east coast and had started in the Midwest, driven down to the Southwest, and then up the West coast. The three of them had quickly become pals even though Leira was nearly ten years younger than either Toni or him.

The subsequent tours for other books had been smaller and less exciting, and the last one for *My Wooded Acres* about his old friend Bill Sims had been a slog. However, while his marriage with Toni seemed to be dissolving slowly before his eyes, his long friendship with Leira seemed to grow stronger. After a book-signing in Portland, they'd lingered over dinner in a Lebanese restaurant. For the first time, Martin had realized the deep feelings he quietly held for Leira—him a married man. Near the end of the evening he had to convince himself that the signals he was picking up from her were all in his head. That, and his strong commitment to Toni, despite the rumors swirling about her and Al, kept him from taking any actions based on his feelings. He'd lain awake for hours that night wondering if he should pluck up the courage and knock on her hotel room door. He was glad he hadn't. The next morning, they were back to normal and survived the rigors of the rest of the tour. Martin always wondered if he'd missed an opportunity but knew that he couldn't have acted any other way and still feel good about himself. He sighed as he turned on the vacuum cleaner.

Chapter 28.

HE'D JUST unloaded several bags of groceries from the car, making a final dash inside through the brief but pounding rain that had developed that afternoon. He was shaking out his coat to hang it up when the phone rang. Martin brushed out his wet gray hair with his fingers as he walked over to the phone and checked the number displayed on the screen. It wasn't one he recognized, but it was from the same area code as Whitefish. Chancing that it wasn't another robo-call, but ready to hang up immediately, he answered.

"Mr. Ropers? Mr. Martin Ropers?" came the question.

"Yes, speaking," said Martin.

"Mr. Ropers, this is Samuel Trinulco, a lawyer representing Ms. Toni Lonzo, your ex-wife."

Martin had been expecting the contact since he'd been forewarned and was wondering what Toni was up to.

"Mr. Ropers, this call is to inform you that Ms. Lonzo is initiating a civil suit against you, and the papers have been filed with the courts this afternoon. In short, you are being sued by her to gain either an equal portion of or full rights to each of your published works."

"What!?" asked Martin incredulously. "She's already getting half of the royalties for the rest of her life. What could she possibly want with the rights to my books?"

"I can only say that she is seeking a fair or full share of property towards which she feels she has made more than significant contributions."

"But she gets half of the royalties!" Martin shouted.

"But not half of the ownership which she feels is her due," said Mr. Trinulco.

Martin was speechless. But only for a moment. "Her due! She's hated everything I've written since the first book! She didn't even know I'd written the last one until it was published! Is she out of her fucking mind??"

"No need to shout, Mr. Ropers. I'm just making you aware of the filing. If you have concerns, you should speak to your lawyer."

"Fucking A, I'm going to speak to my lawyer, you piece of..." the phone was dead. "Shit!" shouted Martin.

He took no real notice of a wind that had come up and the building waves in his left-eye vision as he was immediately on the phone to Stephan, the lawyer who'd represented him during his recent divorce.

"Hello, Martin," said Stephan. "What a coincidence, I was going to call you this afternoon."

"Stephan, I just got a call from that sack of shit lawyer Trinulco, saying that Toni is suing me!"

"Yes," replied Stephan, "I was just made aware of the same thing. But no need to worry, Martin. It's obviously a frivolous suit."

"Can she do that? Is it even legal?" asked Martin. "Even after the divorce?"

"Unfortunately, anyone can sue anyone else at any time," said Stephan. "That doesn't mean that the bases of the claims have any validity."

"Why is she doing this, and does she stand any chance of winning?" asked Martin with a growing apprehension.

"As we'd agreed, I recently filed for an appeal of the divorce terms, especially the royalties that Ms. Lonzo is receiving. She and Mr. Trinulco have obviously taken exception to that and are making a counter-strike." There was a pause. "As to your second question, I'll need to look into the precedents, but I would say that it is possible that she can legally claim the rights to your works."

"What?" screamed Martin again. "She had nothing to do with them!"

"I wouldn't worry, Martin. We'll sort this out, but unfortunately marriage in itself means that she had something to do with your creations. However..." Stephan interjected quickly before Martin had a chance to erupt again, "we'll make sure that they have no chance of obtaining any rights in a court of law."

Martin sighed. He had no idea that going through a divorce meant being married to his lawyer forever. "OK, thanks, Stephan. I guess there's nothing I can do other than feel extremely pissed off." He was about to hang up, but then remembered Leira's question. He explained her wish to alter their existing business contract to Stephan.

"Yes, I think that it'd be a good idea if I was there to hear the details of terminating the contract," said Stephan.

Of course, you would, thought Martin. He said, "OK, we have the meeting tentatively set for 4:00 tomorrow."

"Yes, I should be able to make that. See you then, Martin."

"See you then, Stephan," and they both hung up.

Martin stood and became aware that in his left eye the growing breeze was now a full force gale, almost making him feel that he needed to reach out and steady himself. His intent was to walk to the kitchen while making a pledge to himself not to throw things as he put away the groceries which were still sitting on the kitchen counter. But instead, he found himself somehow rooted to the spot in the study. He tried again to move his feet, but was unable to raise either one. However, in the scene before his left eye, he began walking along the short dunes heading inland toward the huts where lay the paving stones and the cooking pot. He stopped at a flat rock exposed in the sand and raised the staff in his left hand above his head, describing a large circle in the air with the end. The winds seemed to follow the motion and what had been powerful offshore gusts pulling at his long cloak now became a small hurricane with him standing in the calm center. He pointed the staff at the ground and then made an upward motion and suddenly hundreds of the eager little lights zipped out of the surrounding brush and joined him in the eye of the tornado. He could see that his right hand again held the Greek book from his dream, opened as before to the page with a color illustration of a crimson flame shooting red and yellow sparks, all surrounded by Greek words and a deep blue background flecked with golden stars. With the staff in his left hand held high, all of the brilliant specks gathered at the top and followed it down as he drove his staff with incredible force onto the flat rock at his feet. At the instant the staff made contact, there was a terrible boom and all of the specks transformed into live burning embers which exploded as hot sparks into the swirling wind. And then they were gone, and he was left alone in an eerie stillness.

Martin momentarily blacked out but was able to catch himself against his study desk before he fell. He stood shakily and took stock—he could move his feet and hands at will, and his left eye contained the same dusky, calm vista with which he was now so well acquainted. *What in the hell was that all about?* he wondered. *Ah… I'm projecting my anger at Toni. Of course—that burning rage even got to my left eye/right brain.*

He noticed that he was now calm as he put away the groceries and then sat down in his favorite chair, looking out at the suddenly clear weather. *I haven't been that angry in a very long time, absolutely furious, in fact,* he thought, *but now I don't see how I could've gotten so worked up. I survived the divorce, and I can survive this silly action of hers. Still,* he thought, *it could be that this brain injury is affecting my emotions since I flew off the handle so easily.* While he was thinking this, he grabbed a nearby sheet of paper and began to make a list of things that were different to him since the incident. *My vision, of course; a recent bout of depression; several very vivid dreams; headaches; and an outburst of anger. Oh, and mild hallucinations while I'm awake—no, this last one was pretty damn intense.* He set down the pencil and then looked over the list. OK, *well, the depression I'd say is normal for all of the things that seem to have gone wrong lately, and I don't think I'd call it an overreaction. If I was superstitious, I'd say that picking up that staff in Greece has brought me nothing but bad luck, which is ridiculous, of course,* he ended half-heartedly.

He stared straight ahead with another thought. *The hallucinations are so weird. It's like they're me, and yet not me. I can see what's going on in my left eye, but not feel a thing from it—like I'm not really there, so it's not like taking a drug. Now, that kind of hallucination I've had before... and sometimes totally unintentionally,* as he recollected now an almost comically deranged episode from Afghanistan that he'd chronicled in *Faint Trails.*

A short time after the bus left Herat, it unexpectedly stopped in the middle of what seemed to be the vast empty plain that made up western Afghanistan. The only things visible were a tea stall along with some small booths set up next to a lonely mud hut. Some passengers did buy tea at the stall, some relieved themselves behind the hut, some stayed on the bus, but others like Ryan, Audie, and I checked out the stand selling hashish. It was there on display, cheap, and seemingly legal, so we—of course—bought some. None of us had a pipe because the penalties of crossing the border with either drugs or paraphernalia were severe, yet having them in the country wasn't frowned upon. So, the only means we had immediately available to take advantage of our new purchase was to ingest the hashish.

It was the chilly morning of what would become another hot desert day, and Ryan, Audie and I had at least six hours to look forward to on the bus before we reached Kandahar. We all agreed on how much hash it would take to get a nice buzz going, broke off a bit each, and swallowed it. The bus wasn't full, and it was an enjoyable ride. About a half-hour later, none of us could feel any noticeable effects, and so we all decided to bite off a little bit more. In hindsight, that was perhaps a bit too much. We started to notice the effects of the hash a little while later, and quickly began to second-guess having taken the second bite.

The effects: the bus now elevated about six feet off of the road, an organic beast; hot wind streaming through the windows evaporating our sweat the second it formed and us feeling every drop leave; sage and earthy scents floating through the bus on wafting vapors; tires creating a symphony as they hummed along the hot asphalt; the distant mountains now lavender/purple pyramids floating high above the desert floor; me becoming lost in how my hands work. Uh-oh.

Here's the best part. Near the end, I was struggling with a terrible bout of diarrhea, and all my focus was hell-bent on keeping things in place and where they should be. The bus pulled into a crowded square in Kandahar filled with other busses and passengers. Ours was immediately surrounded by Afghans either waiting for someone on the bus or by hotel hawkers shouting out the names of good hotels for any trav-

elers. Men were already on top tossing down the luggage for waiting passengers. I bolted. I tried to ask some of the hawkers where a bathroom was but was met with blank stares and so I grabbed one of them and said "Yes, hotel—now!" and ran in front and then behind as he saw the urgency and directed me down back alleys and streets. At the hotel, I burst in, found a toilet, and finally found relief. I don't remember how I retraced my way to Ryan and Audie, but when I got back to the bus they were clutching our backpacks and staring out into space surrounded by a small crowd—which was just standing and watching them like they would a TV screen, for any signs of life or activity.

Drugs were easier, thought Martin, still sitting in his comfy chair. *No matter how intense, at least there was an end point. What if this damned island video goes on forever?*

Chapter 29.

WHITEFISH LAKE below was reflecting the last of the turquoise evening sky as Martin admired the sunset from the deck with his hands in his coat pockets against the chill when he thought he saw sparks—remarkably similar to the burning embers he'd seen in his left-eye vision—floating on a breeze from the lake and up, over the roof drifting toward the hilltop. He rubbed his eyes and looked again but they were gone. When he thought of it, he couldn't now be positive which eye he'd really seen them with. Then he smelled smoke. This wasn't unusual, given the season when people were allowed to burn brush, but the appearance of sparks was very rare unless the fire was nearby. Martin's first thought was that Caleb was back and had lit an unprotected fire. *Oh, god,* he thought with a start. *I hope he's not trying to burn down my studio!* He dashed inside, put on a warmer coat and gloves, and grabbed a flashlight. Back on the deck he searched his left eye for the dark shape that might indicate Caleb's presence, but everything appeared to be static in the dunes. As he hoofed it down the trail to the shack, the smell of smoke grew stronger, so he knew that it was either from a neighbor's brushfire or from the studio. As he approached, the small shack was dark and, in the faint remaining light, no visible smoke emitted from the stack. He flicked on the flashlight and trained the beam along the roofline just to confirm that this was so. He tramped loudly up the few steps and noisily unlocked the door—sure enough, no Caleb. *Thank goodness,* thought Martin.

He made his way back up the trail, and the smell persisted, so he put it down to the neighbors—probably even Al and Toni trying to prod their huge fireplace into heating their enormous house, which they only did when company was present. He could hear the phone ringing inside and rushed through the door and over to the desk to answer it. "Hi, Dad," came Mandy's greeting. "I tried a second ago and no one answered. Did you just get home?"

"Hi, sweetie," panted Martin. "Nope, I just popped down to the studio to check on it, thinking that Caleb was back, but it was empty. Besides, he'd have to break down the door to get in this time."

"Well, thank goodness, he wasn't there," agreed Mandy. "I just wanted to let you know that I should be home tomorrow around noon, and that I finished all of my assignments today, so I'll have zero school-work to worry about while I'm there. Maybe it's time to set up a puzzle? Go shopping?"

"Sounds good!" said Martin. "We might even be able to fit in a hike if the weather cooperates. I might need one, especially with those holiday calories coming on."

"Exactly," said Mandy. "And maybe still make allowance for a beer! Do you need me to bring anything?"

"I think I have it all covered. There's a chance that Leira will be here tomorrow night, and I've also asked her for

Thanksgiving dinner, if that's OK, although she's not sure about that yet."

"Fantastic!" exclaimed Mandy. "I got to know her so much better in Seattle, and really liked her. The more, the merrier, I say. OK, I gotta go and pack, and Jason wants to take me out for a drink."

"Oh, Jason, huh?" asked Martin teasingly. "Maybe he should come for Thanksgiving?"

"Dad... honestly?" asked Mandy. "We worked on a group project today, and just want to celebrate getting done. He was talking about Thanksgiving with his family over in Billings, so he has plans."

"It was worth a shot," said Martin under his breath.

"What?" asked Mandy. "If you said 'worth a shot' just now, I'm going to sock you in the arm when I get there! OK, I really do have to go. Did you remember everything? Even croissant and turkey sandwiches with cranberry sauce the next day?"

Shit, I forgot the croissants! thought Martin. "Yep, just a little more shopping to do tomorrow morning," said Martin.

"OK, see you soon."

"You, too, and drive carefully," said Martin as he rang off.

Although Mandy was his daughter and he loved her dearly, she was still a puzzle to him. She was smart, articulate, pretty, he thought, and very sociable, yet, she never had a boyfriend for more than a month or two. Nothing evolved into a serious relationship, yet all remained steadfast friends, except for Robert and what's-his-name who'd been real jerks and still were. In an attempt to be objective, he wondered if she had a political, or off-putting, side that he hadn't noticed, but he doubted this was the case. It seemed like no one in her group of friends was interested in any serious commitment in the way that had been common when he was young. *And look where that ended for me,* as Toni sprang to mind.

Chapter 30.

MARTIN HAD spent an hour after breakfast doing some final cleaning and then headed down to the grocery store to pick up some croissants and last-minute items, including the pumpkin ale that he knew Mandy liked. He stood in line at the check-out counter and recognized the young cashier at the register from many previous visits. He even remembered her name—Lauren. "Hi, Lauren, how are you this morning?" he asked as he unloaded the items from his cart onto the moving belt.

"OK," she said in a chilly manner as the groceries bleeped by her station.

She gave him an odd sideways glance and he finally asked, "What's up, Lauren?" as she was scanning the last items. She gave a kind of huff and pointed at the stack of newspapers beside the register. The exposed top half of the Whitefish Pilot read: 'Ropers Assault Number Two?' His shoulders immediately sagged, and he threw the top copy onto the belt. "Lauren, you can't believe everything you read."

"OK," she said coldly as she took his credit card and swiped with a swift downward motion. Handing him his receipt and card back, she said "Have a nice day," without meeting his eyes and turning to the customer behind him.

Great, thought Martin as he made his way out of the store and to his car. It felt as if the entire parking lot was staring at him, but he knew it had to be his imagination. He sat in the driver's seat and read the article. The reporter had taken the police blog: 'Troopers called to 1135 Lakeview Way to investigate a possible assault. After meeting with those involved and investigating the scene, no charges were filed,' and turned it into a scenario that looked very negative for Martin. The reporter had even dredged up an old photograph from the first assault charge by Toni.

The clouds seemed to darken even more as he made his way home. The entrance to the main road leading up the forested hill to his house was blocked by a police car with flashing blue and red lights. *What now?* he thought as the officer emerged from the cruiser at his approach and waved him to a stop. It was Deputy Thompson from a few days before. He rolled down his window as the deputy walked around to his driver's side.

"Hello again, Mr. Ropers," said Thompson. Martin expected to hear something like, "Could you please get out and step away from the vehicle?" but instead the trooper said, "I'm here to give you a warning."

Uh, oh, thought Martin.

"We're allowing everyone who lives on the hill back into the neighborhood, but depending on the direction of the fire, you'll need to be ready to evacuate at a moment's notice."

"A fire?" asked Martin. "What fire?" and Thompson pointed over his shoulder at the ridgeline. What Martin had taken as gathering clouds he could now see were billows of smoke. "What's burning?" asked Martin.

"We're not sure yet, and the first responders are just getting to the reported site," said the deputy. "Since the smoke is white, I'd guess that it's wood—wet wood—maybe a burn pile that got out of control. If it was black, I'd guess someone's dwelling, but I don't think so. The information is just coming in."

There was a murmur on the police radio, and Deputy Thompson went over to listen. "It sounds like a small forest fire has been building on the opposite side of the hill, probably since yesterday afternoon," he said coming back to the side of Martin's car.

"A forest fire?" asked Martin. "How's that possible? It rained yesterday, and we're deep into the wet season of late November. Everything should be thoroughly soaked. We were even under a little snow recently, and besides, open burning is allowed now."

"Well, I don't know how it's possible either, but that's what the report just said," replied Thompson. "Just make sure you keep in touch by phone or radio, and we'll be ordering an evacuation if they can't contain the fire and it heads this way over the ridge."

"You know, I thought I saw…" Martin began, but stopped himself mid sentence. He was going to tell the officer about the sparks he saw the previous evening, but then realized that he couldn't be sure in which eye they'd really appeared.

"You were saying you thought you saw something?"

"Oh, it's nothing. I was thinking of something else," said Martin.

"All right," said the deputy giving him an odd look. "Remember to stay tuned for any updates, Mr. Ropers."

"OK, thanks," said Martin. "I'll keep my eyes and ears open. Let's hope it doesn't spread—although I can't see how it possibly could given these conditions."

Deputy Thompson waved as Martin drove off.

More and more bad news, Martin thought, looking down at the newspaper by his side. *And it all seems to be since that damned trip to Greece.*

Chapter 31.

HE HEARD the tires on the gravel and peeked outside to see Mandy's white Toyota pulling up in front of the garage. A pleasant radiance dawned among the bushes in his left eye. He stepped down to the driveway as she was getting out of the car, a glowing human figure emerging to one eye, and gave her a big hug.

"How was the drive?" asked Martin.

"Fine until I hit our road at the bottom of the hill—they almost didn't let me through their little roadblock until I said that I was your daughter," as she moved to the rear of the car to open the trunk. "The troopers waiting there said it was up to me, but that I might be coming back soon. Apparently, there's a big fire burning just over the hill..."

"They told me the same thing this morning," interjected Martin. "I just don't see how it can possibly keep burning given how wet it's been. If you ask me, it's like a tempest in a teapot and it'll all be over soon. I think the police are just looking for something to do."

"I sure hope so, because I could see the smoke coming off the hill a long way out—way before I hit Whitefish," said Mandy.

"Really?" asked Martin, suddenly concerned. "It didn't seem like anything much just a few hours ago."

"They said to have the radio dialed to KUKL, and to keep our phones charged up and turned on. They must not be too worried if they let me through though," said Mandy.

"Like I said, I just don't see it going anywhere—especially since they're on it now."

Martin helped Mandy carry her bags into the house and then turned on the radio to a low volume, public radio classical music tinkling away in the background.

"This'll be fun, Dad," said Mandy as she set a large cloth bag on the kitchen counter and a small suitcase beside the living room couch. "And you said that Leira is going to be here tonight? What do you have in mind for dinner?"

"I was thinking of something Mexican. And yes, both Leira and my lawyer are going to be here at 4:00," said Martin. "We need to discuss my contract with Leira, and the lawyer is definitely not staying for dinner... or spending the night!" Suddenly reminded, he said, "Oh, and I'd better call Deputy Thompson and tell him to let them both through the roadblock."

While he was looking up the number and dialing the deputy, Mandy removed the perishables she'd brought for Thanksgiving from her bag and transferred them to the fridge. As she was folding the empty bag, she noticed the Whitefish Pilot she'd set the groceries on and picked it up. She was finishing reading the newspaper's front-page article when Martin concluded the call.

"Thompson said that it was iffy whether he'd let them through or not. Apparently, the fire is growing, but it hasn't decided on a direction yet. The reports are coming in that it seems to be easy to put out, but then reignites when their backs are turned. They're now suspecting that it's an underground fire that's been smoldering since the dry season and is alive in the subsoil. They're talking about bringing in some big cats to bulldoze paths down to the dirt layer so that the fire can't cross. I asked if they were worried, and he oddly said that they aren't sure yet."

Mandy didn't respond and was staring at the front-page article. Martin was about to say something when she turned to him with the beginnings of tears in her eyes. "How could they, Dad? How could they fabricate something out of nothing? This makes you look like a serial abuser of some kind!"

"I know, Mandy," said Martin. "Unfortunately, Caleb and Toni are ganging up on me right now, and I'm not sure what to do about it."

"Mom, too? What do you mean? The divorce?" asked Mandy.

Martin shook his head and looked at the floor, then back up into Mandy's eyes. "I'm trying not to lose my temper about it, but Toni is suing me for the rights to my books."

"What?" shouted Mandy. "She already gets half of your royalties, doesn't she? Has Mom finally gone totally bonkers? Both she and Caleb should be locked up in the looney bin— she's totally certifiable!"

"Mandy," said Martin, reaching out and touching her shoulder with his right hand. "I wish I could say that they're both just full of bluff and bluster—but as we know, they're able to land some real punches when they want to, and frankly that pisses me off." He turned from looking at her to staring out the window. "Unfortunately, there's nothing I can do right now but rely on Stephan, my lawyer. It's going to take some time, and money, of course, but both of them will be proven wrong in the end—I'm sure Stephan can handle it."

"Yeah, like that worked for the first charge!" said Mandy, as she brushed past him and went to stow her bag in the loft above the study, visibly trying to calm down.

They set up a card table in the living room and chose a jigsaw puzzle to work on for the holiday—a colorful Italian village tumbling down a steep hillside to the sea. The sleeping arrangements were going to be Martin in the master bedroom upstairs, Leira in the small guestroom below it and just off the kitchen, and Mandy in the cozy loft above the study that she'd chosen as her bedroom years before. They remade the bed in the guest room since Martin couldn't remember whether or not he'd changed the sheets from the previous guest. At 2:30, Martin looked out the windows and noticed that it was becoming difficult to see the shoreline of Whitefish Lake below, although when he stepped out onto the deck, he didn't smell the smoke any more strongly than he had the day before. They'd decided to make chicken fajitas and lentil chili for dinner and he and Mandy started preparing the ingredients. The plan was to start the chili simmering on the stove before the scheduled meeting with Leira and Stephan, and then they'd cook the fajitas after the consultation and the lawyer had headed back to town.

By 3:30, the visibility had diminished significantly, and Martin was beginning to worry, so they turned up the radio. A 3:40 report cautioned all residents to prepare for evacuation, but to stay indoors and await instructions—which they did while each packed a small bag of essentials and left them by the back door.

The phone rang at 3:50 and as Martin picked it up, he saw that it was Leira.

"Hi, Martin," she said, "it looks like they're not going to let me through the barricade. They say it's too dangerous now, and with all of the smoke, I believe it. Are you guys OK?"

"We're fine, and we haven't been told to evacuate yet, so it must not be that bad," said Martin. "How does it look from down there?"

"Strange, if you want to know the truth," said Leira. "I can see smoke rising up behind the hill and then streaming down over the top and clinging to the hillside down to Whitefish Lake. I'm standing at the roadblock, and the smoke hasn't hit here nearly as much. It looks like the main part is being funneled by the wind to not spread outwards, but to flow down and out over the lake."

"Well, it's been getting thicker here, so we must be somewhere in the path below it," said Martin, peering out the main window, "I can barely see the lake from up here now."

"Just a sec," said Leira. "Let me talk to the officer who stopped me."

The phone was muffled while he heard the sounds of walking and then a muted conversation. "OK," she said, "he says the reason I can't drive up is the lack of visibility. They haven't decided whether or not to evacuate you..." The phone was quiet and then Leira was back on. "Officer Thompson wants to speak to you," she said, handing over the phone.

"Martin? Mr. Ropers?" asked Thompson. "I just got the word. The fire doesn't seem to be advancing—at least not very quickly, but they're worried about being able to manage a breakout. Also, the smoke levels are becoming dangerous now. They've just ordered an evacuation of the area. You should leave at once."

"We're packed, and ready to go," said Martin. "See you in about ten minutes."

"Good," said Deputy Thompson.

"Martin?" asked Leira as the phone was handed back to her. "I'm going to try and book a reservation at the Whitefish Inn for tonight instead of going back to Kalispell. Do you want me to book a room for you and Mandy as well?"

"That would be great, Leira—thanks! See you soon," as he hung up.

"OK, Mandy," said Martin turning to his daughter, "they say we need to evacuate. It's not the fire as much as the smoke that they're worried about."

Mandy nodded and headed toward the back door. "Your car or mine?" she asked.

"Let's take mine, and put yours in the garage," said Martin.

Outside, the smoke was rolling past in huge billows travelling down the hillside. They both tucked their noses and mouths into the crooks of their elbows as they made the switch of cars and stowed Mandy's safely in the garage. Mandy was coughing as she climbed into the passenger seat of Martin's Subaru and buckled up. They made it maybe fifty yards. The smoke was so dense that neither of them could make out a landmark to drive by. Martin had edged forward but suddenly felt the front left wheel miss the gravel road and sink into the soft shoulder. He was able to back out thanks to four-wheel drive, but couldn't see well enough to navigate either forwards or backwards. "I think we'd better leave the car here and make our way back to the house," said Martin, with Mandy nodding in agreement. They reached for their belongings and each wrapped a T-shirt across their faces like bandits. Clutching their bags, they left the car with careful steps, feeling along the Subaru's sides until they were on their own in the solid-seeming curtain of eye-stinging white.

At one point, Mandy couldn't see her father when they were within an arm's reach of each other and she gave a small shout, amazed at how close he was when Martin responded. Like having radar or sonar, Martin was always able to see Mandy's location with his left eye. Martin slipped off the road to the right twice on the way back and was going to blame his otherwise useless left eye when Mandy yelped with a sprain after missing the road on the left side. Barely visible in the smoke, he saw her glowing form momentarily hunched over as she reached down to assess her injured ankle. He supported her as she limped their slow, probing progress back to the house. Coughing and teary-eyed they discovered a wall, but it took a few moments to work out where they were in relation to the doorway and find the steps up to the back entrance.

"Oh, my god!" wheezed Mandy as she pulled off the makeshift mask once inside. "Are we going to die up here, Dad? How will we get out?"

"I don't know," said Martin, "but we're definitely not dying. We'll be all right." However, he was immediately on the phone to Thompson. It took several tries to get through. "Deputy Thompson this is Martin...Ropers," said Martin, still coughing and with mucus streaming from his nose. "We may be in trouble here. We tried to drive out, but the smoke was so thick I nearly ran off the road. We could barely see our way to walk back to the house. There's no way that we can make it down to you guys."

"Roger that," said Thompson suddenly sounding officious. "Just a moment."

He was back in two minutes. "Our best advice right now is to stay put. We have some folks on the periphery who made it out, but we've heard from three other families stuck in a situation similar to yours. We sent one team in to help rescue an older couple maybe half-way up your road, but they missed a curve and had to walk back out. The good news is that the fire hasn't yet crested the hill, and so you're not in any immediate danger other than smoke inhalation. Keep your house buttoned up as tight as you can. Put wet towels at the base of all of the exterior doors. The current orders from on-high are for everyone to stay put, but if we declare imminent danger, you're to make your way as best you can downhill to the lake. Just follow gravity."

"Oh, and try not to fall off of any cliffs?" asked Martin, even though he knew that there were none besides the one below the studio between them and the water.

"Yes, that would be best," said Thompson, totally deadpan.

"OK, you know my number," said Martin. "Oh, and here's my daughter's contact information just in case," he said as he read the numbers off the screen on the phone that Mandy was now holding up.

"So, fajitas?" asked Martin as he rang off and turned with a weak smile towards Mandy. She nodded and began to walk to the kitchen with a limp. "Hey, we should look at your ankle first," he said as he guided her to the couch. Mandy protested as he helped her sit and then winced as he slowly worked her sock off. Her ankle was obviously swollen and turning purple near the sprain. "We'd better get some ice on this," said Martin.

Chapter 32.

MANDY WAS letting the ice do its work on her sprain and was checking messages on her phone when Martin remembered that he hadn't called Leira to let her know that they were stranded on the hill. He was just searching for her number when they both heard a loud thump from somewhere outside, followed a few seconds later by another louder thud. "What was that?" asked Mandy. "It can't be the fire... Can it?"

Martin said, "I sure hope not. It sounded like it came more from the downhill side, so I don't think so," and went to the door leading out to the deck. He covered his mouth with his sleeve and ventured outside. The smoke was so thick that he could barely see the railing, but he heard a loud crash in the direction of the studio, and in his left eye he thought he detected a darkening of the scene. Coughing as he stepped back inside, he wiped his eyes and then slowly shook his head.

"Dad?" asked Mandy. "Could you tell what it was?"

"Yes," said Martin. "I think it's Caleb."

"Why do you think it's him? Could you hear him?"

No, I could sense him though, thought Martin, but he said, "I just know it is. That sound we heard was him breaking into the studio."

"How can you be sure?" asked Mandy.

"It was the right sound at the right distance for it to be the studio," said Martin.

"If it's him, I'm amazed that he could find it in all this smoke," said Mandy.

"Me, too," said Martin, and then resignedly, "I think I'd better go check on him."

"Dad!" exclaimed Mandy. "Do you think that's a good idea, especially after what happened the last time?"

"Well, we can't exactly call the police because there's no way they can make it up here, and besides, he could be suffering from smoke inhalation or something for all we know," said Martin, thinking that maybe a little suffering would be good for Caleb.

"But what if he's armed or high on something?"

"Don't worry, I'll be careful and let him know I'm coming. I'll tell him that it's OK for him to stay down there—that we just need to know where he is, in case we all have to evacuate in a hurry... I wonder how he got past the police barricade?"

Martin dampened a scarf and started to wrap it around his lower face when he suddenly put it down on the counter and said, "I have an idea—I'll be right back." He went out to the garage and returned a few minutes later with a coil of rope slung over his shoulder. "I'm going to tie this rope to one of the porch supports and string it down to the big ponderosa pine near the studio so we can find our way back and forth." Mandy nodded, though with a look of misgiving about his decision to go in the first place. He tied on the damp scarf and headed out into the solid bank of smoke.

He felt his way down the path, uncoiling the rope as he went, finding his way by careful steps based mainly on memory. He finally hit a branch from the large pine, felt for the trunk, and worked the rope around it. Pulling hard, the rope straightened, or he guessed that it did based on the tension, and then he tied it off. He knew that the studio was only ten or so feet from the tree and soon found the steps up to the door.

"Caleb!" he shouted from the path. There was no answer. He made his footfalls heavy as he stomped up the steps so as not to surprise the young man. "Caleb, this is Martin! Can you hear me? Are you OK?" He reached the top of the steps and felt for the door, but there was nothing there but empty space and when he finally found the frame, it was splintered where the strike plate had once been. Smoke had entered the room, so it was only marginally easier to see inside. "Caleb? Please don't attack me, I just want to check on you." Still no answer, and Martin vaguely wondered if he was about to be jumped. He stood still for a moment and then could make out a crouched black form nearby on the sand in his left eye and could also hear labored breathing slightly to his right where his good eye found a dim shape was draped across the old couch. "Caleb—I'm coming inside now."

He closed the door behind him the best he could due to the broken latch, and then edged forward until he was within arm's reach of the young man. Martin shook him quickly and jumped back as he did so, just in case Caleb was playing opossum. There was no response at all from the limp form. He backed away to the wall near the door and flipped the light switch up. Caleb had collapsed chest-down across the worn sofa, with his head facing into the small room. His long black hair was matted and caked in blood, as was the sleeve on his old army-surplus coat. Martin could only elicit a moan from him as he tried his best to assess the injury. He found an old blanket in a cupboard and tore some strips from it. Soaking them in water from the small sink outside the tiny bathroom, he set about trying to clean off the dried blood and locate the wound. It soon became apparent that Caleb had a long nasty gash along his forehead just below the hairline, but otherwise appeared to be in good shape. There was a strong smell of alcohol on his breath, and Martin found a half-empty bottle of tequila in the pocket of his coat. The bleeding from the wound had pretty much stopped, so Martin doused some of the tequila on a clean strip of blanket and wrapped this around the wound and his head, Caleb remaining passed out the entire time. Martin felt for a pulse, and to him it seemed to be a normal rate of 57 bpm and strong.

"Not much else I can do," said Martin quietly to the inert form. "Your bleeding's stopped, and nothing appears to be life-threatening. I guess we'll have to see how you feel in the morning." It was darkening significantly outside now as the sun fell behind the ridge somewhere far up above the smoke. Martin arranged an old quilt over Caleb and then decided to leave the light on as he stepped outside and closed the door. It sprang open immediately without the latch to secure it. He found some cardboard from a used pizza box and made a wedge that he set along the frame and pulled the door against so that it held. He reached the tree and found that the rope he'd strung made for a quick and easy hike back up to the house.

"Was it Caleb?" asked Mandy. "I was starting to get worried and almost dialed your cell."

"Yep, it was him," replied Martin as he removed his makeshift mask. "He was passed out on the couch, and his hair was matted with blood. I wiped what I could from his face until I could see that he's had a nasty cut on his head, but luckily, it's stopped bleeding. He must have hit a tree limb or fallen and gashed his forehead on something in all of the smoke. The best I could do was to bandage it as well as I could and leave him sleeping peacefully."

"Knowing Caleb, he'll wake up not so peacefully," said Mandy with a note of heavy skepticism in her voice.

For some reason they both jumped when Martin's cell phone rang.

"Hi, Leira!" said Martin immediately when he answered, "I meant to call you, but something came up."

"Martin, are you guys all right?" asked a worried Leira. "I thought you might've made it here an hour ago, so I called the police and they said you might be stuck, but to wait a while and see if you showed up."

"We're fine for the moment," said Martin, as he then told her about their failed attempt to leave the house in the dense smoke, and of Caleb's unexpected appearance in the studio below.

"The police or the rescuers must be able to do something to get you out of there," said Leira adamantly. "Let me hang up and phone Officer Thompson and then call you back," and she hung up before Martin could reassure her that they were safe.

A few minutes later, Leira rang back. "Hi Martin, I'm sorry I hung up on you so suddenly, but I was just so frustrated with your predicament—I really need someone to DO something to help you!" she admitted. Martin could hear the Spanish trills and clipped phrasing more pronounced in her voice now and loved the sound of it.

"We're doing great here, except for Mandy's sprained ankle..." Martin began.

"Sprained ankle?" asked Leira before he could finish. "Is she OK? Can she walk?"

Martin glanced at Mandy curled on the couch with the ice pack on her foot. She gave him a big smile back. "She's fine, and I think it's only a minor sprain," said Martin. "So, what did Thompson say?"

"He said that they're working in the dark—literally now. He meant it as a joke, but I wasn't amused, and so he explained the situation. The fire's advancing but hasn't crested the hill yet. It seems to be generating a lot of smoke for a blaze of its size and starts up again after they put it out. Their major concerns are smoke inhalation and any changes in the wind that will send the fire down the hill towards more dwellings. Actually, they're hoping for a predicted shift from west-east winds to east-west. It's happened everywhere around us but not in our area, and they're not sure why. There are a dozen families like yours who are stranded, and they've made several attempts to send in rescue crews only to have them become lost and then emerge somewhere else around the perimeter. He said that your ex-wife is stranded as well and is making life miserable for them by her constant calls and demands for action."

"Yeah," said Martin. He was about to say, "I know all about her making life miserable," but stopped himself. He didn't need to burden Leira with the fallout from their fractured relationship.

Sensing too long a pause, Leira said, "I know that she made things difficult for you, Martin. I'm sorry I phrased it that way."

"Oh, no," said Martin, thinking quickly. "I was just wishing that we all had walkie-talkies and night-vision goggles so that we could just waltz right out of here. I'm sure this will all be over by tomorrow—are you excited about your talk at the U of M?"

"I might not attend after all," said Leira. "I called and let them know about the fire situation outside Whitefish and that you might be trapped. I just realized that even though I can't do anything from my hotel, I'd feel terrible if something happened to you and Mandy while I was off in Missoula giving a talk. They understand, and said that we could re-schedule."

"I'm sure we'll be fine, Leira," said Martin. "I'd hate for you to miss your lecture."

"Thanks, Martin, but I'm certain I'll feel better just knowing you two are safe. I'm going to keep in touch with the police and with you until this fire is put out."

"Thanks so much, Leira" said Martin, his throat suddenly feeling tight. "That means a lot to me—us."

"Of course, Martin," said Leira. She was just about to hang up when she said, "Oh! I just remembered. I expected to run into your lawyer at the base of the hill where they had the roadblock, but he never showed. I looked up his number and called to say the meeting was cancelled. He said that he figured it was and then asked me out to dinner tonight to discuss the contract, but I got a weird vibe from him and said that I'd meet with him when you did. Anyway, he knows that you're stuck for the time being."

"Thanks, Leira, we'll keep you posted."

"Stay safe," said Leira and hung up.

Chapter 33.

MARTIN WAS sautéing the fajita mixture for dinner and
gazing ahead at the black kitchen window. All he could make
out was his own reflection in the glass but nothing of the
smoky conditions outside. He was suddenly overcome by a
blinding headache and he gripped the edges of the counter
and dropped his head in reaction. His left eye became his sole
focus, and he was standing again before the three huts and in
the middle of the square next to the cooking pot now boiling above red-hot embers. He held the Greek book again, this
time turned to a page showing a frothing sea, and he had the
staff held in the other. Two specks of light came to his calling
this time and at a flick of the staff they entered the steam rising off the pot. The vapors immediately thickened, and he was
soon staring at a miniature vision of a stormy sea, whitecaps,
and at the far edge, a three-masted ship with sails stowed trying to weather the storm.

In a moment it was as if the event had never occurred,
and he struggled to remember what had just happened. Setting
down his spatula and feeling a little dazed, he grabbed a flashlight and headed to the back door to see if by chance the
smoke and fire had passed. He stepped outside, flicked on the
beam, and pointed it towards his garage. There was nothing
to be seen but reflected white, pulsing where denser clouds of

the smoke hit and rolled over the house. Back inside and tending the fajitas, it became even more apparent to him that the smoke trapping them meant a major fire burning just above them on the ridge which he hoped wouldn't end up turning into a serious physical threat. The sudden unbidden thought of his house and body in flames brought back a chapter from *Faint Trails* about the funeral pyres he'd seen in India.

Benares is a beautiful and interesting city, calmer and more centered than any of the cities nearby, so it's a big relief for us. The focus here is on spirituality and death, but in an affirming way. I thought tonight what the city would be like if they had a similar spot in the West: churches lining the riverbank with spotlessly clean granite steps leading down to the river; caskets, some with a lid open, some closed, lined up for ceremonies with ties and suits, black dresses and veils, shiny black shoes; white lily floral arrangements displayed on ornate stands; perhaps a sleek barge pulling up to accept the coffin, or a windowed hearse driving a circuit down to the river and back to the graveyard.

Here everything unfolds at once: a busy street with shops and stalls across from the ornate and varied temples that line the river; crowded occasional openings providing access to the broad steps descending to the river's edge; small fires at the top of the steps or ghats, cooking food for meals or offerings; the devoted heading down the steps to bathe in the sacred Ganges, heading up the ghats soaked and perhaps carrying a jug of the holy water; a mix of nearly naked sadhus, *pilgrims in white* veshtis *on the men or simple saris on the women, local villagers in normal wear coming down to bathe; orange and yellow flowers in garlands on the blessed or floating on the river surface; the funeral ghats—a pyre being built, one with a wrapped body laying atop in the middle of a ceremony, another with a blaze already begun.*

We hired a small wooden boat to take us out on the Ganges near sunset. It was so peaceful and the river so calm. We saw, I swear, a pink porpoise swimming upstream. Nearing the busy bank again—burned wood, charred cloth, flowers, smoke drifting downriver as the orange sun sets.

An old grandmother—barely a bump in the binding
Fresh-cut brown-barked wood from a neem tree
Thick pink resin incense in ornate orbs
Oil pooled in a red-clay butter lamp
Dried cow dung gathered from a far-off field
The concentration of a forest gone now a million years
The petals of marigold flowers
All enter me, become me
I take a breath
All enter, as if of smoke

His reverie faded as he concentrated on dishing up the last fajita when he heard a faint sound outside. It was the wrong direction to be Caleb, and he turned his ear to the window and detected a far-off cry.

"Hey, Mandy, I think I hear something—or someone," he said turning to look at her.

Seeing him turn towards her she smiled, head bobbing to a song playing through her earphones. As he took a step towards her, she reached up and pulled them out.

"What is it, Dad?"

"I'm going out on the porch for a second," he said, "I thought I heard someone calling out there."

Mandy got to her feet and, easier for her now, limped over to the door with him. "Do you think it's a rescue crew?" she asked.

"I don't know, but I hope so. Just a sec," he said as he opened the door, stepped out, and quickly pulled it shut behind him.

"Hello," came a far-off call. "Hello, is anybody there?" it rasped again.

Martin cupped his hands and shouted, "Hello! We're here!"

Now Mandy, coughing in the smoke like Martin, was on the steps as well. "Is someone coming?" she asked. Before he could answer, they both heard, "Hello! Keep shouting so we can find you!"

Martin and Mandy, coughing in spells, kept up a string of "Hellos." After a minute or two, they paused and waited for a response. Now, much closer, came some shouts of, "Are you still there?" One higher pitched voice suddenly sounded familiar to Martin. "Toni?" he asked himself aloud, with a sinking feeling.

"Martin!" came the weak reply. "Thank god we found somebody!" But Martin could hear in her voice "Too bad it was you."

Martin and Mandy kept up the 'Hellos' as the party drew nearer when suddenly a deeper voice shouted, "We found your car!" It was about this time that Martin, still shouting and coughing, was jolted by what he saw with his left eye as the memory of a few minutes before came back to him. The scene was an exact replica of the miniature storm that had been conjured from the boiling pot, only this time the little ship was listing terribly on what must have been a reef and was being smashed by waves. A head was slowly emerging from the waves some ways out from the foamy beach. As the callers picked their way along the road in the blackness and thick smoke, a body slowly rose up out of the water—a dark profile, and now that more of it was exposed, he saw that it was a woman. Martin seemed to make out faint words being spoken and the shape slowly lost its opacity. He could now see the action of waves rolling through the shape—as if it had become a shadow. When the lost party was about twenty feet out from the house, Martin had the oddest display before his eyes: glowing orbs of moving flashlights through the dense smoke in his right eye, and a hovering shadow that seemed to refuse to come out of the water, standing knee-deep and coming no nearer in his left.

Now they heard footsteps crunching on the gravel. "Martin, thank god!" coughed Toni when three shapes finally emerged from the dark only feet away from them. "We made it! No thanks to this idiot," she thumbed as Al lumbered up the steps with her and Ferny, Al's daughter, right behind them. Martin opened the door whereupon the three burst into the house and collapsed into any available chairs, panting and gasping with tears streaming black, sooty lines down their cheeks.

"God, I thought we were going to be lost out there forever!" wheezed Toni. "I was sure we were goners—no thanks to Al!" looking over at her sweating husband who now glared back.

"Hi, Mom," said Mandy, limping over and giving her mother an awkward hug.

"Hello, Miranda," said Toni without acknowledging the brief attempt at affection. "I see you're stuck here, too. Martin, do you have any water for us?" Seeing her mother's pointed disinterest, Mandy retreated to the couch and propped up her foot with a grimace.

Martin grabbed some glasses from the cupboard, filled them, and handed them to Toni, Al, and Ferny. Ferny thanked Martin and went over to say hello to Mandy and sit with her while Toni launched into a detailing of their misadventure. Martin's attention turned to what he saw with his left eye—a softly glowing form to the side where Mandy sat and a shadowy woman standing up to her knees in the pounding waves as he stared at his ex-wife.

Toni was hacking and blowing her nose while she ranted. "I said we should stay put like the police warned us to, but no, Al was worried that the fire was closer to our house than any of the others and we might not have enough time to evacuate if it suddenly took off. We couldn't see a thing when we left home, but Al had me drive while he walked ahead to show where the road was. That worked until we must have taken a wrong turn. Or maybe we didn't—I don't know. We just couldn't figure where the hell we were. I lost sight of him and swerved off the road a little, only to have him jump down my throat for that…"

"Jesus Christ, of course I yelled!" said Al. "I told you to stop the car while I looked ahead and checked the road, but you decided you had to follow, and look where that got us! Swerved off the road a little? The car's in the fucking ditch!"

Toni was defiant. "Nothing would have happened if we'd stayed put in the house, god damn it! Anyway, we knew we couldn't remain in the car, so we took our best guess and started walking. It was like an orgasm when we heard your voice and found your car."

"Jeez, Toni," said Al.

"Well, it was," said Toni, turning to Mandy and Ferny. "Excuse me, girls, I thought I'd never say that about Martin again."

They both shook their heads. "Whatever, Toni," said Ferny. "You keep forgetting that we're both adults now. And you need to respect our host and chill a little bit, don't you think?"

"Chill?" asked Toni. "Our beautiful house could be a pile of ashes by now for all we know, and you want me to chill?" and she sank back into her chair with a sad sigh.

What a changed woman she is, thought Martin, unhappy to be again in her presence. As the years went by, Toni had made the transformation from a full-blown flowerchild to a blue-blooded socialite, from a free-love commune type to a vampire capitalist, from heart over head to head over heart. In fact, he couldn't think of a person he knew who had changed so utterly.

Mandy had weathered the creeping distortions in her mother the best that she could, but had only been able to go along with them up to a certain point. She was in love with the Toni who'd played games with her, spread finger paints all over the paper and their faces, woven honeysuckle into her hair, kept her up at night laughing, argued with the teachers for requiring prayers in school, taught her to turn pots, knit her sweaters. The intermediate Toni, who would have sudden temper tantrums, be upset at spilled juice, needed to have the best brand of jeans, gossiped about the neighbors, and sniped at Martin had been tolerable to Mandy who'd still clung to the previous version. The current and final installment of Toni was an unapproachable level for her daughter—the final word in fashion, the decider of who was in and who was out, the sneerer at the less well-to-do, the vice-president of the Chamber of Commerce, the senior partner at Lonzo Realty, the eager candidate for mayor, the queen on the hill—an upgraded version that wasn't compatible with Mandy's old operating system. The two had drifted apart since Mandy was fourteen, and had hardly spoken since the divorce.

Ferny, on the other hand, was only really acquainted with the latest version of Toni and had set up a workable arrangement with her new stepmother. After some initial rows, the two had tacitly agreed to never discuss politics, current events, other people, Ferny's life or pretty much anything. Ferny demanded her autonomy in exchange for a grudging tolerance of Toni.

When Toni excused herself to use the bathroom, a formality the old Toni who would pee in the bushes would never have shown, Ferny asked, "What's up with your foot, Mandy?"

"I tweaked it in the ditch when we were making our way back from the car," Mandy replied. "I couldn't see a freaking thing. In fact, I'm surprised that you guys were able to make it through all of that smoke unscathed."

"Well, not entirely unscathed," said Ferny pointing at Al. Her father sheepishly pulled up the torn knees on his pressed pants and then thrust forward a scraped elbow.

"Tumbled down the ditch twice," he admitted.

"I want to check out that elbow, Dad, but first let me look at your ankle, Mandy," said Ferny, gently raising the leg by cradling Mandy's calf. She slowly pulled off the loose sock Mandy had found in her father's drawer to keep it warm, supporting the foot the entire time.

"Are you through with school?" asked Mandy.

"I've only really just started," said Ferny.

"But I thought I heard you were qualified to be an LPN, now," said Mandy.

"Yeah, I just got my license," replied Ferny. "But that's only a place-holder. I've applied to the pre-med program at the U of M to be a physician's assistant and I'm waiting to see if I can jump-start classes in the spring, or find out if I have to wait till the fall semester to enter."

She bent over the foot, pressed lightly on the swelling, and tried some small motions in each direction, one resulting in a little jump from Mandy. "Yep, a light sprain," said Ferny. "I have a compression wrap that should keep it from moving, but it shouldn't take long to heal, especially if you keep icing it." She retrieved a small bag, extracted the elastic bandage, and began to wrap the foot. "Oops, forgot the secret cure," as she bent over and gave the spot a little kiss. Mandy let out an unexpected giggle and wiggled her toes. "Works every time," grinned Ferny. "See? It's better already!" and the two laughed.

Toni was emerging from the bathroom when Martin exclaimed, "I nearly forgot! Ferny—there's someone else who could really use a nurse. Caleb's down in the studio with a big gash on his head."

Al immediately rose and turned on Martin. A head taller, he loomed over him and set his two feet squarely. "Martin, if you've attacked Caleb—again—I'll kick the shit out of you from here to Sunday."

"Dad!" "Al!" screamed both Ferny and Mandy at once.

"Al," Martin replied calmly a moment later. "Like I told you before, I didn't touch Caleb the first time, and I've only seen the results of whatever happened to him this second time—not the actual event." Al relaxed some and took a step back. "We heard a noise down at the studio, and when I checked, there was Caleb passed out on the sofa with a big cut on his head and a half-empty bottle of tequila in his pocket. I cleaned the wound and sterilized it with the tequila and left him to sleep it off."

"Good thinking," said Ferny. "But I'd still better go see him."

"I'll go with you," said Al.

"No, you stay here, Al," said Martin. "I know the path, and you need the rest."

Ferny gathered her kit and some items from her backpack while Martin found a flashlight and dampened two kitchen towels to use as masks. As he led Ferny down the steps from the deck, he wondered how she would feel about treating her younger brother. Caleb had been a handful since he was a toddler, but his aggressive tendencies had become glaringly obvious when he'd tried to set his sister on fire when he was seven and she was nine. They'd been in their pajamas next to the firepit and had finished making s'mores when Caleb had grabbed a burning stick and set Ferny's gown alight. Luckily Al had seen Ferny start to dash across the lawn screaming and had immediately jumped off the porch, tackled her, and put the flames out. Ferny still had scars on her calves and the backs of her lower thighs as reminders. The incident had destroyed their sibling relationship, and despite professional counseling, Caleb had remained on a downward path ever since.

"Here, Ferny, take hold of my shoulder and this line," said Martin following the rope as he searched for the path with his feet, his right eye, and a mainly useless flashlight. When they entered the studio, Martin saw the black mass twisted tightly into a ball and tucked beneath a bush in his left eye.

Caleb was still unresponsive, except when Ferny shook him hard and got him to open his eyes for a moment. She immediately shown the flashlight on them to watch the reaction of his pupils and said, "No apparent concussion," after they closed again. Martin ferried basins of fresh cold water over to Ferny, and toted red-stained basins back, as she gently rinsed the blood out of his hair and off his face. "He needs stitches," said Ferny, "but even though I have the right suture supplies, I'm not going to attempt sewing him up without an anesthetic." *Why not?* thought Martin immediately, but remained silent. "These steri-strips should hold things together until he can see a physician," she said as she blotted his hair dry, "but it's going to be a hell of a scar, regardless."

When she was finished, she stared down at her brother with an expression that changed as she swept through various emotions, finally settling into a gentle smile. "The poor guy. If he could just let his guard down and trust people, his life would turn around. He doesn't know all the love that he's missing." She patted his cheek and tucked the blankets in around him. They stepped out of the studio and started to make their way back up the hill to the house, using the rope again as a guide. Martin's thoughts were still on Caleb as they felt their way through the smoke. Caleb had let his guard down once and fallen for a girl in high school—and that girl was Mandy. Although his daughter had never reciprocated his advances, and in fact had sought intervention, the boy had obsessed over her to the point of becoming her stalker. When she had been asked to a dance by another boy and accepted, her apparent straying from a non-existent commitment to Caleb had resulted in Pete's broken jaw and a subsequent arrest for assault with a year in juvenile detention for Caleb—the best reduced sentence Al could manage. Martin wasn't sure of all the love Caleb might be missing, but was impressed that Ferny still treated him with some affection.

His mind heavily on Caleb and the road he'd chosen, a part of his novel came back to him by way of a strange association. Instead of seeing Caleb as an aggressive fighter, he oddly formed an image of a slowly drowning young man. The chapter floated up as he slowly climbed with Ferny through the smoke.

Some never come up.

There's no guarantee. We can try our graceful best, and still not make it.

Dietrich, Katrina, and I felt that Vai Beach on the island of Crete was just too crowded for peaceful camping, even though we loved the taverna *with blaring music situated where the road ended at the bay. We hiked up over the promontory of rocks that jutted out to the south end of the beach and down to the next secluded cove. Only one other group was camped there, and the spot was just what we had sought: soft sand warmed by the sun nestled between two big rocky ridges protecting it from the wind, bells on the grazing goats in the mornings to wake us, a ten-minute hike over the ridge to the taverna for food and wine, and swimming in the calm waters off the narrow beach.*

We could dive off the rocks into our cove, but the best diving was from the rocks facing Vai Beach. There were several natural platforms and the height only depended on your courage. I liked fifteen to twenty feet at the most, but there were some who went to insane heights. The rocky floor was clearly visible, so it was not bottomless, but the salty water buoyed up every diver before they reached the bottom if they planed up soon enough, which everyone did. Hiking, diving, and the taverna had become our daily routine.

After Vai Beach, I'd left Katrina and Dietrich behind and was travelling in southern Turkey. I arrived at Pamukkale with its warm and healing mineral springs spilling out down the valley in a series of white inverted mushroom pools that held the sapphire water back, flowing gently from each to each. There was also a swimming pool that had been built and filled with some of the spring's effluent and was an attraction mainly for the water's medicinal qualities.

I swam some in the pool and then got out and went to the elevated diving board. Taking measured steps, I paced, sprung off the board and cleanly entered the water. Though I planed up at the end of the dive, I surprisingly continued down to the bottom meeting it with the full force on the bridge of my nose. I hadn't thought about the difference in buoyancy between salt and fresh mineral water! Not for one minute. I lay stunned on the hard concrete, vaguely wondering what had happened. I must have been down for a while because when I finally pulled myself into a ball and pushed off from the bottom, there was someone swimming towards me as I broke the surface. Embarrassed, battered, and bleeding, I made it to the edge of the pool and clung to the side, waiting for the healing properties of the now slightly red water to kick in.

We all dive beautifully, we all dive deeply, some just never come up.

Maybe Caleb has done just that, thought Martin, holding onto the rope and taking another step. *Maybe he's one of those who's gone too far—he's misread all of the signs and yet somehow thinks he'll come out on top. Most likely he's sinking and will never find his way up to join the rest of us.*

Chapter 34.

CHOKING AND teary-eyed, Martin and Ferny reached the house and through stuffed noses slowly realized they were being greeted by the odors of a Mexican meal. Mandy had set the chili on the stove to cook and had the fajitas reheating in the oven. She'd found some chips and salsa, and Al and Toni had obviously found the ingredients for margaritas. *One would hardly think we're trapped in a house in danger of a forest fire,* thought Martin, though glad that the mood in the room had mellowed while he and Ferny were patching up Caleb. As Al blended the drinks while talking on his cell phone and Toni was dipping the rims of the glasses in salt, Martin realized that this was the first time they'd all eaten together since before the divorce, and he wasn't sure how comfortable he was with it.

There had been plenty of parties when they were younger, and Al and his wife Geena had been frequent guests, especially when they'd finished building their nearby mansion at the top of the hill. Al had always tolerated Martin, but any chance of a real friendship had waned as Martin's success as an author and standing in the community had diminished. Ferny had put up with Mandy, but since she was in middle-school and Mandy was still in elementary school, the cultural gap between them was too great for them to become playmates.

There seemed to be little to draw the two families together, however, even Martin couldn't miss the attention that Al paid to Toni, and she was the reason that Al and Geena kept showing up at gatherings even though the Ropers were rarely invited up to the Lonzo's estate.

Al pressed his phone to his chest for a moment, sipped the drink Toni had slipped into his hand, and asked, "How's Caleb doing, Ferny?" as Martin and she moved toward the kitchen.

"The cut should be all right now, but it could really use stitches to help it heal without much of a scar," said Ferny. "He's feeling no pain now, but later could be a different story. Martin and I cleaned him up pretty well, and he's sleeping."

"That's good, and thanks for going down there and taking care of him," said Al. "We'll need to get him to the doctor as soon as this smoke eases up," and he raised a finger as his attention was drawn again to the phone. "I know they're on the fire-line, but I need my house protected! I demand at least an armed guard stationed outside—as a lookout. There are valuable things in there!" He paused and then nodded to the person on the other end of the line. "Then they can sit in their car so they don't breathe it," and listened again. "No, god damn it. If anything happens to my property, I swear, I'm holding you personally responsible!" and hung up—without the dramatic effect it might have had were it an old solid, wired phone that could be slammed down. "Gotta know how to talk to 'em," he said with a sly grin.

"Oh, hey, Dad," said Mandy catching Martin's attention. "Frank called while you were down at the studio—he wanted to make sure that we were all right. I assured him that we were OK for now, but that we're prepared to feel our way downhill if the fire takes off and we have no other choice. I said there was no getting out of here by the roads."

"Did he want me to call him back?"

"No," said Mandy. "He said that he'd tried to call earlier but couldn't get through, and out of concern for us he thought he'd try and reach us in his four-by-four truck. He checked out the main road, but it was under a total lockdown. Then he tried some of the back roads he knew up behind the hill, and they were all plugged with emergency crews and equipment. He said that things are fine everywhere else, but that it was like we were on an island in the fog. He called it the 'Mysterious Island'."

"He would," said Martin with a laugh. "Thanks, Mandy."

Mandy and Ferny chose to have some of the pumpkin ale that Martin had bought, and settled on the couch, chatting away. When they had each reached high school, Ferny had seen Mandy struggling both with snowboarding and with fitting into the crowd when Frank had first brought her up to learn the sport, and she'd taken Mandy under her wing with encouragement from Frank. During Mandy's first two years of high school, Ferny had picked up Mandy nearly every Saturday during the winters to take her up to the resort. Her influence had brought Mandy out of her shell, and she was adopted as part of the snowboarding scene by the time Ferny went off to college.

Martin accepted a margarita from Toni as Al joined them at the small kitchen table holding the chips and salsa. Martin thought about asking Toni the reason for the lawsuit she was filing against him but set the idea aside as Al spent the next half-hour telling them about his business dealings, the golf enterprises, how proud he was of Toni for being elected as vice-president of the Whitefish Chamber of Commerce, and of her now running for Mayor. "I keep telling her that she's going to be a shoo-in," he said as he poured himself another green-colored drink.

"And, I'm stoked about running," said Toni, slowing her speech so as to not slur these words. "We can sure afford it." Turning to Al, she said, "Did I tell you that the head of the party called me yesterday..." as Martin got up to help Mandy and Ferny get the dinner ready and laid out on the table.

Martin had switched to water after the first margarita and thought this was odd—his desire for alcohol seemed to have diminished with each day since his accident. It was nearly 8:00—late for dinner, and both Al and Toni, on the other hand, were showing the effects of too many drinks on empty stomachs. The chili, fajitas, grated cheese, sour cream, hot sauce, margarita pitcher, bottle of red wine, and a salad Mandy had thrown together were all crowded into the center of the small table, and the five squeezed in around it. Martin noticed that Mandy and Ferny seemed to have renewed their friendship, and their slight age difference was no longer the factor it had been when they were in grade school. He watched Toni take a bite of chili, and closing his eyes momentarily, he saw at the left that her shadow had retreated out to waist-deep water, and that Mandy appeared as a human shape glowing even brighter than before.

Martin was halfway through his meal when his phone rang, and apologizing, he moved into the study to answer it with a couple of tortilla chips in hand. "Hi, Leira," said Martin as he partially closed the door to the study. "How are you? What's up?"

"Do you have some time, Martin?" Leira asked. "I have something interesting to tell you."

"Sure, I was just eating, but no problem," and he took a bite of a chip.

"It can wait, although I thought you should hear this," said Leira. "It's about Toni and her lawyer—your lawyer too as it happens."

"Believe it or not, Toni and Al are here in the house as we speak," said Martin. "They tried to evacuate without waiting for a rescue party but got lost and ended up at our doorstep."

"Oh!" said Leira, obviously very interested. "So, as you listen, remember that I might have misinterpreted things I'm going to tell you—you might not want to mention this discussion to them."

"OK," said Martin. "What's the story?"

"I went looking for a place to eat and ended up at a pizza and pasta restaurant near the old train station. I was seated at a table above a sunken section of the floor, with some plants serving as a divider between the levels. Two gentlemen came in and were seated just below me, so I couldn't help but overhear the beginning of their conversation. One was named Stephan, whom I worked out later to be your lawyer and the other was named Sam, who must be Toni's lawyer. They sounded like they'd been to one of the nearby taverns before dinner.

"Anyway, I was sipping my wine and they shared some small talk, and then one said to the other, 'So, how's business?' and the other says, 'Oh, making it paycheck to paycheck.' And they both burst out laughing, like it was a common joke between them. They looked to be well off, so I thought that was a pretty obnoxious comment and so it drew my attention. Then one says, 'I understand you're hitting Ropers with another suit.' 'Yep, gotta pay the rent,' says the other. 'Was it your idea?' asked the first. 'Nope, it was Toni. She wants herself made whole after the divorce.' 'Pretty good timing, too,' said the first, and then, 'I didn't want to get into inventing billable hours.' 'I know, right?' asked the other. 'For now, they're the gift that keeps on giving.'"

"And then they both broke out laughing again, but of course, they were drunk. So... Martin, I don't mean to pry, but what the heck kind of suit were they talking about? What did that mean about making Toni whole?"

"Oh, I guess Toni is filing a lawsuit to try and get half of the rights to my books is all," he hissed in a sarcastic manner. Martin took a deep breath and then sighed into the phone. "Sorry about that, Leira. Stephan said that it was nothing to worry about, but now I'm not so sure."

"What? I thought she already gets half of your royal..."

"I know, I know. Apparently, she wants more, but it will probably be up to the courts to decide."

"How could Toni possibly..." began Leira, but then she paused. "Well, the lawyers certainly seem to be happy about it."

"Why should I be surprised?"

"But then again, for all I know, that could be normal talk for lawyers," and Leira continued, "it didn't sound like they were being completely deceitful or anything. Just boastful. It still creeped me out though. But it was something I heard a little later that really got my interest."

"What was that?" asked Martin.

"They were well into their second bottle of wine when the one called Sam thought he was lowering his voice, but I could hear him blurt out, 'That Toni is a fox!' Stephan then snorted, 'Why, you old dog!' at which point Sam choked on something and they spent a minute laughing. 'That's not what I meant!' said Sam. 'I meant she's as sly as a fox!' He then went on to whisper that Toni had asked him on the q.t. to begin gathering divorce papers against Al."

Martin peeked around the edge of the door as she said this and watched Toni take another sip of her margarita. "Will she never change?" he asked himself in a whisper.

"And then I missed some words, so I don't know if I heard them correctly because they lowered their voices even more. From what I could tell though, Sam said he'd just received a phone call from the County Prosecutor's office. He said that

Stephan should expect a call, too. There was going to be an announcement made tomorrow morning about the Ropers' case."

"That's what they said?" asked Martin quickly. "'The Ropers' case'? What's the announcement? Is it good news or bad?"

"I don't know," said Leira, "and I don't know the timing of the announcement tomorrow either, but I thought I'd find out and show up at the courthouse and see if I can get in to hear it."

"Thanks, Leira," said Martin and paused. "It sounds like Stephan will be there and can handle it—I don't want to impose on you..."

"Martin—are you sure you can really trust that guy? I know he's your lawyer and all, but after the way those two talked, I'm not sure I'd rely on him to represent you fairly. I'm going to be there, just in case you need an objective ear for what's announced."

"OK, if you don't mind, that might help. Now I'm wondering what's going on and what case they're talking about. Isn't it odd that neither lawyer seemed to know anything about it? Is Caleb filing a suit after all?"

"Why would Caleb be filing a suit?" asked a confused Leira.

Martin quickly filled her in on the altercation with Caleb and his friends from the previous day, and explained his worries that Caleb was seeking legal revenge.

"My god, you're awash in lawsuits, aren't you?" asked Leira. "Don't worry, Martin," she said in an attempt to ease his mind, "I'll let you know as soon as I find anything out."

"This sounds corny," said Martin. "But I hope I'm not going from this thick smoke into the fire."

"Is it still bad?"

"It's terrible, and so is eating dinner with Toni and Al, but I'll survive," said Martin. "Thanks."

"See you, and don't worry, I'll keep you posted," said Leira as she hung up.

Chapter 35.

MARTIN HAD thought he'd noticed raised voices while he was talking to Leira and expected to find Al and Toni going at one another as he came out of the study. Instead, an agitated Al was on the phone and Toni appeared to be in a state of shock. Martin gave her a questioning look as he came up to the table, seeing now that Toni was nearly at the point of tears. "The police are on the phone," whimpered Toni. "They said that the fire has made it to the edge of our property and destroyed our garden shed—and our beautiful gateway to the driveway." Martin would hardly have used the word 'beautiful' to describe the ostentatious entry facade with its two carved grizzly bears on each side, a wooden bald eagle with its wings spread across the lintel, and 'Lonzo Acres' carved into a gigantic cross-section of what must have once been a sequoia.

"I'm sorry, Toni," he managed.

"Oh, like you care!" she spat at him.

"Is the fire out of control? Is it coming our way?" asked Martin.

"That's what Al's trying to find out now," she said in an exasperated tone.

Coming to the rescue, Mandy walked up with only a slight limp and said, "So, I think we've worked out the sleeping arrangements, Dad. To make room for everyone, I think that

Mom and Al should sleep upstairs in your master bedroom, you can have the guest room, and Ferny and I will take the loft. She'd insisted on sleeping on the couch, but I showed her that there's a bunch of room up there."

"Sounds like a plan," said Martin. "And we need to change some bedding."

After she and Martin had seen to it, and set out fresh towels for everyone, Ferny and Mandy said good night and retreated upstairs above the study while Toni and Al had a nightcap on the couch with Martin joining them from his favorite chair. Toni had calmed down considerably, and Al appeared to be in a mellow mood.

"What a hell of a day," said Al with a yawn. "They said that the fire's out for now and they're trying their best, but that it's the weirdest fire they've ever seen. I demanded to talk to the head honcho instead of the police, and Fire Chief Francisco, a buddy of mine, said that it reminded him of fighting fires in interior Alaska. There, he said, the peat layer can be pretty thick in places and you think you have the fire out, but it keeps burning underground through the peat and jumps up somewhere else. He said it's just like that—only there's no peat to be found on our hill. The soil here shouldn't be able to sustain a fire like that. They promised they'd call if anything changes, but they can't even get a truck up there to water down the house because of the thick smoke that keeps coming from somewhere."

"I guess we can't do anything but sit tight," said Martin.

"That's what I'm trying to do," said Al while raising his glass. He had another shot of brandy and then headed unsteadily for the stairs to the master bedroom without another word.

After listening to Toni moan again about her beautiful house and then recompose herself, Martin couldn't help but ask, "So, Toni, I understand you're suing me?" With his left eye, he watched the shadow in the water move towards the shore and stop in knee-deep water.

Toni took a slow sip of brandy and then gave him the little wink and raised eyebrow that used to be so playful and charming. "A girl needs to look out for her self-interests," said Toni.

Martin had thought ahead about this exchange and vowed to keep his temper in check. He didn't need another assault charge or claim of verbal abuse from her. "But why sue me? And why do you need the rights to my books?"

"Because I know you, Martin," said Toni. "The only way I'm getting anything more from you is to sue. You know, you think you're the only one who put any effort into those books, but I did too."

"Toni, you didn't even know I'd written the last one until it was nearly published," said Martin in a soft tone but gripping the arms of the chair.

"But I was there, Martin. I was there to inspire you and watch after Miranda while you puttered away in the studio. I read a lot of what you wrote and gave you ideas and feedback. I was in or inspired every one of them, and I think I should own at least half of the rights, if not all of them on some of the books."

"Toni," began Martin in a raised voice, "you already get half of the royalties—that means half of everything they'll ever earn."

"I doubt you'll be publishing anything more, but what happens if you should write another? What if it miraculously becomes a best seller? Will I get any royalties from that? Any rights to it? No. I need to claim what's mine while I can."

"But you and Al are already the wealthiest people in town," Martin said more quietly, trying to keep his rising anger under control. He wanted to attack her about her upcoming plans for divorce from Al, but clamped his teeth firmly together instead.

"It's not about money," said Toni stabbing the arm of the sofa pointedly as she stood up, "it's about what's mine. It's about what's right." She haughtily made her way over to the stairs and climbed to the bedroom without saying good night, following Al's example.

Martin closed his eyes in exasperation. His head was throbbing. He hadn't noticed during the exchange that both wind and waves had risen at the island. He could see the staff in his hand, and he held it towards the shadowy figure that was now only ankle-deep in the surf. The waves passed through her as they broke on the beach. Nothing touched her. He felt that the 'him' on the island wanted to do her damage, but then he turned and walked to a low rise nearby to create some distance. It was obvious that she couldn't come ashore, and he was glad for it, both on the island and sitting on the couch.

Chapter 36.

HE'D HEARD a helicopter far overhead in the darkness outside, and hoped it was a positive sign. Things needed to change. That damn fire had to be extinguished—he didn't know how he could spend another day trapped in the house with those two without losing what little goodwill he had left. He even idly considered moving down to the studio the next morning and spending the day with Caleb as a break. While he lay awake in bed, however, he'd come up with a plan of revenge on Toni, and it wouldn't require a lawyer, courts, or physical harm. The revelation occurred at the same moment that he recognized what his next novel was going to be about. He was going to write a story that would feature a character so like Toni that he'd probably be sued again—this time for libel—but it would be worth it.

He'd paint her as she'd created herself in this life—a beautiful creature transformed, by her own doing, into a horrible, grasping monster. He was going to ensure that the reader had absolutely no compassion or sympathy left for her at all by the end. And any readers with even the slightest familiarity with Toni, especially those in her inner circle, would know exactly who the character portrayed. He wasn't yet sure on the direction the novel would take—a different twist on *Beauty and the Beast*? A retelling of *Macbeth* of some sort? A recasting of actual events? Her recent aspirations to rule the town started making *Macbeth* seem like a sure bet.

As he thought of possible plots, he veered off to wondering about how she perceived his own changes through the course of their relationship. Here he'd been, a thin young man freshly back from exotic India with tales to tell. He was into meditation and poetry and was a person, she'd said, who seemed to exude a calmness and gentleness that she hadn't seen in many men. He'd loved the same things she had, the same music, the outdoors, marijuana, the same foods—once he'd introduced her to curries. And early on he was mildly famous, drawing attention everywhere he went.

Then what had he become? Someone whispered about as a has-been and humored at parties? Someone prone to self-doubt and worried about success? Someone who'd tried and failed to keep operating at the same creative level? Someone with a dwindling income? Someone gaining weight, drinking, prone to depression, looking for excuses to keep away from her?

He drifted into sleep with these thoughts counterbalancing what had seemed like sweet plots of revenge. The waves pounded, the wind buffeted him, and the shadow lingered, now off in deeper water.

Chapter 37.

MARTIN AWOKE with a start and reached out for the alarm clock that he kept by the side of his bed. His hand hit empty air—the clock wasn't there, and he couldn't feel the nightstand either. Then he remembered that he was sleeping in the guest room downstairs. He lay back on the warm pillow and closed his eyes again when he heard what must have awoken him in the first place. Rustling sounds from the living room or study. *Probably Mandy getting some water,* he was telling himself when he thought he heard the click of a filing cabinet closing. *If Toni is going through my papers, I'm going to kill her,* he thought as he got out of bed and pulled on his pants.

He saw it as he was opening the door and stepping out into the living room. On the darkened beach near the now-calm seas was a black shape, scuttling around at the edge of the bushes. *Caleb,* thought Martin in a moment of panic. *What in the hell is he doing up here? Maybe he got hungry?*

But Martin knew instantly that Caleb wasn't in the kitchen—he was in the study, and so he approached the door quietly. There was the faint light from the weather display on his desk and the glow of LED lights from the router, so he could make out a shape even with his right eye. Martin didn't turn on a light, but entered the study and in a hushed voice so as not to wake the others said, "Caleb—what are you doing in here?" The outline of Caleb visibly started and turned towards him in his right eye while the dark shape on the beach slithered up towards him. The intruder was clutching a portable hard-drive, Martin's laptop, and several folders of paper in his arms as was evident to Martin's 'good' eye.

Caleb stared at him with a face that seemed, in the shadows, to be that of an old man with sunken eyes, but the sneer on his mouth looked just the same. His hair was stringy, and he still wore the stark white bandage Ferny had fashioned across his head. He slowly set the items on Martin's desk and then was upon Martin before the older man could react, pressing him hard against the wall next to the door. Martin could smell that Caleb had continued with the tequila, and by the harsh whisper in his ear could tell that the younger man was in a rage.

"This is mine!" Caleb hissed, pushing Martin into the wall again with a thump. "You can leave now healthy, or you can leave later hurt, but this is mine, Marty, and it's staying with me."

Martin stupidly asked, "What's yours, Caleb?" and this brought an immediate sharp blow to Martin's abdomen, while Caleb continued to hold him up so that he couldn't buckle over. The pain brought tears to Martin's eyes, and he suddenly felt like he was going to vomit. He gasped for breath as his stomach muscles tried to relax.

"You've taken everything from me, and now I'm taking it back," said Caleb. "You and that witch who cast a spell over my dad."

Martin wheezed with closed eyes. The wind was up, the waves were suddenly thunderous, and he gripped his staff against them.

Caleb took a step back. "It's your fault!" he hissed loudly. The black shape rose up from the sand, and a dirty finger was brought up just under Martin's nose. "You brought that bitch into my dad's life and she thinks she can take everything from me. My inheritance! Toni should own at least half of this land—you don't deserve it, and it should go to me. You never even use what ought to be my studio anyway, so it's rightfully mine—by squatter's rights! I've got the deed to the property now, so let's see how you like that!" He gestured to the pile of treasure on the desktop.

"Caleb," said Martin shakily, trying to follow the young man's twisted logic. "You're not making any sense. I've done nothing to you. And why do you need my laptop?"

"Toni's taking from me, and I'm taking from you," he sneered. "Besides, you won't need it when you die in flames. If the fire doesn't make it down here soon, I'll make sure you go up in blazes anyway."

It was then that Martin noticed the small plastic jug of gasoline on the other side of the doorway. "You're not thinking straight," said Martin. *Neither am I,* he thought as he suddenly shouted out loudly, "Help! Caleb's here!"

"Yeah, like who's gonna to hear you, you stupid shit?"

"Help!" shouted Martin again. He gave a weak smile. "There's something you don't know—your folks and Mandy are all upstairs, trapped here by the fire," Martin turned to the door and yelled, "Wake up, everybody!"

Caleb suddenly shrank back to the opposite wall and set himself to run or fight. They both waited a few moments, but there was no response from the household. No footfalls coming down the stairs. "Wake up! Mandy! Al! Help!" Still nothing. Caleb became emboldened by the silence. No one stirred.

"Hah! Either you're lying, or if they're here, they're cowards!" said Caleb, now in a louder voice.

What's going on? thought Martin. *Is everyone drugged? Did he kill them all?*

He stepped towards the doorway to make his escape, but Caleb countered by moving in closer. "Going somewhere, Marty?" he asked with a hoarse laugh. "You attacked me in the studio, and I let you get away with it. Not this time."

Martin took another step toward the study door when there was an unfamiliar click. *What was that? The filing cabinet?* Martin asked himself when the answer suddenly presented itself as the switchblade in Caleb's hand.

Martin's reaction stunned the both of them. He stretched out his left arm with the palm outward as if to placate a savage beast. In his left eye, Martin saw the raised staff that he pointed in the blob's direction. Caleb's response was swift, and with his right eye, Martin suddenly saw the black hilt of the knife standing out of his forearm, yet he felt nothing. Blood had spattered up his sleeve. On the island, the staff waved menacingly in his left hand. Then, with his right eye he saw Caleb's hand seem to tremble as Caleb twisted the knife that had penetrated the flesh and muscle between the radius and ulna bones of his forearm. Still, no pain.

Seeing Martin's lack of reaction, Caleb jerked out the knife, flipped it in his hand and then thrust it towards the older man's stomach. At the same instant, the man in his left eye raised the staff up high and then aimed the thick end commandingly down at the squirming black mass which immediately shrank from him. Martin expected immense abdominal pain from an entering blade, but he felt nothing and instead he heard something clatter on the floor and bounce away. The arc of the knife had never completed its deadly path. With his right eye, he saw the blade glinting on the floor and noticed his bleeding left arm continue to extend forward until his hand was resting on Caleb's right shoulder. "Caleb," he found himself saying in an unexpectedly gentle voice, "this is not the way." Caleb backed away until he was stopped by a cabinet and Martin kept pace the entire time. "The enemy isn't me. It's inside yourself." Martin vaguely wondered who was doing the speaking.

Caleb instinctively tried to bend over to pick up the knife, but seemed to be halted in mid-motion, unable to complete the grab. He straightened again and looked back with a face now filled with panic. In desperation, he reached up and drove a finger into the wound he'd created in Martin's arm. Martin still didn't react. His left arm didn't move. The scene he saw with his right eye had become somehow detached from reality, and the focus was now on what he was seeing with his left. The black mass was taking shape into the cowering, miserable figure of a man.

Caleb's finger pushed and twisted in the wound, and he was shocked by the lack of response from Martin. He brought out his red-soaked finger, staring at it and the blood pouring from the gaping hole in amazement. He attempted to shove a knee into Martin's groin, but they both heard the pop of his hipbone clicking momentarily out of its socket, forcing a sudden cry of pain from Caleb.

Martin gently gripped Caleb's right shoulder and gazed into the frenzied eyes of the bewildered young man. "Caleb," he said again. "This fight of yours is over, and the bigger battle has to end, too. And by that, I mean your battle against life. There is no oppressor, there is no one out to get you. Life is balanced, and you are not being treated unfairly."

Caleb attempted a final lunge for freedom but found himself riveted to the spot. The island-bound Martin saw a man in rags bowing before him on the beach, and suddenly sinking to his knees. "You must change, Caleb, or you will die—and I know death is really what you fear the most. It will be all right. Change is not easy, but you'll find that everyone will accept even the slightest efforts you make to better yourself. However, you must do it now, or you are lost."

The broken man on the beach slowly rose with a bowed head, while Caleb simultaneously slid down the cabinet to the floor, slipping in the blood at their feet. Both figures were weeping and muttering indistinct phrases. "I will help you," said Martin as he removed the hand that had remained on Caleb's shoulder the entire time. Caleb slowly raised himself up from the floor with tears streaming down his face. "I'm sorry," he muttered as he edged toward the study door and then bolted for the entrance to the deck, throwing it open, and disappearing into the seemingly impenetrable night. The pathetic man on the beach crept away and soon disappeared behind a dune.

Martin walked over and closed the deck door, wondering who had actually uttered the words he must have spoken during the exchange. As he turned back, he noticed the dark trail that led back to the study. He looked at his left arm with his right eye and realized that he was bleeding severely, but there was still no pain. He went to the bathroom and tried to wash the wound as best he could and then wrapped it tightly with layers of gauze and then with a towel. He took another towel and tried to mop up the drops, pools, and foot-tracks, but found the mess in the study to be too overwhelming. He was exhausted and left the bloodied towel on the floor as he stumbled to bed. Collapsing onto the mattress, he noticed that the staff was gone from view and that there was not a breath of wind. The sea was like glass.

Chapter 38.

Martin awoke to a high-pitched scream followed quickly by a throaty moan. "Dad! Oh my god!" He heard her pleading, "No, no, no..." as Mandy burst into his room. She gaped at the bloody towel around his arm and then broke into tears. "You're alive?" and then as he shook his head trying to get his bearings, she shouted, "What happened? There's blood everywhere!" Her arms were around him as he sat up in bed. "I thought you were dead!"

"I'm OK," said Martin. "I just had a little scuffle with Caleb last night."

"Little scuffle?" she wailed, "it looks like the scene from a horror movie in the study!"

Ferny appeared at the door and immediately ran for her medical kit. She returned, giving Mandy's hand a squeeze of support on her way past and then sat at Martin's other side, trying to unwrap the towel to examine his wounds. "Please don't let it have been a severed artery," she muttered under her breath, trying to maintain pressure while easing back a layer of towel at a time. When the layers were thinner, she opened her kit and set out some necessary supplies.

The doorway filled with Big Al who stood blinking at the crimson towel and the spatters of blood on the floor. "What the hell happened?" he demanded.

"Just another encounter with your son," said Martin.

Al followed the trail of blood across the living room and into the study. After a pause he erupted. "A knife!" he shouted. "If you've hurt or killed Caleb, I'll see you crucified!" he shouted storming back into the guestroom.

"He's fine," said Martin at the same time that Al said, "I'm calling the police."

"Don't Al." said Martin firmly.

"And why shouldn't I?" asked Al.

"Because they'll find that I was the only one hurt, the blood was all mine, and it won't look good for Caleb. That's why."

Toni was there now as well, absorbing the scene and the implications. "Maybe that's exactly why we should call the police," said Toni. "If that's true, he needs to be taught a lesson."

Al stared at her in amazement and was about to say something, but then slowly nodded his head in agreement. He pulled out his phone to make the call when Martin said, "Don't. It won't do any good. I won't press charges."

"Dad," said Mandy. "You have to—look what he's done to you."

By then, Ferny was down to the final layer of cloth and gently pulled it away, a sterile gauze pad ready in the other hand to try and staunch any further bleeding. "What?" she asked in surprise as she stared down at his outer forearm. Martin looked as well. Where a gaping wound had been the night before, there was now a deep gash—angry, red, and still seeping blood, but hardly displaying the level of trauma that had been inflicted upon it earlier. The site where the knife had entered was surrounded by purple bruising. She turned his arm over and there was a similar gash on the inner side, but not nearly as deep looking as the first. She examined this inner cut and tried gently to pull it apart to find the extent of the wound. It appeared to be superficial, but suddenly separated enough to begin bleeding again. Ferny immediately covered the area with a gauze pad and searched Martin's face with a wince. "I'm sorry, Martin! Did that hurt?"

Martin had watched the process and said "No," somewhat surprised. "Isn't that weird? Maybe a nerve was cut?"

"I guess that's possible, if it was very deep, but your fingers still work, and I don't see how the surface nerves could have been so affected," replied Ferny as she opened a gauze packet to apply to the top of his forearm. "I still don't understand—did he cut you twice?"

"No," Martin said, confused. "I know it's hard to believe, but the knife went in through the top and came out the bottom. It was sticking all the way through—I saw it." He reached out with his right hand and gently touched the area—he could feel his fingertips on his own skin, but there was still no pain. *How can this be?* he thought to himself.

"I don't see how that's possible," said Ferny, perplexed. "The muscle tissue looks damaged, but not badly torn, and evidently the artery wasn't touched—so, where did all of the blood come from? These aren't deep enough to produce all of that," indicating the towel with her finger. Martin sat bewildered, thinking of the black knife hilt he'd seen standing up out of his arm just hours before. "You're going to need stitches though."

"I infect easily, Ferny," said Martin. "Could there be an inner infection that's closed up the wound?"

Ferny examined his arm again and shook her head. "No, Martin, I don't think so. If there was an infection that severe there would be redness, swelling, discharge, and it would feel warm to the touch. I don't see any of those things around the wound site."

"But how could it heal that quickly?" he asked.

"I have absolutely no idea," said Ferny.

"The blood must have come from Caleb then!" growled Al as Ferny began to wrap the dressing. He glared at Martin, "I knew it, you bastard!" he spat.

"But look," said Mandy, "the only blood is on the towel and in the study, and the path between the two."

Al had his head down and found drops leading to the porch door where Martin had walked to close it, along with two bloody footprints from Caleb's boots, and that was all he needed. "You're lying! I think it was Caleb who was wounded," he snarled and headed outside to follow the path leading down to the studio. "He'd better be alive," he said in warning as he left, vanishing into the blanket of smoke.

Toni had also disappeared—upstairs with her cell phone. Mandy and Ferny set about cleaning up the blood on the living room floor and gasped again when they reached the study. Martin had joined them to reassess the damage. "I just don't understand it," marveled Ferny. "There had to have been a severed artery to produce this much blood. Look," she continued, pointing at the ceiling and wall, "that's a spray exactly like what would occur when a major artery is cut." She examined Martin thoughtfully, "Are you certain that Caleb wasn't wounded?"

"I'm positive," said Martin. "I find it hard to believe myself, but last night I was standing right here with a switchblade sticking through my arm." He suddenly felt dizzy and had to grab the edge of the door to steady himself.

"You're as white as a sheet," said Mandy. "We'd better get you to lie down for a while, you may have lost a lot of blood after all." She led him to the spare bedroom and helped him stretch out to rest. Not much blood was seeping into the bandages, which was a good sign, but he still felt drained, both physically and mentally. As he closed his eyes, the severity of the situation he'd been in with Caleb the night before became glaringly obvious. He'd just survived a knifing and was now aware of how lucky he was that Caleb hadn't succeeded in sticking him in the stomach or chest. As he started to drift off to sleep, he thought, *What kind of a person wields a staff that can calm a black blob, and at the same time tame Caleb here in the house? What if my left eye vision is more real than I thought?* He felt as if the cloak he wore on the island was laid over him as he fell asleep.

Chapter 39.

HE AWOKE a short time later to the slamming of the porch
door and a murmured exchange just outside the guestroom.
Al and Toni were evidently in a huddled conversation interrupted by fits of coughing from Al. Standing near the open
doorway, Al noticed Martin stir in his bed and was the first
to speak. "I guess I owe you an apology, Martin," he managed before turning and hacking into his fist. After a breath
that didn't trigger another event, he continued, "I just got
back from the studio. Caleb is fine. The only damage to him
is that cut on his head that Ferny treated yesterday. He let me
look him over pretty closely—we washed the blood off his
hands and there wasn't a scratch on him." Al and Toni moved
into the guest room as he continued. "He was asleep when I
went in and claims that he doesn't remember a thing from last
night. He seemed genuinely shocked to see blood on his hands
this morning. I mean, he even squirmed he was so uncomfortable. When I related what I'd heard happened up here, he
was stunned and then became sheepish, as if he did remember
portions of it but didn't want to admit it to himself." Al then
shifted on his feet and looked awkward for the first time that
Martin could recall. "He asked if you were OK, and I told him
I thought so, and then he asked if we'd called the police, and
I told him that you didn't want us to. He actually wept for

a minute, and then pulled himself back together. But it was strange—there wasn't that instant backlash or those defiant excuses that I've come to expect from the little shit. Anyway, I want to thank you for not threatening to accuse him, and I'm glad we didn't call the police."

That's when Toni spoke up. "Too late," she said.

Al looked at her in surprise. "What?" he asked loudly.

"I called them a little while ago," Toni replied in a defensive tone. "I figured if Martin hurt Caleb, we'd want them here, and if Caleb really did stab Martin, we'd want to teach Caleb a lesson once and for all."

Al stared dumbly at Toni, over at Martin, and then back at Toni. "Are you out of your mind?" asked Al.

"No, Al, either way one of those two needs to face the consequences of their actions! You can't just knife people and spill blood all over the floor and do nothing about it, now can you?"

"Toni, there was no need for that," said Martin. "Somehow I think that Caleb's learned enough from last night's episode. Jail time's not the kind of thing that's going to help the boy." Martin listened to himself speak and was surprised by his own words. *Why am I suddenly feeling so forgiving towards Caleb?* he wondered.

"Well, I don't agree," said Toni flatly. "He's out of control and has been for a long time. Anyway, I've called the police, and they said that they'd be here as soon as they can find us. In fact, they said that they're already looking for him."

"Why would they be looking for Caleb?" asked Al. "Has he done something else we don't know about? Is that how he got the cut on his head?"

"I don't really know," said Toni. "They only said that they needed to talk to him about an ongoing case."

"What case?" asked Al and Martin in unison.

"Like I said, I don't know."

Martin sank back in the bed. *Just what I need,* thinking to himself about the stabbing and the earlier incident down in the studio, *more court time, more headlines, more false accusations.*

"Well, they might not be here for a while," said Al. "The smoke out there is just as bad this morning as it was yesterday evening when we ended up here."

"Oh, and that's the other thing," said Toni. "I also called to ask about the fire situation. They said that there was a huge flare-up last night that lit up the sky. The fire jumped up around its entire perimeter and forced all of the fighters back." She went over and hugged Al. "They expected our house to be just a pile of ashes, honey, but when they made their way to it this morning, it was fine—it looks like the fire stopped about twenty feet from the house. Now everything is just smoking like it had been before."

"Thank god!" said Al and hugged her back. "Any word if they're finally getting that sucker put out?"

"They said that they don't know when, but they feel better about the flames retreating," said Toni. "They'll 'keep us apprised of the situation' is what the officer said," making quotation marks in the air with her fingers.

The smells of coffee and bacon on the frying pan drew them all into the kitchen where Mandy and Ferny were fixing eggs, pancakes, and toast to round out the meal. Martin was suddenly starving and noticed that it was already ten o'clock. He felt refreshed from his brief nap, and his arm still felt no pain.

"Hey, Dad," said Mandy pouring coffee for everyone, "there's enough food here for breakfast, but I'm not sure what we'll have for lunch or dinner. We might want to think about roasting the turkey and using the Thanksgiving supplies. The turkey should last us for two days, and hopefully we'll be out of here by then."

"That's a good idea," said Martin knowing Al's appetite. "I'll start getting the bird ready for the oven after breakfast." He was taking a sip of coffee with his left hand, completely forgetting about the wound, when his cellphone rang, and he answered it with the right.

"Hi, Frank," he said, getting up from the table so as not to disturb the others. He spent the next five minutes reassuring his friend that he and Mandy were safe after the fire's over-night flare-up, and that they were just waiting for the blaze to be extinguished and the smoke to clear. He said nothing about the stabbing. Martin had just finished the conversation with Frank when his Santana *Black Magic Woman* ringtone blared again.

"Hi, Leira," he said, "you're lucky—I just hung up from another call."

"Hi, Martin," said Leira, "is this a good time to talk then?"

"Sure, we're just starting breakfast," said Martin.

"This late?" asked Leira. "I always seem to catch you at meals, don't I?"

"That's OK, we're getting a late start…" began Martin wondering whether to tell Leira about the previous night's events, but he decided to wait. "What's up?" he asked instead.

"Well, first off, I wanted to let you know that I introduced myself to your lawyer, Stephan, at the courthouse this morning. He seems to be all right after all, and since you're stuck up on the hill, I'm going to have a lunch meeting with him to discuss our contract, just to get some of the preliminaries out of the way. I talked with Chatham-Grant this morning, too, and they said they're still excited about your joining them, so everything should work out on that front."

"Oh," said Martin, seemingly at a loss for words, "that's fantastic."

"Yes, I hope so," responded Leira. "And the other thing was, I went to the courthouse this morning at the appointed time. They were scheduled to make an announcement right about now, but they just informed us that it would be postponed until around four o'clock this afternoon."

"Any clue what it's about?"

"They're not saying much, only that new evidence has come forward that may have bearing on the case of your assault on Toni. I cornered the County Prosecutor for a moment and asked what that would mean, and he wouldn't say another word about it, especially since he didn't know me."

"Do you think it's damning or helpful?" asked Martin.

"I tried to get an answer to that very question, but I don't have any idea right now," she said. "Sorry."

"That's OK," said Martin now covering his mouth and moving farther away from the others. "I wouldn't be surprised if they came up with some other phantasm to add to the fabricated story in the first place. Probably something to help with Toni's new lawsuit. Especially now that she's running for Mayor and wants favorable publicity."

"Who knows?" asked Leira a little too brightly. "It could go the other way, too."

"Yeah, right," said Martin. "We can only hope."

"So how are you all doing up there?"

"Oh, fine," said Martin. "We had a little excitement last night, and that's why breakfast was delayed."

"What kind of excitement? Was it the fire? Is it near you now?"

"No, I guess the blaze flared up dramatically overnight, but still hasn't progressed over the ridge. I'll tell you all about the events here later, but we're all OK."

"OK..." echoed Leira. "Well, I'll try and call after the meeting with Stephan and let you know how it went."

"Sounds good," said Martin. "Talk to you then."

He padded back over to the table carrying his coffee mug and sat down to join the others. *It sure is going to be empty around here in a few days,* he thought to himself unexpectedly, *no Leira, no Mandy, no...* Toni was reaching over to slap Al's hand as he reached for another pancake, *no unwanted relatives—once the fire is put out and we're not all trapped here, that is.*

Chapter 40.

AFTER BREAKFAST, Martin helped pick up the lighter items to clear the table and then reached into the refrigerator to lift the turkey out when Mandy stopped him. "Dad, I don't think that's such a great idea after all you've been through," she said. "And think of your arm. Ferny and I can handle the kitchen—you should go rest." She and Ferny jumped into preparing a stuffing which they decided to cook separately from the turkey. Not particularly tired, Martin brought his laptop to the kitchen table and began surfing for news of the fire while the ladies chopped and mixed ingredients. Toni had received a phone call from her lawyer and took it upstairs, and Al opened a bottle of white wine. Martin expected him to be on the phone for business as well, but Al had discovered the jigsaw puzzle and settled into it. Each in his or her own world, they all jumped when there was a loud pounding on the door.

Martin slid his chair out and was moving over to answer the knock when in stumbled Deputy Thompson and another deputy behind him, coughing and teary-eyed. Martin recognized Jim Duggins, the deputy who'd accompanied Thompson on their previous visit. They set down their small oxygen tanks and some equipment, and then immediately choked out a request for water and a sink to wash their eyes and faces. Mandy was immediately there with water, and Ferny guided them each back to the bathroom and helped them flush their eyes and clean up.

"How did you make it through all the smoke?" asked Martin.

Thompson sat in a kitchen chair and took another gulp of water. "It looked like things were letting up. We were making some easy progress along the road when suddenly the smoke rolled in thicker than ever. Seeing any sign of the road ahead became hopeless and so we had to abandon our vehicle. We had oxygen with us, so we decided to hike out. Somehow, we ended up walking in circles and came back to the cruiser when our oxygen was almost gone. We decided to make one more attempt and came across your car when the tanks ran out of air. Thank god we guessed right about which way to go after that."

"Why were you trying to drive in before the danger was over?" asked Al who'd abandoned the puzzle for now, but not his wine glass.

"Like I said, from the perimeter, it looked like the smoke was clearing. We needed to check on families and give assistance if they required it," said Thompson. He then twisted in his chair to fully face the elder Lonzo. "And we're looking for your son, Al."

"And why's that?" asked Al, expecting an arrest warrant to magically appear in Deputy Thompson's hand.

"The County Prosecutor wants to talk to him about some prior charges," said the policeman. "And he's put some urgency on his request. That's not the main thing though. While we were out, we received a call about another assault here at the Ropers' residence from Ms. Lonzo—your wife. Now where's Caleb? As you can see, we need to talk to him on both counts."

Al started to deflect the question, but sighed instead and pointed at the porch door. "He's resting down in the studio."

Thompson turned to Martin. "The one where you have your altercations?" he asked.

"Only one was down there. And it wasn't an altercation," said Martin to a somewhat dubious look from Thompson, "but, yes, down the hill."

"OK," said Thompson. "Where was this second altercation then?"

"Here," said Toni coming down the stairs. "Over there in the study."

Both Martin and Al glared at her, and Thompson caught the looks.

"We'll check that out, but we need to see Caleb first. We're going to bring him back up here for some explanations. The prosecutor might be able to discover the information he needs over the phone."

Both deputies rose and headed for the door to the deck. "I strung up a rope to make the path easier to follow," said Martin. "It'll be on your left. Oh, and take these," as he wetted two kitchen towels to use for masks.

"Thanks, Martin, we should be right back," and wrapping their mouths, the two disappeared out the door and into the smoke.

Mandy threw a crooked smile at her father. "Good thing we're making the turkey," she said. "There may be a couple more mouths to feed."

Martin sighed inwardly. *Another day cooped up with Al and Toni, and now two police officers. Perfect—just perfect!*

Following a whim, he stepped out on the deck and looked down towards the studio, concentrating on what he saw with his left eye—to try and detect Caleb's presence. There was no black blob to be seen anywhere on the now serene beach. He walked back inside and wondered why he hadn't noticed it earlier—Mandy's glowing shape was there as always, but next to it was another faint, but very visible shimmering form, corresponding to where Ferny stood.

Chapter 41.

THE TWO officers were back in ten minutes, entering the living room just as Mandy was returning the basted turkey to the oven. Deputy Duggins went over and started unpacking what turned out to be an evidence kit while Deputy Thompson addressed the group, "Caleb's gone. The studio's empty, but it's obvious he's been there since my last visit. When was the last time any of you saw him?"

The room was quiet. "Anyone?" he asked again.

"I think I was the last one to see him, and that was this morning around ten or so," said Al.

"And no one's seen him since?" There was a shake of heads around the room. "He can't have gone far in all of this smoke, but there was no trace outside the studio of which way he headed. We did find blood on strips of cloth though. Can anyone explain that?"

Ferny spoke up. "Caleb had a nasty cut on his head when we got here yesterday. He was passed out down there in the studio, but Martin and I cleaned him up and treated the wound."

"So that wasn't the result of an assault?"

"Not that I know of," said Martin. "He showed up down there with the gash just after the smoke rolled in."

Deputy Thompson turned to Toni. "Ms. Lonzo, can you please tell me about the assault you phoned in this morning then?"

"Toni," said Toni.

"OK, Toni," said Thompson. "What happened?"

Toni described the bloody mess they'd awoken to—the splatters, the pools, the knife, Martin's wound and claim of being attacked, and the clean-up. Deputy Thompson quickly looked at the spare bedroom, the living room and the study. "Where's the knife?" he asked. Mandy pointed to it on the desk where she'd placed it while cleaning. "I'd accuse you all of tampering with the scene of a crime if I knew exactly what happened last night. Jim, you gather all the evidence you can, and take plenty of pictures." Turning to the others, he said, "I want to interview each of you individually. But first, I need to examine your wound, Martin."

Martin was sitting at the kitchen table at this point and self-consciously covered his left forearm sleeve with his right hand. He then spoke up, courageously as he saw it, in an attempt to protect Caleb. "I'm afraid you're going to need a search warrant, or something like that, to look at my arm, Deputy."

Thompson was just in the middle of saying, "I don't need a warrant to…" when Martin's left arm withdrew itself from under his right, reared itself back and slapped his own face soundly across the left cheek. The entire room gasped and then all exchanged surprised looks.

"What the?" asked Martin, bewildered himself.

"Dad, are you nuts?" asked Mandy. "What'd you do that for?"

That was just like the dream I had the other night, thought Martin for a moment, rubbing his cheek with his right hand. Aloud he said, "I think I wanted myself to do the right thing."

She furrowed her eyebrows and asked, "What do you mean?"

"I guess I want the Deputy to look at my arm after all," as he began to roll up his sleeve and reveal the slightly bloodied bandage underneath. Ferny came over and began to help him unwind the gauze as both deputies stepped up to the table for a better look. Ferny removed the final sterile pads and examined the cuts. "I think they look even better than before," she said. "The bleeding seems to have stopped completely, and it doesn't look nearly as raw."

"This happened last night?" asked Thompson, leaning over for a closer examination. "It sure doesn't look that new—more like it happened at least a few days ago." Pointing at the bloody bandage he said, "And this doesn't look like much blood, but it does look like it should have come from a fresh wound; it's still damp. Was this worth calling us for?"

Martin didn't answer, but Toni found her voice. "There was blood everywhere, officer... I mean everywhere. And the gash on his arm looked even nastier this morning. It had to be either him or Caleb who bled so much, but Al checked out Caleb this morning, and he was fine. Wasn't he Al?"

Al said nothing, but nodded in reply.

Toni walked them over to the bathroom and the small pile of blood-soaked towels that had been temporarily placed in the bathtub. "See what I'm talking about?" she asked.

"Jesus," said Thompson looking over again at Martin. "I think we need to find Caleb to check him out. Unfortunately, that appears to be impossible right now, doesn't it? I personally don't see how you could have produced all of this last night, Mr. Ropers."

The deputies spent an hour collecting statements and evidence: they took photos of Martin's arm before Ferny re-bandaged it; they took pictures of the bed, and kept the red-splotched pillowcase and sheets; they gathered scrapings of blood from between the floorboards and from the ceiling and placed them in evidence bags; they stowed the knife; they took the two or three towels soaked in blood and put them in a plastic garbage bag; they drew a sample of Martin's blood; and they recorded a witness statement from each person in the house.

Deputy Thompson was sitting at the kitchen table, gratefully sipping a cup of coffee while Duggins was finishing up, and told Martin and Al, "This is absolutely the most evidence I've ever collected where it's hard to prove that a crime has been committed. And for now, I'm believing you about Caleb's condition because Duggins says the samples we've taken here in the house match your blood type, and they don't match the samples found on bandages down at the studio. This would normally be enough blood to constitute a murder scene, so you can see why I might consider this all to be a little bizarre, though, Martin," he said turning to face him, "I'd ask you how it is you could heal so quickly, but suspect I wouldn't get an answer that I'd believe. Plus, you've already told me that no matter what we find, you won't press charges, regardless."

"Nope," said Martin.

"But I'm still not clear why Caleb allegedly attacked you in the first place. You say he had your laptop and some files when you found him in the study?"

"He had a harebrained notion that some of this land should belong to him, and he thought that holding the deed would make it so. Remember," added Martin, "he was drunk and not thinking straight."

"And the gas can in the study?"

"Like I said, I don't know anything about it," said Martin and then changed the subject. "Hey, you guys are stuck with us, and we're going to be eating an early Thanksgiving meal as soon as the turkey comes out of the oven—would you and Duggins care to join us?"

Thompson took a deep appreciative breath and said, "I was hoping you'd ask," with a smile.

Chapter 42.

THEY SPENT the next hour occupied in their own ways: Deputy Thompson wrote out reports on a tablet and was in several phone conversations with headquarters, being especially interested in any news on Caleb's whereabouts; Duggins finished up his duties and joined Al at the jigsaw puzzle; Toni was on the phone, both upstairs in private, and downstairs so she could include Al in the conversation; Mandy and Ferny were kind enough to see to the cooking, and also spent time playing cards at the kitchen table; and Martin sat in his most comfortable chair, either with his eyes closed or staring at the dense smoke that had become a perpetual feature of his once-spectacular hillside view.

Martin's plans for a revenge novel from the night before seemed to be fading from his awareness like trying to grasp the tails of an ephemeral dream when one first awakens. The more he contemplated ways to get back at Toni, the more he realized that this resulted in one of two things occurring—either the left-eye perspective would overwhelm him and he'd be thoughtlessly staring over the barren landscape hoping to catch a glimpse of a darting point of light to relieve the boredom, or his mind would sabotage his malicious thoughts and he'd find himself thinking of something completely different.

He dwelt on his damaged brain. *Had what I remembered from last night really occurred? What was with the staff in my left hand, and why can't I always see it? How do I come to have a book in my right hand at different times? Why do only certain people show up in my left eye?* And, more disturbingly, *How could my arm possibly be healing so quickly? Why haven't I felt any pain? Why did my left hand slap me—once in a dream, and now in public? How could it have a life of its own? Am I finally losing it?* Martin let out an audible sigh. *I've always had a sense of who I am, haven't I? Is that sense of self collapsing? Am I becoming somebody else?*

He closed his eyes and recalled part of a chapter written long ago. It was from a time when he'd been prone to frequent self-examination but had always remained full of youthful self-assurance. Just like a fairy tale, things would work out fine in the end, of that he'd had no doubt.

Ryan and I were sitting on the temple steps in Durbar Square, Kathmandu, in the shade, watching the world pass by—to me it was like picking up a kaleidoscope and slowly spinning the wheel: a couple fresh off the bus, wide eyed and carrying goose-down parkas, toting shiny new backpacks, and wearing boots that they'll soon find were too hot and too stiff— staying close together and walking quickly; a laborer bent forward with a load held by his neck muscles alone—a strap from the bundle running up his back and then to the padded band across his forehead—barefoot and leaning forward and perhaps, like so many with similar burdens, waking up not to breakfast, but to a nice stiff belt of the rakshi *rice liquor before shoving off; a monk in burgundy robes and carrying a* mala *of brown wooden beads, following a path through the crowd that he's been on since childhood—the path; a western junkie, either happily playing a flute and bouncing around the square, or joining the beggars off to the side—here for a day, here for a week, here for a year, not here for the high altitude, but here for the High; a businessman in a Nepali hat, off to have a cup of chai with a friend, chat about politics and the influx of foreigners, and then back to the store, the wife, the radio, or possibly a rare TV; the beggars—trained to it as a job, or absolutely hopeless—smart and street-savvy or clutching a child at the edge of desperation. I'm like everyone else— defining myself by whom I'm not.*

"What are we becoming?" asked Ryan, and neither of us knew. We were hermits, making conversation only occasionally and with only a few, because in this country of millions, we don't speak the languages. We were gypsies or dandelion seeds, changing course by wind or whim. We were vagabond hoboes—carrying only what fit on our backs, and light at that. We were also prisoners, locked up by our color, our attitudes, our past. Compared to many, we were literati, able to read and write and discuss what we'd read or written. And we were lonely and homesick at times, but desperate—never.

He thought about his situation when he'd written those words. He'd been back in familiar surroundings and was beginning a new life with Toni, a home giving him the luxuries of comfort, distance, and hindsight. Now, he knew that he'd overlooked some aspects of their travels, like how exposed they'd been, and how this vulnerability had permeated each day, lurking just below the surface until some event slapped them into awareness of their frailty. How little it really took for things to go awry. There was that bus ride in Nepal where the driver had swerved from a head-on collision at the last second to end them up in the ditch, but intact. They'd made it through the entire journey pretty well unscathed, and it was probably their positive, or naïve, outlook that had made that happen. When he'd written *Faint Trails* he'd still been leading a life where there was little of the negative to weigh him down. *However, so much seems to have gone wrong lately, and those seem like halcyon days in comparison,* he thought morosely, and then sat up straighter in his chair. *But have I reached the point of desperation?* He listened to the conversations, and heard Mandy say, "I think this is almost done, take a taste," and then laugh as Ferny must have had either too much or too little. He sensed the comfort of his chair, sitting in his own house, on his own land. *Not hardly,* he thought. Then as the vision in his left eye again became prominent, *Not yet.*

Something was pricking at the back of his mind, and he got up and went into the study, booting up his computer. Opening a fresh document, he began to type.

We carve our place in the world
Sparks fly off the blade as it sharpens
Reflecting on only a single side

We hone it for our daily use
A myriad of cuts to fashion infinite lives
A keen divide each time
He bumps her coffee and they chat
  He misses the cup by a whisker and doesn't notice
She stumbles on the step and misses the train
  She slips in just as the doors slide shut
He ducks under the water and never comes up
  He bursts up gasping for air
They see the cat and screech to a stop
  They see the small black shape too late
Each side a new world
Each cut the right one

Startling him, his phone rang in his pocket and he answered. "So, are you eating?" asked Leira. Martin burst out laughing as the oven timer for the turkey dinged in the kitchen.

"Not yet—perfect timing! The turkey's done. Let me see if they need any help in the kitchen, and then we can chat."

"The turkey?" Leira began, but Martin had already set the phone down next to the computer, hustled into the kitchen, and watched Mandy pull out the bird. "Is there anything I can do to help?"

"I think we have it covered," said Mandy with another tray in her hand, "I'm just going to broil these Brussels sprouts, and warm the rolls, and that's the last thing."

"Wow—good job!" said Martin as he gave her a hug and headed back to the phone. He noticed that Duggins was starting to hover around the turkey. Al and Thompson were talking about football next to the card table.

"Hi, I'm back," said Martin picking up the phone again.

"Sounds like a crowd there," said Leira.

"You have no idea," said Martin, walking slowly around the study. "Toni and Al are still here, and so is their daughter Ferny. Plus, we have two policemen who showed up and are now stranded. Luckily, Mandy thought it was a good idea to cook the food for Thanksgiving today to be able to feed everyone. We're actually just about to sit down to a Thanksgiving dinner."

"I thought you were inviting me to Thanksgiving tomorrow!" said Leira with a laugh. Then, "No, really, but I wish I was there."

"Um, are you sure? Think about it: my ex-wife, her magnate husband, and two police officers? The only bright spot for me is Ferny—she and Mandy have renewed their friendship, and she's an excellent nurse as well."

"A nurse? Why do you need a nurse?" asked Leira.

"I'm just saying... OK, that's something I can tell you about later. So how are things in the real world?"

"The County Prosecutor has reported, once again, that they're going to make an 'official' announcement at 3:30, a little earlier than expected—in about half an hour. I've tried to be as nosey as possible, but their lips are still sealed."

"And how was your meeting with Stephan?" Martin had jumped into the question, despite not wanting to hear the answer.

"It was a good meeting," replied Leira, "and he's not near-ly the creep I expected him to be."

"Well, that's a relief," said Martin, having known the man for two years and thinking him to be decent.

"Yes, and very straightforward, too. He looked over the contract and said that it's only binding if we want it to be. I know that sounds weird, but there are no penalty clauses for changes or termination of the contract. The contract itself is binding, but if neither of us contests it, we can change or cancel it at will."

"OK," said Martin. "What does that mean for us?"

"I explained the situation to Stephan, and he said that, keeping your best interests in mind, as long as you found a situation you were comfortable changing over to, the contract could be binding to that point and then terminated when the new contract came into play, assuming we both agree. What do you think, Martin? Does this sound good to you?"

I'm opening her cage, and she's at the door, he thought. "That sounds like the perfect solution," he said, trying his best to sound chipper. "Now we just need to find out more about Chatham-Grant's ideas, and if they like me, I'll slide over un-der their umbrella."

"Oh, good," sighed Leira. "I was hoping that's how you'd feel."

"Definitely," said Martin. "So, you'll call after the announcement?"

"Will do," said Leira, and rang off.

Chapter 43

MARTIN WAS overcome with an incredible sadness from their conversation as he walked over to cut the turkey. Remembering his bandaged arm, however, he deferred the task and watched Duggins expertly carve and layer the slices onto a platter. The busy activity and boisterous table soon made him forget his melancholy. Al poured wine, which even the deputies accepted, and they were the most adamant in their toasts and thanks for the meal. As they chatted and the forks clicked against the plates, Martin admired the spread before them and took a bite of the mashed potatoes. Seeing the plenty on the crowded table caused him to think back to a time when a simpler meal was welcomed happily.

Dried apricots, nuts, and apples were laid out on a woven wicker platter. After days on the truck, munching jaggery, and skipping meals, this was heaven. And it was—the sparsely populated Hunza Valley opening as a fertile little pocket below the towering Karakoram range and reachable, before the new road was put in, only by narrow paths up the precipitous sides of the Hunza River. And visitors were still a novelty— a small crowd gathered to meet us and show us to a room in a little mud house we could rent while there. No one was shy—women and children coming up to say hello. An old man brought us a photo of himself and a certificate in English say-ing that as a soldier he was a reliable fellow. We were told that the Mir was out of the region at the time, otherwise he would have wanted to meet us. The men wore what we called 'Hunza hats' that we had seen on others on the way up the river and we each bought one—a wool tube with one end cov-ered, rolled up till the roll met the top—wonderfully warm.

We spent several days wandering the area—along irriga-tion ditches and through fruit tree groves, across a swaying narrow suspension bridge to hike up the other side of the river, to the two-story palace of the Mir of Hunza further upriver, to the old fort in Baltit. The days started with late sunrises and ended with early sunsets because of the season and the height of the mountains surrounding us—north now of Rakaposhi and under Ultar Sar shouldered by its huge brothers, all over 24,000 ft. tall.

One evening we were proudly served some duck curry. We were starving and ate packed in close with a little family in a warm room. We're pretty sure this was where we picked up giardia. We still managed to make it around the area for more exploring, but we were all pretty sick and were treated for the parasite when we got back down into India. A most unpleasant thing—like farting through your mouth. Maybe in all heavens there is a little hell.

The memory of that taste came back to Martin, and he quickly sloshed some wine around in his mouth. *Ooh, that duck,* he thought, but for the first time he realized that the giardia could really have come from anywhere. They'd endeavored to be so careful during the whole trip, but ended up getting sick several times with dysentery and other ailments, regardless. Bottled water was rare then, and they avoided tap water in most places, so their main source of liquid was from tea or soda pop. They tried to see that the sweet tea and milk combination had boiled, and when they were served, they would slosh the steaming liquid so that it slopped over the rim, cleansing the lip that had been washed in who knew what kind of water. And they always wiped the top of the Fanta bottle well, because they didn't trust the source of the ice the pop had been sitting in. They ate mostly with their hands, well washed if possible, as did most of the population, and avoided cutlery. Except for in remote Hunza, they never ate raw fruits or vegetables unless they could be easily peeled, so they ate a lot of bananas. *No wonder we lost so much weight,* thought Martin, as both he and Ryan had come home as thin as rails. He looked down at his now-generous stomach, but still gratefully took another bite of turkey and gravy, smiling at a joke Duggins had just told.

Chapter 44.

FOUR PHONES rang at almost the same instant at 3:35. Martin, Toni, Al, and Deputy Thompson each stood up and moved to a different part of the house so that they could hear the caller above the other conversations.

"Is it the fire?" Ferny immediately asked Al who listened for a moment and then shook his head.

Martin was soon across the room and pressed the button to answer his call. "Martin!" said Leira breathlessly. "You're not going to believe this!"

"What is it, Leira?" asked Martin, hoping for good news of some kind, but fearing the worst.

"The charges against you have been dropped!"

"What? What charges?" he asked, thinking they must be the one's recently made by Caleb.

"The old ones! The ones made by Toni two years ago!"

"You're kidding!" yelled Martin.

"What?" he heard Toni scream at the other end of the room.

"The charges, the sentencing—everything! You've been cleared of assault!"

"But... How is that possible?" he asked.

"A video was discovered clearly showing what happened that night on Halloween. It took them awhile to verify it, and that's why there was such a long a delay, but now they're sure it's authentic and it proves your innocence." Leira took a breath and continued more slowly. "Apparently a teenager had borrowed his parent's video camera to take movies of his friends Trick or Treating that night, and afterwards he was playing around with what he could do with the camera—taking pictures from weird angles, and in different lightings. He's older now and was going through old footages before tossing the tapes. Anyway, his yard was a few houses away from the parking lot where Toni said you hit her. The boy was experimenting with the black and white setting and happened to film you two without really realizing what he was seeing—just a couple of old drunks trying to get into their car—as he described it. But luckily, he remembered all the publicity surrounding your trial and the relevance of the tape clicked with him. He took the film into the police who handed it over to the County Prosecutor. The film distinctly shows Toni trying to take a swing at you, missing, bumping against the car, and going down on her face while you try to stop her fall. It's all there!"

"What?" was all Martin could think, say, or feel for a moment. Then, "I can't believe it! This is fantastic!"

He glanced across the room. Al was still listening to his caller but staring first at him and then at Toni. Deputy Thompson had hung up his phone and was walking towards Toni, and Toni was in tears, sobbing into the phone.

"Yes! You're in the clear, Martin," said Leira, nearly laughing. "And they want to bring in both Toni and Caleb and talk to them about giving false testimony and lying under oath. Of course, this also brings into question Toni's suit against you for the rights to your works. The County Prosecutor didn't sound very happy with her, to say the least."

The sudden drama in the room had brought Mandy over to Martin's side where she peered at him inquisitively, while at the same moment Ferny was over trying to speak to Al. "What?" Mandy mouthed silently.

"Leira—I can't thank you enough for being there and calling me," said Martin. "This is going to take me some time to process, and Mandy's right here. Can I call you back after a little bit?"

"Absolutely, Martin." said Leira. "I'm so glad that you've finally been cleared of all of this—talk to you soon!"

Martin put away his phone and gave Mandy a long hug while she asked "What is it, Dad? What's going on?" He held her at arm's length, and nearly teared up.

"They finally know that I was telling the truth!" he said. "I can't believe it, but there's now proof that I never struck your mom. She made the whole story up, just like I've said." The two sat down on the sofa together and he told her what he'd learned from Leira.

Mandy grinned as he finished, throwing her arms around him and hugging him fiercely. "Thank god, this is over!"

Across the room he happened to catch Toni's eye and she shouted, "You bastard!" as Thompson stepped in front of her to calm her down.

"I'm still in shock," said Martin, "and I've got to speak to your mom," as he returned her hug and stood up from the couch. He'd intended to walk over and talk to Toni about dropping her latest lawsuit when he froze. He suddenly couldn't see the room—only the deserted beach with a distant shadowy figure up to its neck in utterly still water. To his surprise, instead of continuing to watch the shadow he turned on the sand and walked over a dune and up a small path. He was back at the spot in front of the huts where he'd summoned the tiny points of light and seemingly turned them into fiery sparks. He held out his staff and dozens of what he now thought of as glowing fairies joined him, and with the staff raised, he sent them out in all the directions of the compass. They zipped out several meters and then began to fly in a counterclockwise circle, driving a wind before them. When he felt that the gale-force winds were strong enough, he waved the staff out away from the huts, and each point in turn flew out from the cyclone in the indicated direction. The swarm had nearly faded from view when the lead fairies swung around in a gigantic arc and headed back straight towards him. He heard a low moan which quickly grew to become an ear-splitting howl as a huge cloud of dust and sand bore down on him driven by an incredible wind—in a moment he was engulfed, holding steady to the staff that he could now see he'd driven deeply between the paving stones for support. The blast hit and almost knocked him over and was just as suddenly gone. In the blink of an eye, he was alone on the square looking out on a calm, clear day. There was something new though—the background sound of broken bits of glass tinkling as if from a hanging mobile in the huts.

Someone was shaking him as he opened his eyes, and he heard Mandy saying, "He was standing here and then just fainted." Her face was in front of him. "Are you all right?" she asked with a look of concern. He could see clearly with his right eye again as several arms helped him stand up.

"I'm OK," he was saying when suddenly the house shook violently. They all gaped at each other as the walls rattled again and their eyes were drawn to the shuddering main window. *Another earthquake?* thought Martin immediately. He then realized the cause was a fierce wind driving down the hill towards the lake and shaking the house and the surrounding trees that were slowly becoming visible. They all gathered at the window and watched in amazement as the smoke that had choked them for days was being blown down the slope, out across the lake, and dissipating against the far shore. In minutes the stark white tops of the mountains across the lake stood out in sharp contrast to the clear blue sky now above them.

"What the …?" asked Al and, "Yes!" shouted Ferny.

Deputy Thompson's phone rang, and he took the call while opening the porch door and walking out onto the deck. The others followed into the cleansed, cool air. He was soon able to give a report. "The fire's out. Completely out. And the Fire Chief said that it has a lot of them scratching their heads. There's burn damage and ash where they've been fighting the blaze, but it's like the fire completely disappeared. There's no more smoldering, no hotspots—heck, they can't even find any warm spots. It's as if the fire happened a month ago, instead of last night. Anyway, we're all cleared to go, and all of the roads are now open. You're free!"

Yes, I am, thought Martin as he leaned against the railing and took in a long deep breath of fresh air. Thompson must have read his thought because he walked up and gave Martin a hearty pat on the back.

Martin found that he had to go back in and sit on the couch for several minutes with a massive headache until some ibuprofen kicked in. Feeling better, he called Leira while the others gathered their things and prepared to leave. Deputy Duggins was helping Mandy deal with the leftovers. Al was on the couch consoling Toni, who wouldn't even look at Martin. She'd laid into him with another string of profanities after the skies cleared, but had since withdrawn into herself.

"Hi, Leira," said Martin as she answered. "You won't believe what just happened."

"What? Toni fainted from the news?" asked Leira.

"No, but it looks like I did."

"Really?"

"Well, maybe not from the news—anyway, this is just as strange as the new evidence. Are you outside, or near a window?" asked Martin. "You should take a look at the hill my house is on."

"I'm in my hotel room and it faces the wrong way. Just a sec," said Leira as she walked down the hall and stepped outside.

"Oh, my god!" she exclaimed. "The smoke's gone! How did that happen so quickly?"

"This huge wind stirred up and blew it all down the slope towards the lake, but I don't see any traces of it left, even down there," said Martin. "It was the oddest thing."

"I'll say," said Leira. "The day is just full of surprises, isn't it?"

"I'll say," echoed Martin. "We're free to leave our houses now, so in just a bit we're going to walk the short distance to my car and then drive up the road and see if we can locate either Toni and Al's rig or Deputy Thompson's patrol car. Hopefully both. I might make a run into town after that. Do you need a place to stay tonight?"

"No, thanks, Martin. I'm already checked in for another night here, and it'll be getting dark soon anyway."

"Maybe we could get a drink or a bite somewhere? I just have to get out of here."

"That sounds like fun—and like you deserve it," said Leira. "Call when you get into town?"

"Will do," said Martin.

Chapter 45.

"*ARE YOU* sure you need this?" asked Martin. He had the black garbage bag that had been filled with bloody towels slung over his shoulder and they were walking to his abandoned car.

"You know regulations," said Deputy Thompson, "gotta follow them." He looked over at Martin. "But don't worry, I don't see this going anywhere at all."

They reached Martin's Subaru which was now covered with a fine layer of gray ash, stowed the officer's bags and oxygen tanks in the trunk, and then everyone piled in as best they could—Thompson in front, and Toni packed in between Big Al and Deputy Duggins. Toni had been quiet during the short walk to the car and remained silent in the back seat. Her eyes were puffy, and her self-assured manner was seriously deflated.

Martin drove toward the main branch in the gravel road that lead either into town or further up the hill to the Lonzo residence. "Hey, Martin, stop," said Duggins suddenly from the back seat where he'd been staring down the steep incline below them. Martin halted in the middle of the road and Duggins opened the door and climbed out. "Hey, Thompson," he yelled over his shoulder as he faced down the slope, "I think we've found Caleb's Jeep." They all got out and looked down at the vehicle that had left the sharp shoulder and lay with its front end smashed against the base of a large pine. Duggins slid down the embankment and examined the Jeep. Once he'd scrambled back up to road level, he informed them that the keys were still in the ignition and that there was some dried blood smeared along the driver's side window that had been partially rolled down. "So that's where Caleb got the gash on his head," said Al. Then, "Sorry for blaming you, Martin." Martin merely nodded as they all got back in the car and he put it in gear.

They turned up the road towards the Lonzo's mansion and soon found the Escalade with two wheels planted firmly in the uphill ditch. With Thompson's and Duggins' help, Al was able rock the Escalade free and drive out. Deputy Thompson admonished Toni that he expected to see her at the courthouse on Friday morning as she got in beside Al who then backed the car up the road towards their house since there was no convenient way for him to turn the huge car around.

The police cruiser was found one-hundred feet down a side road that they'd missed seeing on the first pass. "Now, how the hell did I get off the main road?" asked Thompson, and Duggins shook his head. The policemen transferred their equipment to the back of the patrol car and waved to Martin as they headed into town. Martin managed to turn his car around without incident and returned home, enjoying the quiet and solitude during the short drive.

Ferny had stayed behind to help Mandy clean up the mess after the huge meal. Martin parked his car in front of the garage and, opening the back door to the house, was shocked to find Caleb sitting at the kitchen table with a bite of turkey in his mouth. Most of what had been on his plate was gone, but Ferny was already spooning another helping of mashed potatoes onto it. Caleb stopped chewing, fork in hand, and stared at Martin with wide eyes.

What happened next was totally unexpected to Martin. Caleb chewed quickly and grabbed a glass of water to wash down the food. He wiped his hands on his napkin as he got up and approached Martin who at first feared a confrontation. Standing in front of him, Caleb said, "Mr. Ropers... I'm so sorry about what happened last night, and I can't believe what Ferny told me." He looked at the floor. "Well, I guess I can believe it, the way I've been acting, but I don't remember a thing about it." Martin started to raise a hand to comfort him, and Caleb instinctively took a half-step back, continuing to stare at the floor. "I saw the blood on my hands this morning, and Dad helped me wash it off, but I was so afraid that I'd killed someone or something. Ferny says that your cuts aren't really that bad, so I don't get why my hands were covered in the stuff."

"I don't get it either, Caleb," said Martin. "But I'm OK. It really is healing up surprisingly well."

Caleb nodded at Martin's bandaged arm and said, "Good."

"You know that the police want to talk to you?"

"Yes, Mr. Ropers," Caleb said in a weak voice.

"And you know that it's not really about last night? That little interaction is between you and me and won't amount to anything. They want to talk to you about your statements concerning Halloween when you said I hit your stepmother."

"Ferny told me," said Caleb. "They want to talk to my stepmom, too." He paused, still failing to meet Martin's eyes. "The funny thing about it is that I don't really recall much of that night either. I was high on something, and I kind of remember you two arguing. I sort of woke up in the car outside the hospital and decided to split. I found another party. The next day, Toni said I had to say I saw you hit her, or she'd tell Dad about me being stoned. I figured it was no skin off my nose." He looked Martin in the eyes now. "What do I tell them?"

"Tell them the truth, Caleb," said Martin. "That's always best. Why don't you finish eating, and then I can drive you back to your dad's house? Oh, by the way, where were you this afternoon?"

"I knew I was in trouble, so I snuck back up here and hid in the garage. I figured nobody would be using a car today." He headed back to the table and then turned around. "Mr. Ropers, could you not take me back to my folk's house? Could you take me to the rehab center instead?"

Ferny came up and put an arm around part of Caleb's big frame. "We've been talking while you were taking Dad and Toni back to their car. Caleb's decided to try and make a new start—on his own—without Toni or Dad involved."

"That's great, Caleb," Martin said, looking at the young man with a measure of hope.

"He said he had a friend who went through the rehab center and had good things to say about the personnel. I called, and they said that they're open and could take him today. He just needs a sponsor to help sign him in."

Caleb looked at Martin, and Martin nodded back at him.

"But what about the police?" asked Martin.

"They can interview him at the center as well as at home," said Ferny. "We both think it's best if he stays away from Toni and Dad for now."

Martin nodded again. "OK," he said, "I was going to drive into town in a bit anyway, so this is perfect." He thought for a moment and looked over at Mandy. "I'm going to meet Leira for a celebratory drink downtown—would you and Ferny like to join me?"

The two women exchanged glances. "I have to get home to clean up and do some packing," said Ferny. "What do you think, Mandy?"

"Yeah, I think I'll join Dad and visit with Leira. But I'll see you tomorrow?"

"Definitely," said Ferny with a smile.

"OK, then," said Martin. "As soon as Caleb is done eating... You must have been starving, Caleb. I can drop Ferny up at the Lonzo's, take Caleb to rehab, and then Mandy and I can visit with Leira. Sound like a plan?"

Everyone nodded and stood for a moment watching Caleb begin on another full plate before each moved off to other things.

Chapter 46.

CALEB SLUNK down in the back seat while Mandy and Ferny got out of the car and said a few words on the walkway leading to the front door of the Lonzo estate. There was no sign of Al or Toni and the house appeared dark and empty. Martin noticed in his left-eye vision that the two human forms now in front of the stone rooms on the island had glows of equal intensity. *How odd,* he thought. *I wonder if I'll ever figure out what's going on in my left eye—my right brain?* The two gave each other a quick hug, and Ferny let herself into the house while Mandy settled back in the front seat.

On the way down the hill towards town, Martin asked Mandy, "Ferny said she wanted to stay at her house to pack. Is she going somewhere?"

"Something to do with pre-med school has come up," said Mandy. "I can tell you about it later."

Martin wanted to say, "We have time now," but decided that would be prying.

Caleb had been quiet for most of the trip, but just after this exchange he said, "Ferny's really a nice person, isn't she? I never paid her much attention, since she's my older sister and all, but she's really got it together, doesn't she?"

"Yes, she does," said Mandy. "She's a very good person." There was a long silence, and then Mandy added, "And you are, too, Caleb. You're a good person, too."

Mandy's cell phone rang at that moment and they heard "Hi, Jason!" when she answered. "Ready for Thanksgiving? You wouldn't believe mine so far," as they drove into Whitefish.

They pulled into the parking lot at the Whitefish Rehabilitation Center with Mandy still deep in conversation, and both Caleb and Martin got out of the car, Caleb stretching out his large frame once he was standing on the sidewalk. But the young man was obviously nervous, and as they approached the entry doors he turned aside and took a seat at one of the outdoor benches. Martin followed and saw that a normally surly and defiant Caleb was quietly crying.

"I don't get it," sobbed Caleb, his big shoulders quaking, "I don't get what's happening."

Martin sat down next to him, not sure if he should pat Caleb on the arm, but decided to do so anyway. "We don't have to go in if you don't want to, Caleb. I can take you back to your folk's house or drop you at the police station. Heck, I can even drop you off with some of your friends; it's up to you."

"No," said Caleb earnestly, "that's not what I mean. I want to go in. I need to go in."

"Then I'm not sure what you do mean," said Martin.

"I think I'm losing my mind," said Caleb anxiously. "What if I killed one too many brain cells? Or a lot too many? What if I had one of those brain thingies?

"An aneurism?" asked Martin.

"Yeah, one of those!" exclaimed Caleb and hid his face in his large hands.

"Well, what's wrong?" asked Martin.

"Look at me!" said Caleb, and Martin withdrew his comforting hand and did look at him. "I'm sitting here with you, for one thing!"

"So?" asked Martin.

"Don't you see?" asked Caleb. "I've hated you. Your wife replaced my mom. I came to believe you really did attack my stepmother. I thought you attacked me in the studio!"

Martin sat back, ready for Caleb to lash out, even physically.

"But here I am sitting with you, and you're the person I trust most in the whole world right now." He looked over at Martin with glistening eyes. "Isn't that crazy?"

Martin returned his gaze and then gave a little smile. "I know a little about crazy," said Martin. "Try having a knife in your arm, and a day later it only needs a light bandage." He wanted to tell Caleb about the visions he saw with his left eye, but decided that would be too much information for now.

"I am so sorry about that, Mr. Ropers," he said sincerely.

"That's OK, Caleb. Everything has worked out just fine. Oh, and it's 'Martin.' You should call me Martin."

"No," said Caleb shaking his head. "That's too close to 'Marty', and I don't like the sound of that. It's Mr. Ropers for now."

"OK," said Martin as they both stood. Caleb turned and gave him a crushing hug.

"Thanks so much, Mr. Ropers," he said, "for everything," and they both walked in through the doors to the admissions desk.

Chapter 47.

MARTIN HAD chosen The Fireplace since it was a cozy spot to relax during the cold months approaching winter. Leira had let him know that she was running late with a conference call, so Martin and Mandy found a small table near the well-stoked fire and ordered some wine. "A bottle?" asked the waiter. They looked at each other and Martin said "Why not? Leira will be helping us with it soon anyway." When the waiter left after pouring their initial glasses, Martin lifted his own to his daughter. "To Mandy," he said. "To Martin," she said back with a grin, "and to freedom," to which he toasted back.

"You know, I'm so glad that you're at the age where we can sit and have a glass of wine together now," Martin reflected. "It's so much better than your sneaking wine from the bottles I left down in the studio…" and she laughingly slapped his arm.

"You never said you knew!" she exclaimed.

"Now, remember—fathers know everything," he chuckled back.

They talked about the days stuck in the smoke, but to Martin, Mandy was behaving oddly. *Maybe fathers don't know everything,* he thought.

He poured them each some more of the Chardonnay when Mandy, twisting the glass in her hand said, "Dad, this is weird—very weird, but I need to tell you something."

Martin set his glass down, now more serious. "What is it, honey?" he asked.

"Well, I... I'm in love," said Mandy with a bashful face.

Finally! thought Martin, but he said, "It's that Jason character, isn't it?" thinking about the long phone call while he was admitting Caleb.

She twisted her glass another time and then in a low voice said, "No, it's Ferny."

He sat back and let this sink in. "So that's why!" he said, not realizing that it was aloud.

"Why what?" asked Mandy, cautiously, but leaning forward at the same time.

"You remember that I said that I saw images in my left eye? That I could see you as an illuminated form?"

She nodded and said, "Yeah, how strange that is—but I almost forgot."

"Well, I was watching you and Ferny preparing the Thanksgiving meal, and I swear I could see both of you glowing. Somehow that totally makes sense now." He took a sip of wine. "So... tell me."

And Mandy did, beginning with, "I don't know why, but you know I've never been able to keep a boyfriend. Sure, they've been great friends, and I like boys, but I never really felt anything like, you know, in here," holding her hands over her heart. "Take Jason for example—he's a great guy, funny, smart, and he's going places, I can tell you. But something's always held me back. Like, I can't do that—it's fun, but it's not love."

"I've known Ferny for a long time, but she's a little older and so hung out with a different crowd. We snowboarded together early in high school, and when we've been at parties during the summers, we always joked around. But now I know I've found the one. And she feels the same way—like she's been waiting and realized that I was standing right in front of her the entire time."

Martin nodded. Ferny had been in the group of snowboarders Frank had introduced her to when she was fourteen and he now remembered the stories that Mandy had brought home about their antics on the ski slope and about the older girl.

"Mandy," said Martin, and he couldn't get the words out in time.

"Oh, Dad, I know what you're going to say," she began.

"No, honey," he finally managed. "I think that's the greatest thing in the world." Mandy looked up at him. "To find someone like that is beyond special. I couldn't be happier. For both of you."

Mandy jumped up and gave him a huge hug.

"Ah, so that's why Ferny is packing!" said Martin after reciprocating. "She's going to Missoula until she's accepted into pre-med?"

Mandy laughed, "You're right," she said, "father's do always know what's going on!"

Well, not always, thought Martin, as he laughed with her.

"What did I miss?" asked Leira as she walked up and put her coat across the back of the waiting chair.

Within a few minutes, Mandy was filling her in on all the details. Martin poured a glass of wine for Leira and sat back, watching two glowing forms dancing and swaying about on the little paved square in front of the stone rooms that were his home now on the island.

Chapter 48.

THE TURKEY was gone, but Leira had said that she'd bring all of the fixings for a Thanksgiving Day meal, and the smells emanating from the kitchen were wonderful although completely out of context. Martin had started a new puzzle and contentedly sought out another edge piece while Mandy and Ferny excitedly helped Leira make the paella she'd decided on. They peppered Leira with questions about growing up in Murcia, Spain and going to school in Barcelona. Before the rice was done, they'd decided that they were going to put a trip to Spain on their must-do list.

Martin closed his eyes. Concentrating on his left-eye vision, he watched as there were now three luminous bodies on the small square of paved stones that lay before the three-room stone structure. He'd discovered something new: he could now move around a little in this strange world. Willing himself, he could navigate about the confines of the square and also enter any of the three rough rooms, but his movements felt unnatural, like he was floating rather than walking. In the room to the left he'd discovered cooking utensils and a firepit, in the room to the right were two sleeping cots and a few tattered clothes, and in the center room with the tapestry door, as he knew there would be, were a desk and piles of books. He'd looked at the two texts that lay open on the desk, but couldn't read either of them. The one portraying a shipwreck was written in what looked to be Italian, and the other appeared to be in Greek, and it was turned to a page illustrating a stylized wind blowing at clouds. Mostly hidden by the Italian volume lay a handwritten sheet of paper with what looked like the word 'Prosper' written in a bold hand, and more illegible script below it flowed beneath the book. He'd tried to turn the pages or pick up any of the treatises without success.

Martin was just thinking, *Survival might be possible on that island, but I think prospering would be impossible...* when there was a knock at the door. He went over and opened it and in strode Frank, a bottle of champagne in one hand and a home-made pumpkin pie in the other.

"Gonzo!" shouted Mandy in greeting.

"Hey! This doesn't smell like turkey!" he whispered loudly with a grin as Martin took the offerings in his hands and the others laughed. Mandy ran over and wrapped herself in his arms.

"Glad you could make it, Frank," said Martin. "We sort of ran out of turkey, what with the crowd we had trapped here."

"That's OK," said Frank. "Whatever this is smells delicious!" and he wandered over with Mandy to inspect the dinner and meet Leira. "Always a pleasure to meet such a beautiful lady," he said taking her hand and giving Martin a sideways wink. "And little Ferny! I haven't seen you since you were up on the slopes."

"Hi, Frank," said Ferny also giving him a quick hug, "you're looking fabulous as always."

Frank stood as if at attention, took a hand and brushed from his forehead to his ponytail in a dramatic fashion, bringing laughter to the group. "OK, now tell me about this dinner," as the ladies filled him in on the paella preparations.

Martin was sitting at the table, and Ferny came over to him with her medical kit before they ate. "I think it's time to change those bandages before dinner," she said. The steaming paella had just been taken off the stove, and the others came over to watch out of curiosity. Ferny gently unwrapped the bandages, lifted off the gauze, and raised her eyebrows in surprise. They all stared at what appeared to be the nasty scratch of a one-clawed cat where there had been a seeping gash the day before. "What the…" said Ferny as she turned his arm over and saw a raw looking scar on the inner arm. "But how is this possible?" she asked. "If I hadn't seen the cuts yesterday morning, I'd never have believed that this is the same wound."

Martin looked at the scratch and knew that his healing had something to do with the potent staff in his left-eye vision, but how it was able to impact his life in Whitefish he wasn't quite sure. He reached out to the formerly substantial wound with his right hand.

"I just don't understand," said Mandy, watching as Martin rubbed the scratch with his fingers. "It doesn't even need a bandage anymore. Does it?"

"No, I don't believe it does," said Ferny. "And to think I was of the mind that it needed stitches before."

Leira reached out and lightly touched the scratch as well. "Now, tell me again what happened..." she started when Frank interrupted.

"Yeah, what the hell are we talking about?" he asked, and Martin filled them both in on the right-eye version of his encounter with Caleb while Ferny and Mandy arranged the place settings.

"You're kidding me!" said Frank when Martin finished, and Leira chimed in, "Martin! It's a wonder you're alive!"

Frank was indignant. "You mean to say that Caleb stabbed you in the arm and then tried to plunge the knife into your stomach? That's attempted murder, Martin! He should be locked up!"

"Nope," said Martin. "Something happened that night—to both of us. Caleb doesn't remember a thing from the incident and has completely changed—he's like a different person. You should talk to him, Frank, and see if you don't agree. It's not just the words he says, it's how he says them—his whole attitude has flipped. And for reasons I can't explain, I've lost all bad feelings toward the boy, and will never press charges."

Frank shook his head. "Or, maybe you're still in shock and not thinking straight."

"OK, everyone," said Mandy bringing over the last dish, "Thanksgiving dinner is served—for the second time in as many days," with a smile. The paella was delicious, since they all loved seafood, and Leira was in heaven. "This is just like having a special occasion back home with friends and family," she said. "All that's missing is some flamenco music."

"We can fix that," said Martin, and soon there was Spanish music playing through the computer speakers in the study.

Leira poured the Tempranillo she'd brought and said, "To friends and family!" "To friends and family!" they echoed back, clinking glasses around.

After some eating and small talk, Frank and Leira both turned the conversation back to Caleb and the knifing episode. Martin was curiously silent, toying with his fork, and eventually all conversation around the table ceased. Martin emerged from his thoughts and looked up to find everyone staring expectantly at him. "I realize that I haven't been very forthcoming about all that's going on in my head, and things might become a little clearer to you if I explain. It's not easy, because you'll probably think I've gone nuts. I can't say I really understand what's happening in there myself, but here goes." And first he described to Frank the physical trauma he'd undergone, leaving his friend shaking his head.

"So, now for the bizarre part. Some of you know that I can see most of you as shapes in my left eye out on that strange island. Mandy, Leira, and Ferny show up as glowing beings, Toni is there as a dark shadow—always in the water, and Caleb emerges as a sort of hideous black blob." Turning to Frank he now saw, as expected, a gnarled tree at the edge of the square behind the other shapes. "Frank," he said, "I don't know why, but I noticed that you show up as a tree."

"A what?" asked Frank. "Why a tree of all things?"

"Don't ask me. Because you're solid? Because you're rooted? Because you're gnarly?"

"Ha, ha—dude," said Frank, and they all burst out laughing.

"Anyway, I can't seem to see any people other than you guys. Not the police officers, not Al, nobody. When the images first appeared, I was stuck looking out at the ocean, glued to one spot, but since then I've moved to a paved square with three huts and I can move about them now. One room has two cots, one is a makeshift kitchen, and the other's a kind of study or library with a pile of books. I seem to have a staff that I can wield to some effect, and I also seem to get some spells or something from a book in Greek that has appeared in my hand.

"In my first run-in with Caleb down in the studio, I held up the staff, which I could see in my left eye, and made the black blob recoil. I don't know how, but that seems to be what caused the real Caleb to stumble backwards and fall into the table. I never touched him physically—I swear. Then, when I heard the news about Toni's lawsuit, I was so pissed off that I somehow made burning sparks fly up when I slammed the end of the staff into the ground, and I know it sounds crazy, but I think those were the ones that started the fire that caused all of the smoke. Next, when I learned that I'd been cleared of assault charges, the staff created a huge windstorm on the island and, amazingly, a big gust just like it seemed to blow away the smoke here in Whitefish. When Caleb attacked me in the study the other night, I used the staff to subdue the blob on the island once again and ended up speaking to him here in the house in words I wasn't really consciously saying. For some reason, he listened to me and stopped the attack."

"Martin, how can you live with that?" asked Leira, "being in two places at once?"

"Yeah, and how is it that you don't really know what that other self is doing? What its thoughts are?" asked Frank.

They were both answered with a shrug of the shoulders from Martin.

"So, how do you feel, Martin?" asked Ferny. "Is this impacting your life? Your mental acuity? Do you feel it's changing in character—for the better, or for the worse?" Mandy and Leira looked at Ferny oddly and she shrugged saying, "I am in health-care, after all."

"That's all right, those are all good questions," said Martin. He thought for a moment. "I have to say that I'm worried lately. Just seeing a hallucination as a picture in my eye would be one thing, but it's the other changes that have me wondering if I might be succumbing to something."

"Like how so, Dad?" asked Mandy worriedly.

"Well, I have a persistent low-level headache. I've passed out a few times. I hear a sound in my left ear now, like tinkling wind chimes, and it never goes away. My left arm sometimes takes on a life of its own—no pain from the knife wound, healing quicker than normal, and slapping me if I do something it doesn't think is right. And sometimes if my thoughts go off in the wrong direction, the vision takes over so that I can't concentrate."

"Wrong direction?" asked Leira.

"Yeah, like if I start brooding, or… Oh yeah, I was trying to think of a way to get revenge on Toni for all that she's done to me, and my left-side vision simply wouldn't let me go there. It completely took over."

"Wow!" said Ferny. "It's like having a judge sitting on your shoulder the whole time."

"Exactly!" said Martin, shaking his head. "And it's driving me absolutely crazy!"

Frank had been quietly listening to his concerns, but then spoke. "Like I said when you first told me a little about it, Martin, I think you've been shoved over into another reality, and the two are bleeding into one another. You should pay special attention to what you learn there. It could help you with the next stage."

"The next stage?" asked Martin.

"Who knows what happens when we die?" asked Frank in reply, "This could all be in preparation for something important coming up." There was a thoughtful silence with some taking this statement better than others, and then Frank said lightly, "How about some champagne?" which was greeted with some enthusiastic nods.

After dinner, they had the pumpkin pie and all sat around the puzzle chatting. Martin realized how happy he was in spite of his brain injury, especially in being able to spend the day with Leira. He was delighted when she sat up with him for a while after Frank said his farewells and Mandy and Ferny had wished them good night.

"I'm worried about you, Martin," she said gently. "Especially after you described what's going on in your head."

"Thanks, Leira, but I'm coping."

"But what's happened to you is serious, and now it sounds like things have changed significantly with your headaches and blackouts. I don't think you should wait for your scheduled doctor's appointments. I think you should see someone soon."

He sighed, "Maybe you're right. I keep thinking that it's stabilized, but when you put it like that, it might be a sign of something else going on."

"I'll be away for a few weeks, but if you need a place to stay in Seattle, I could leave a set of keys with you."

"Where are you going?" asked Martin.

"Oh, Doug Bateson, my client with the new best seller is doing a tour of Washington and Oregon, and I need to be there to help him promote his book, plus I have to court a publisher for another book he's just completed."

"Ah," said Martin.

Leira noticed his reaction. "But if you need help with any appointments or anything, I could leave him on his own for a day or two."

"No, I should be fine," said Martin. "So, anyone significant in your life lately?" he was just dying to know.

She looked at him questioningly and then said, "Oh, um, no. Not since Charlie." She gave a conspiratorial smile. "The bastard." Charlie and Leira had been together for ten years, and then about the same time that Martin was dealing with the assault charges, she'd come home to find Charlie in their bed with another woman. She'd soon learned that there had been others. She'd been devastated and had fled from Portland to her rental in Seattle. Martin nodded in sympathy.

"Martin," said Leira after they'd been silent for some time. "I hope you don't take it personally that I'm asking for a severance of our contract. You mean the world to me, and you were my first client. I'd never do anything to hurt you, so you should tell me if you're not OK with this. I never thought I'd say it, but I'm completely overwhelmed with work right now."

Martin smiled back, *Such a wonderful lady,* he thought. Then he said, "You know, for the first time in months I actually wrote something yesterday. It wasn't much, but it was something. I'm not concerned about the representation; I'm concerned about the writing. As long as I have someone who treats me fairly, and it sounds like Chatham-Grant will, I'm not worried." He wished that he'd started a fire in the woodstove. It would have been nice to huddle around it. "I just don't want to lose you as a friend," he let slip out.

Leira immediately put her hand on his shoulder. "That will never happen—and I hope you know that," she said warmly.

"I do," he said and put his own hand over hers for the briefest of moments.

Later, Martin padded upstairs while Leira retired to the guest room. He realized this was not what he wanted, but it was how it was to be.

Chapter 49.

H**IS** **HEAD** was killing him when he awoke so he quickly downed two ibuprofen and waited for the pain to pass. *And I hardly drank anything last night,* he thought. Feeling better, he showered, dressed, and started in on breakfast preparations. The only foods remaining in the refrigerator were mashed potatoes and eggs, and in the pantry were the croissants that had been meant for leftover turkey. He fried potato patties, set the croissants in the oven, and awaited orders for eggs while the aroma from the coffee began to permeate the house. "This might take some time," he realized.

Leira emerged, looking lovely in his eyes—both in the left and the right; accepted a cup of coffee; and disappeared into the bathroom for a shower. She was out and dressed by the time Mandy and Ferny stumbled down the stairs. Everyone requested an omelet, so he found cans of olives and mushrooms, and a jar of salsa and did his best.

Within an hour, he was the last in a line of three cars. In the lead, were Mandy and Ferny heading down to Missoula in search of a new apartment. He could already sense their commitment and thought of the life together that stretched out before them. He almost slammed on the brakes as he realized what it would mean if they ever got married. He'd be related to Big Al through marriage in two ways, and he'd be related to Ferny as a daughter-in-law and as an ex-stepfather, or something like that. Toni would be his ex, his daughter's mother, and his daughter-in-law's stepmother. It didn't bear thinking about.

In front of Martin drove Leira, heading back to Seattle. He knew he'd visit her again in a few weeks when he was back in the area for more tests, but that was the last he might see of her again for quite some time. The further they drove down the hill, the emptier the house behind him seemed to become.

In Whitefish, the others took the road south towards Kalispell and their homes while Martin turned off at the grocery store to replenish his decimated stocks. He ended up in Lauren's checkout line, and when he reached her, she initially ignored him. Finally, she came out with an abashed, "Good morning, Mr. Ropers, how are you?"

"I'm doing fine, Lauren," he said. "Did you have a nice Thanksgiving?"

"Yeah," she answered. "Ate too much, though," and with a smile, "of course."

He grinned back, and as the last items were checked, he threw the local newspaper on the conveyor belt.

"Have a nice day, Mr. Ropers," said Lauren with a welcome cheeriness after he'd paid.

"You, too, Lauren," he replied.

Knowing he was returning to an empty house, Martin decided to have a cup of coffee in the Grizzly Den before he headed back up the hill. He'd only glanced at the headlines and wanted to see what the paper had to say about the events of the last few days. Nothing had changed in the café with the exception that Toni's campaign poster had been removed from the door. The unfamiliar waitress was curt, and he still received the evil eye from several of the patrons. Then it dawned on him that it would never change for some people. He was now the cause of all of Toni's woes.

He added cream to his coffee and took a sip as he read the cover page under the headline 'Toni Lonzo Held for Alleged Perjury.' The article detailed the new evidence showing that Toni had lied to investigators and perjured herself on the witness stand. There were intimations that she had also coerced a false testimony from her stepson, and that she was being accused of filing a lawsuit under false pretenses. He scanned the entire paper. So far nothing specific about Caleb, and he hoped it stayed that way. The poor guy had been through enough. The other big item was the mystery fire that had prompted some evacuations, trapped households, had no discernible cause, and had inflicted minor damage while disappearing without a trace. Already, a local UFO group was claiming that they'd seen strange lights and sparks up on the hill during the night before the blaze. The head of the group maintained that aliens had set up a test landing site at the top of the hill—and used the smoke as a screen to cover their activities. The wind had apparently been generated by a huge spaceship taking off from the ridgetop.

Chapter 50.

AFTER TWO weeks, the headaches were becoming more frequent and were unbearably painful, although luckily they were intermittent and only lasted an hour at a time—usually just once or twice a day. Martin had noticed them becoming increasingly powerful after Thanksgiving, and they seemed to be growing in intensity with each bout. When they struck, the vision in his left eye would become so dominant that it would essentially blind his right eye to the point that he had to quit what he was doing during a flare-up. *I wonder if these are really migraines, and I should be treating them as such?* he'd asked himself more than once. He'd tried a darkened room and pain killers, but neither seemed to help.

Following the first major episode of debilitating pain, he'd entered the central room on the island and noticed that the page in the Italian book had been shifted from one featuring an etching of a foundering ship to one of a drowning man with arms flailing amid tall waves, woefully far away from the rope that was being tossed to him. The book with Greek letters had been turned to a page with the illustration of two open hands and a bird launching into the blue background. He'd looked expectantly at the books after the subsequent headaches, but the pages never changed.

He'd used an online translator to read the Italian and it was a simple description of storms that ravaged ships and the pitiful plight of the sailors who had never been trained to swim. The Greek volume was impenetrable, and he reasoned that it must be an older form of Greek, not accessible to non-scholars. The only word that he found a translation for was *eleftheria*—freedom.

They'd all been through court proceedings, again, and Martin had been exonerated, at least by the legal system. He'd given the same testimony as he had two years prior—Toni taking a swing and missing, him trying to break her fall and taking her to the ER with Caleb all but passed out in the back of the car. Caleb had given testimony that he'd been very stoned at the time and remembered little except for finding Martin's car downtown and climbing in and then waking up in the hospital parking lot when he then left to search for another party. He admitted that he hadn't wanted his condition to be known and so had followed Toni's strongly suggested series of events. Toni's lawyers had been working overtime and painted Martin as abusive when out of the public eye, the video evidence as misleading and inadmissible, the kid who took the video as emotionally disturbed, and Martin as an author who rewrote history regarding Toni's contributions to his novels.

The court's ruling was swift with Martin free and clear of all charges, Caleb in the proper place for rehabilitation, and with Toni facing three months of house arrest and one year of community service. The judge had emphasized that being the vice-president of the local Chamber of Commerce did not count toward the service requirements. It was a coincidence that Martin had found the translation for *eleftheria* on the very morning of the ruling.

Chapter 51.

CALEB HAD insisted on helping Martin clean up the studio. They'd stayed in touch, with Martin dropping in for visits now and then when he was in town on errands—and it soon became apparent that taking care of the mess he'd made had become a major issue for Caleb. Martin welcomed his assistance and signed him out for the day, the two of them driving up the hill with the sun shining on newly fallen snow from the previous night. They found the rope Martin had strung between the house and the studio to be a very useful support as they made a new set of tracks down to the small building.

The hunched figure in rags that Caleb had become in Martin's left eye after the attack had slowly morphed over time, so that the image Martin now saw in that eye perfectly matched the image of Caleb he saw in his right eye, except for the clothing and surroundings. The stature, gestures, and size of both Calebs matched so well, that it was as if Martin never really saw him on the island anymore. They had merged into a single person.

The initial stage of the cabin cleanup had been rough, but mainly on Martin. "Caleb, are you sure you want to be around all these bottles?" he'd asked. "We even found this baggie of marijuana. I don't want to be impacting your recovery. This has got to be tough on you."

"Honestly, Mr. Ropers, it's not a problem for me at all," said Caleb. He threw a mostly-empty bottle of tequila and two more beer bottles into a black plastic trash bag. "And you really don't have to worry about me."

"If I had to give up wine and there were any bottles of the stuff around me, I can tell you it would be a problem," said Martin sympathetically.

"Remember when I said that I thought I was going crazy when we sat outside the Center?" asked Caleb. Martin nodded. "Well, I think I'm really there…" and he perched himself on a nearby stool. "But in a good way. To tell you the truth, I'd been raiding my dad's liquor cabinet since I was twelve, doing coke, oxy, and smoking pot since I was sixteen—there wasn't a day since I was twelve that I was sober. But I woke up the morning after the knifing incident—again, so sorry about that—and it was like I had a root canal in my brain or was pithed. I honestly have zero desire for any drugs anymore. I don't even think about them." He put his elbows on his knees and spread his hands open wide. "It's like I've been straight my whole life. Now, how do you figure that?"

Martin shook his head. "What a weird world, huh?" he asked and patted Caleb on the back.

"Sorry for the mess, and thanks for letting me come down here… Martin," he said.

"Yes! Martin! I like that," smiled Martin. "But please, no more apologies—I don't think I can handle any more."

Caleb grinned up at him, grabbed a broom and began sweeping up more of the detritus.

In total, they lugged five full bags of trash out of the small studio. "I can't believe that you and your friends partied so... hearty," said Martin on the last load.

"Neither can I," said an impressed Caleb.

Martin left Caleb to more cleaning while he made ham, cheese, and tomato sandwiches for the two of them in the main house. When he arrived at the entrance to the studio with lunch and a thermos of coffee, the place was spotless, and Caleb was sitting staring out the window over the snow-lined lake. Martin admired the look of total calm on the man's face.

They ate in silence, Martin next to the small woodstove, and Caleb on his perch appreciating the view. "This sure is a great spot," said Caleb as he finished his sandwich, "why don't you use it anymore?"

"When we were raising Mandy, it was a place where I could retreat from the family, and into myself, to write. Then when things began to fall apart between Toni and me, I'd come down here to be away from her. Maybe that's why the marriage disintegrated in the first place." He stared out the window. "Anyway, now that I have the house to myself, I find that I don't need to come down here to get away."

"What did you write?" asked Caleb. "I heard it was some book about the seventies?"

"Yeah, that, and I've written a couple more," said Martin. "One was about the guy who used to own this very land before we built the house on it."

"Really?" asked Caleb, "I'd love to read it."

"I'll see if I can dredge up a copy in the house when we head up there," said Martin.

Martin was lost in thought as he drove Caleb back down the hill to the Rehabilitation Center through lightly falling snow. Caleb sat beside him, thumbing through the copy of *My Wooded Acres* Martin had given him. Looking at the newly snow-blanketed hillside Martin was flooded with a memory he'd recorded in another chapter of *Faint Trails*.

We'd hiked for a day out of steamy-hot Pokhara in Nepal and made the arduous climb up to Poon Hill near Ghode Pani where a surprise awaited us. Our goal was to trek up the Kali Gandaki River to Mustang, and on the lower sections of the river the gorges were too steep for a trail to be built along the banks of the river, so the journey meant hiking up and down the high ridges on either side. There was a small wooden cabin near the top of Poon Hill, and Ryan, Audie, and I laid out our gear near nightfall after stopping at a tiny tea shop along the trail for a bite to eat. We'd begun the trek in sunshine, but the clouds had been gathering all through the day. That night was incredible. The temperature plummeted, and we'd never seen thunder and lightning during a snowstorm before. We didn't sleep well—it was cold, the floor was hard, and the thunder kept us up well into the night.

We awoke to nearly a foot of snow blanketing everything. What was tropical now became alpine, but we were exhilarated. After packing up and eating a few biscuits for breakfast, we headed out, Ryan in his huarache sandals, and Audie and I in our worn canvas sneakers. The air was still, the ridge perfectly silent, and the morning sun was shining brilliantly off the fresh snow. We didn't know it at the time, but this was to be the only significant snowfall that we'd encounter in our two years away from home. Being addicted to hiking in the mountains and skiing back in Washington, this morning made us feel more at home than any other time in our travels. We lingered in the white solitude but had other destinations in mind. It took several missteps along a precipitous ridge to find the trail, but eventually we were in ankle-deep snow and then back to the rocky trail that snaked down to the warm valley below.

There were many more climbs up ridges, some with stone steps or steps carved into the solid rock, and then we were back down to the main river as we headed up to Mustang. We'd entered another climate, another terrain. The narrow gorge we'd been skirting disappeared and the valley opened up into a glacial moraine, sometimes a quarter of a mile across with a constant cold wind blowing down off the glaciers. Beyond Tukuche and Marpha, the path became difficult to discern as it snaked across the broad silty valley, the trail often leaving the churning milky river as we headed up the valley between the peaks of Dhaulagiri and Machhapuchhare, then past Annapurna. Here and there, we could make out small vil-

lages clinging to the mountain walls high above where some valley or other dropped toward the riverbed.

At one point, Ryan pointed out some tiny figures making their way downriver, well away from the path we were following. He was curious, so we fell in step behind him. They were a pair of Tibetans driving a team of yaks laden with burdens down toward Pokhara. We had a friendly non-verbal exchange with them and then both parties went their separate ways. Bells on the yaks becoming steadily fainter, the snow level descending with each mile we hiked upriver, we continued on to Mustang.

It was the snow that had produced this memory, but Martin had the curious feeling that he'd recalled it for a different reason. Heading up into the barren windswept expanse of the silty gray braided Kali Gandaki River valley, was surprisingly similar to the desolate windswept island in his left-eye vision. Both were remote, foreign, and virtually unpopulated.

The approach of an intersection busy with traffic brought Martin back from his reverie. As the car was stopped before entering the main road into town he asked, "Hey, Caleb, how long are you going to be staying at the Center?"

"They say I can leave in February or early March," said Caleb. "But I may hang out a little longer—I'm starting to like it there, and they let me help the newcomers get settled in."

"You know, if you need a place to stay when you leave, you're welcome to use the studio."

Caleb sat and stared straight out the window. "You're not kidding, are you—after all of the trouble I caused down there?"

"No," said Martin. "If you like the place, it might be good for you. Maybe you'll find some inspiration there, too."

Caleb turned to him with a smile. "Thanks, Martin. I'd like that."

Chapter 52.

MARTIN HAD barely made it aboard the plane in Kalispell before collapsing in his seat and writhing in pain. The flight attendant checking for fastened seat belts had noticed his condition and questioned whether he should be on the flight, but he'd managed to reassure her that he suffered from migraines and that his medication should soon kick in. He prayed that would be the case, and in reaction to the pain, passed out for most of the flight. The tinkling of glass chimes on the island had been joined by the constant roar of surf, though he was far inland. He could make out the sea from a portion of the small slab-covered quad in front of the huts, and from that vantage-point the green waters always appeared to be calm. Compared to the weeks before, things remained oddly uneventful on the island. The extreme headache vanished as quickly as it had begun one-half hour before the plane landed in Seattle.

Leira was in town for his arrival, but was trapped in meetings, so he caught the new Link Light Rail into downtown, killed an hour in a coffee shop, and then walked with his carry-on bag the few blocks uphill to the hospital. "I've scheduled your MRI for immediately following this appointment," said Dr. Powell when Martin stepped into his office. "I'm glad that you called me last week and described your change in symptoms, and I want to see what's going on in your head as soon as possible. Have you had any of those episodes recently?"

"Yeah, I practically fainted… well, in fact I did pass out on the plane ride over here. They nearly kicked me off the flight when the pain hit, but I convinced them that I was suffering from migraines. These episodes happen daily now, but not at any specific time of day."

The doctor checked his eyes and ears, blood pressure, and heart rate. He also duplicated some of the tests he'd given him before—Martin deftly catching a ball again with his right eye closed. For the rest of the meeting, Martin described as well as possible the events that had occurred over the past few weeks, both on and off the island, and it left the doctor shaking his head. "I still don't know what could be causing these detailed hallucinations. Do you mind if I look at your stab wounds?"

He examined Martin's left forearm and could make out the faint scars that remained on either side. "If it was all in your head, that would be one thing…" said Dr. Powell trailing off as he became lost in thought and turned to his computer as Martin left for his MRI scan.

Leira picked him up after the appointment, which had stretched into the early evening due to a delay in radiology, and drove them to the same Italian restaurant where they'd eaten during his last visit. Her mood was subtly changed and not as light as Martin was accustomed to seeing. They ordered an appetizer, and Leira toyed with her garlic mushrooms more than ate them. The waiter brought a bottle of Chianti, and after they approved of the sample tasting, Martin thought to lighten her mood by saying, "Here's to your new direction and the best agent I've had," but found Leira suddenly in tears.

"What is it, Leira?" asked Martin, putting his hand on her forearm. "Did I upset you?"

Shaking her head, Leira quickly glanced around to see if anyone noticed and dabbed at her eyes with the corner of her napkin, looking embarrassed. "I'm sorry," she said, "I don't know where that came from." Martin waited, thinking that she probably did. She finally took a sip of wine and then said, "It's a lot of things combined." She took a deep breath, and that seemed to calm her. "The tour with Doug Bateson was a disaster—no, Doug Bateson is a disaster. The book he wrote is so-so, and he already has an entire series in mind—with an eye to making as much money as he can from it. He doesn't care about the quality, and just wants to sell as many books as possible in the shortest time frame. He's all flash, grins, and ego. Plus, every night I had to fight off his suggestions that I join him in his room. It was the worst tour ever.

"Do you remember our tours, Martin?" she asked, looking at him with sad eyes. "Those were my first, and I thought that's how they all were. We took our time, had great interactions with people, and had fantastic material to work with. We had fun, didn't we?"

Martin nodded, and again tried his salutation, "Like I said, to the best agent I've had." Leira finally relented and clinked her glass against his. Detecting something else, he said, "It totally makes sense why you need to move on, Leira. I'll manage just fine."

She looked at him gloomily and said, "I know, but aren't I being just like Doug Bateson? Putting myself and business first?" Before he could answer, she continued, "And I find myself so worried about you lately! Those strange events over Thanksgiving, and now these terrible headaches—what if they can't fix it? What if something happens to you?"

Dinner came and they both poked at their dishes. "We should know more tomorrow when the MRI results come back. I'll meet with Dr. Powell at one o'clock, and we'll see where to go from there. I'm sure it won't be anything to worry about."

Leira gazed across the table at him. "Like on top of a disappeared corpus callosum, visions in your left eye, strange noises, and severe headaches?"

Martin smiled back. "Yeah, like that," he said.

Chapter 53.

"I'D OPERATE today if I could," said Dr. Powell the next afternoon. "As it is, I've scheduled you for surgery in two days, if you agree. I'd like to be able say with certainty that what you have is not life-threatening, but I fear that's not the case. The sooner we operate, the better for you."

"What am I seeing?" asked Martin, stoically peering at the scans on the computer screen, but knowing that it didn't look good.

"Do you remember your previous scan, where I said it was like the corpus callosum had shriveled up into a little stick shape?" Martin nodded and recalled the image vividly. "Well, it appears that your stick has grown into a small log. See how much thicker it is? And it's elongated here," he pointed, "and here. I believe this is where your pain is coming from—the structure is pushing the rest of your brain against the inside of your skull. In fact, I'm amazed that you're not in constant pain, but instead only have eruptions occasionally during the day. Frankly, I'm also amazed that you're able to function as well as you do. We should be seeing incredible mood swings, changes in personality, difficulty with fine motor skills."

Martin nodded thinking about the pain. He'd had a severe episode that morning, with Leira trying whatever she could think of to alleviate his agony. Ice on his temples had helped the most. But, strangely, seeing her glowing shape on the little stone veranda in the middle of the island had been comforting in itself, and took his mind off the torture in his skull. "Are there any other options besides surgery?"

Dr. Powell shook his head. "I don't think so. We could try and slow down the progression of the mass with radiation therapy or drugs, but, honestly, it's growing so rapidly and has advanced so far that none of those treatments would produce results nearly quickly enough."

"And what are the chances of success if I do opt for surgery?" asked Martin.

"Martin, I hate to say this, but I have to admit that your chances for a normal life, or life at all for that matter, are very slim. This growth is so massive and impacting so much of the brain now that separating one from the other will be difficult to the extreme. The only truth is, if we let it progress, I think you have absolutely no hope at all."

"So, it's either operate or not with the same likely outcome?"

"I'm afraid so."

"How much time do I have to think about surgery?" asked Martin.

"Until the day after tomorrow," said Dr. Powell. "I've scheduled you into the operating theater and will keep to that schedule even if you try and cancel. I realize it's a difficult decision, and I've known people who have vacillated till the day of the surgery in extreme cases like this. I want to keep both options of whether to proceed or not open to you, but I strongly urge you to consider the surgery. And don't eat anything the night before, just in case you make a last-minute decision."

Martin thanked Dr. Powell and left his office in a daze.

Chapter 54.

HE WAS back in SeaTac airport waiting for his departing flight that same evening. Leira had picked him up from his consultation with Dr. Powell and on the way to her townhouse, Martin had said "Hey, let's go for a walk in the UW Arboretum." Although there was a low cloud-cover overhead, the drizzle had stopped, and Martin had needed to clear his head and think about the two choices that lay before him. Leira had parked the car and they'd donned their raincoats before selecting a path to stroll along.

"So, you're certain that those are your only two options, Martin?" asked a distraught Leira.

Martin nodded and said, "If you'd seen how much the area of the corpus callosum had changed in the past two months, you'd have been shocked, Leira. Just viewing those images has made my head feel completely different. Like I'm walking around with a brick up there. Dr. Powell said the only way to treat something that aggressive is to try and surgically remove it, or for me to just wait it out and see what happens. And they both have the same likely outcome. He did say in the end though, that if I elected not to have surgery, he'd start me on an intensive radiation therapy as a last-ditch effort."

"Oh, Martin," she said, turning and gripping him in a tight hug, burying her face in his chest, "I'm so sorry!"

And suddenly Martin was on his back in the wet grass. He had the sense that Leira was crouched over him, but all he was aware of was the scene in his left eye. He'd walked away from the huts and over the pavers to the rocky, sandy soil that lay beyond. With book in hand, opened this time to a page depicting a landslide, he held the staff vertically out in front of him and several of the little fairy lights flew out and met it at the top. With a little shake of the staff, they spiraled down the shaft, continuing down till they hit the ground and then disappeared beneath the surface. The sand slowly collapsed into the shape of a long crack, very similar to the one that had appeared on the island of Kos following the earthquake. More specks of light flew down into the crack and then they all emerged in a formation resembling a stick, or a miniature staff. They rose until they were level with his face, hovered for a moment, and then suddenly flew straight for his eye. Martin awoke with a start—staring now at Leira's tear-stained face. He knew what he had to do.

"Martin!" gasped Leira. "What the hell happened? Was it another headache?"

"No, it was… How long was I out?" he asked as he sat up shakily.

"For a couple of minutes," replied Leira, "I was just about to go for help when you finally came to."

"Whew," said Martin, "you're not going to believe this." And he told her about the vision he'd had. "I know it sounds crazy, but I have to catch the next possible plane to Athens. I don't feel like I have much time."

They'd driven back to the townhouse and checked for available flights on the computer, finding one that left at eleven that very evening. Leira had insisted on accompanying him to Greece, but Martin had firmly declined, finally winning out in the end. His unexpressed worry was the thought of her having to deal with his dead body in a foreign country. *Let the locals deal with it,* he'd thought, *not her.* They'd debated whether or not to tell Mandy, and Leira had eventually convinced him that she didn't want to be the one to spring this bad news on his daughter.

Mandy had been furious with him at first for not telling her immediately how seriously his condition had deteriorated, but soon understood where things stood. She also wanted to fly to Athens with him, but he explained how urgent it was for him to return to Kos as soon as possible, and that he was leaving this evening. She was devastated, but had to make do with his promise that he'd call often and let her know how he was, and that he would check himself into a hospital if his illness became debilitating.

Instead of dropping him off at the airport entrance for departing passengers, Leira had parked the car and walked with him into the terminal, holding his hand as he neared the TSA screening area. They said their final goodbyes and Martin was pleasantly shocked when Leira pulled his face down and gave him a long, meaningful kiss. "You come back," she choked. "You just come back," and then turned, wiping her eyes as he entered the short line. Martin watched her go with the oddest thought. *This is the best day I've had in a long, long time.*

Chapter 55.

THE PLANE was four hours into the flight when he almost screamed at the pain in his skull and gripped both armrests until his fingers turned white. He had an aisle seat, and the man next to him was so engrossed in a movie, he didn't seem to notice Martin's sudden discomfort. As the initial shock of the searing headache passed, he dug into his pocket and found two extra-strength pain killers, flagged down the next passing flight attendant, and waited in agony for her return. The water sloshed in the cup from his shaking hand as he took it from her, and he immediately downed the two pills under her concerned gaze. "Just a migraine," he said as she nodded and headed to the rear of the plane.

He slept for three hours straight after the medication kicked in, and awoke feeling somewhat better, but still traumatized from this recent attack. *This must be it,* thought Martin. *I may really be down to my final days.* He'd survived another life-threatening experience when he was younger, but by comparison it had seemed like floating—a so much more gentle experience. He recalled a chapter from *Faint Trails* that had made a pivotal mark in his life at the time he wrote it, but now seemed almost pedestrian by comparison.

We stayed for several days in a room off of a tea stall at Tato-pani, or 'hot water,' in Nepali. The place was like a displaced chalet from the Swiss Alps—a weathered-brown wooden house with a slab-stone roof built beside the road and next to the Koshi River. Our room was an open-beamed ceiling, with smooth wooden floors and benches built into the wall under the glassless window openings that looked out onto the river rushing just below it. We could throw the wooden shutters open and sit on the benches watching, reading, or writing as the Koshi flowed over and around the huge boulders that made up its bed.

The mosquitos were bad, especially on the rainy days and at night—tiny little darting barbs of terror. We were used to the mosquitos in the Northwest US that were bigger, slower, and easier to swat. These Nepalese mosquitos even made it through the netting that we tried to keep draped over ourselves at night, their high-pitched whine penetrating the hot darkness. And the leeches were miserable. The first full day at Tatopani, we took a hike up a trail and I found one stuck on my foot. We jumped and laughed at that until each of us raised our loose cotton pants to find our legs covered in them, the blood flowing in streams as we pulled them off one by one. On the way back down the trail, we could make them out—thin, black, tubes wavering on wet grass blades, waiting for something passing to attach themselves to. We stuck to the roads or more open paths for the rest of the summer.

Still, it was paradise. There was little or no traffic, since we were within a mile of the check-post for the tightly controlled

Chinese border, and the road wasn't yet well-used. We could take walks, relax inside our room and enjoy some Tibetan tea—black tea with salty butter—or bathe in the hot springs. One day, out of sight of the border, we found a crossable point in the river and leapt from boulder to boulder to land on Chinese soil and stand in a different, forbidden country for a few minutes.

But we'd really come for the hot springs. Each day Ryan, Audie and I would walk a few hundred yards up the road to a narrow bridge fashioned by bundling bamboo to form a large log. Balancing, we'd cross the Koshi and make our way back downstream, still on Nepali soil on that section of the river, and weave through the sand and boulders to some small pools that contained the hot springs—the water rising and spilling over the lips and flowing down the banks to join the Koshi. We'd soak in the pools until the heat became too much, and then splash or dip in the cold river water to cool off. Repeated as necessary.

I'd gotten out of the pool with my heart pounding in my head from the heat, made my way over sand and boulders to the edge of the river, waded in, and dipped my entire body underwater into the blissfully cold current, letting it float there for a moment. Some ways upstream from us, a gigantic boulder thrust out from the banks into the river, and some ways downstream another boulder did the same, the water forming rapids around them. I'd forgotten about the swift current. As I sought footing and was raising my head up for a breath of air, I found that I'd floated underwater downstream and was pinned under the huge rock. I fought the current with the boulder against my back but couldn't make any progress to the surface. A moment of panic. I didn't see my life flash in front of my eyes, but I did think This is how it happens in the movies, *and saw the image of a newsreel playing against a screen in a darkened theater. I tried once more straining against the pressing course of the river with all my might, but was no match for its power. Then something changed.* Wait a second, this water must go somewhere, *and I let myself go with it. I was forced down under the boulder, spun around, and came up gasping for air ten yards downstream from it, making it ashore another ten yards further along. I stood up shakily to find a panicked Ryan and Audie running down the riverbank frantically searching for me.*

The person next to him laughed out loud at the comedy he was watching, suddenly bringing Martin back to awareness of the present and being on a plane. *That trial had seemed to be by water,* floated up into his thoughts, but with the relentless throbbing in his head, this current trial seemed to be by fire, and he felt he might be losing. *Perhaps I've been fighting this long enough now,* he thought, *maybe it's time for me to just let go.*

Chapter 56.

I GUESS every time is different, thought Martin as he set his small carryon suitcase down in the shabby room of a pension situated a quarter of a mile from the luxury resort he'd stayed in a few months before. It had rained all morning on the ferry ride over, and low clouds nearly touching the flat seas had continued throughout the gray day. The Regal Inn resort in Kefalos was closed for maintenance and repairs, as were many other buildings in the aftermath of the earthquake, and the few open hotels had been booked for the night. The only remaining options had been a few bed and breakfast homes and this pension boarding house. After unpacking, he closed and locked the door to his comparatively rustic room and headed immediately toward the beach, following the straight streets flanked by low walls and dotted with white single-story buildings. He accessed the beach from a lane near the Regal Inn and walked along the wet sand towards the old basilica.

The light at day's end was beginning to fade as he made his way around some large rocks and reached the flattened area that comprised the ancient shrine. Walking forward he saw that the pillar toppled during the earthquake was in the same broken position as before. He easily found the column he'd stood under the night of the earthquake and to his relief, the wide crack still emanated out before it. *Finally,* he thought, *this will be the end of things.* He stared down at the fissure which he could see had accepted some bits of litter and blown leaves. *But why couldn't Mandy find the crack? Had she looked in the wrong place?* he wondered and then, *Now, how do I get this hole to accept the damned staff back?*

He checked to see that there was no one around—he didn't want to look like a madman, after all. Standing over the crack he raised his left arm high and concentrated on what was happening in his left eye. Nothing. In that eye, he stood before the huts and was gazing out over the dunes toward the sea in the distance. He tried with all his might to spark some activity in his left eye, but the scene at the little square remained static. *OK, it's up to me,* he thought. He thrust his left hand out and shouted, "Now!" Nothing. He squeezed both eyes shut and willed his left hand again to take some action on the deserted island—to bring the staff into view. He felt like he was going to pop a blood vessel in one of his eyes. Nothing. He lay down on his stomach next to the crack and reached down with his left hand as far as he could, scraping the bottom of the fissure. Nothing. The same actions on his right side had no result. He stood and stamped the ground. Nothing. "Come on, god damn it!" he shouted as loud as he could. The scene in his left eye was unchanging. "Fuck!" he shouted and squeezed his head between his hands with all his might. The pain didn't approach the level of the headaches he'd been experiencing. In desperation, he grabbed the column erected beside the fissure, tilted his head back and cracked his skull against the hard marble. "Shit!" he gritted his teeth and held his head. It hurt like hell, but still nothing like the headaches. He put his hand up and, feeling a knot beginning to swell, sank down next to the pillar and began to weep.

Half an hour later in the now nearly complete darkness, he picked his way carefully along the beach, up a road, and toward a *taverna* he'd visited two months previously. He'd received some strange looks from those seated when he arrived, but after returning from the restroom where he'd washed his face and then drinking a glass of wine from the carafe he'd ordered, he felt like he was a little less of a mess and the world was more in focus. He found two ibuprofens in his pocket and downed them with another gulp of wine. Martin felt defeated, but oddly comfortable with his fate. His mental state brought to mind a prisoner struggling with, but finally resigning himself to the firing squad he was facing. *This isn't how I thought it would be,* he reflected, slowly shaking his aching head. *I was sure that the message was to return the staff to the crack opened by the earthquake. How could I have been so wrong?*

He made two phone calls as he worked his way through another carafe of wine and dinner. After reassuring them that he was fine and apologizing for leaving so suddenly, he said essentially the same thing in both calls. "Just before I left, I think I told you about the vision I had where I was on the island and created a fissure like the one from the earthquake and then all of a sudden these points of light gathered in the form of a staff and came streaming straight at my eye. I was positive this meant that I was to somehow return the stick pieces I'd taken back to the fissure, even though I don't have them physically. It's like they're in my head. I'm certain they combined to form the staff that seems to perform its magic on the island. I went to the crack just now and tried to return the goddamned thing, but nothing happened. I tried everything I could think of, and all I got was another headache," not telling them about smacking his head against the pillar.

Both Leira and Mandy had made similar replies. "I should never have let you go there alone."

"It's something I absolutely must do by myself," he'd replied, "I started this alone, and I thought the universe was saying that I had to finish this alone."

Both had expressed concern, and he'd said, "Don't worry, this might be crazy, but I'm going to try again all day tomorrow, and will call and let you know how it went. If worse comes to worst after that, I'll fly back to Seattle and see what Dr. Powell can do." Outwardly reassuring, he'd turned to inwardly drowning in doubt.

He made his way to the pension through the darkened lanes, opened the door, locked it behind him and collapsed onto the bed. He had the strangest dream that night and he revisited it during his fitful attempts at sleep in the early morning hours.

In the dream, he'd just fallen into bed when he was jolted upright by two strong arms pulling him out of the bedroom. He looked around and there were two swarthy men holding him and guiding him through what appeared to be a palace. There were tapestries, paintings, urns, and shelves of books in elegant rooms with polished marble floors. He was jostled into a waiting coach and a small child, a girl, was thrown in beside him. The horses clattered through the streets, stopped, and he was yanked out of the carriage at a harbor—dark except for some burning torches to light the way. He was dragged up a gangplank and onto a sturdy ship, only to be led below-decks with the girl and locked in a small room situated against the hull. Time was ephemeral, but he remembered being fed decent food by candlelight. Just before dusk on a following day, he and the girl child were taken up to the deck and over to the railing. Below on a choppy sea lay a leaky dory with a chest stowed in the middle. He and the child were lowered into the small craft and he heard laughter as the line connecting the dory to the frigate was cut. They were adrift with no oars.

Again, time morphed in the dream. They'd been floating for what must have been days, and it was a cool night. Both he and the girl were asleep when a hard thump awakened them. They'd struck a single rock along a stretch of beach; they climbed out of the dory onto what appeared to be an island. After exploring the area, he'd found a cave near the center of the island and spent what seemed like months stacking flat stones to make additional rooms. They'd dragged the chest to the spot, and used what clothes, tapestry, pots and books were in it to make the best of things.

He'd noticed a dark shape that lurked around the periphery of this odd landscape, and it never approached, and yet it never retreated either, becoming a fleeting fixture to the dreamscape. One day, out gathering wood he came upon a dead tree—one of the few, living or dead, on the island.

Sensing something inside it, he'd taken his staff and with a command had split the tree in two and out had leapt a blazing thing. There was an immense flash of light, and that was the end of the dream.

Chapter 57.

HE LAY in his bed the next morning feeling both mentally and physically numb—from lack of sleep was his guess. He recalled the trials of the previous day and the strangely vivid dream he'd just awoken from. *And it was straight out of* The Tempest, *Leira was right,* he admitted to himself. *I'm trapped in a Shakespearean nightmare… but why?* He was thirsty, and his tongue felt thick. *That was smart,* he thought, remembering how much wine he'd had the night before. He expected a headache but had none, at least nothing to compare to his most recent bouts.

Deciding it was time to rise, he attempted to push himself up from the bed but only his right arm cooperated, and he fell back on the mattress. *My arm must have fallen asleep,* he thought and then reached over to rub it awake. His right side felt fine, but he soon found that he couldn't feel most of his left. He was able to move his left leg, but that corresponding arm was as if frozen in place. He reached up to his face with his right hand and felt that his left cheek was numb and covered in drool. Martin managed to sit up and eventually to stand. He shuffled over to the mirror and saw immediately that his mouth on the left side was sagging. *I've had a stroke,* he thought resignedly, *on top of everything else, now this.* He vaguely realized that his response was as if he were a detached observer and he was oddly unconcerned. He cleaned himself up with his right hand as best he could and was now glad that he hadn't undressed the night before. *It'd be impossible to put my pants on in this state,* he thought, yet he remained ambivalent about his drastic change in condition. Surprisingly though, the impulse to revisit the crack at the base of the column and to try and return the staff was stronger than ever.

It took him more than twice as long to make his way to the basilica on this attempt. His vision was clouded so that nearly everything that registered was through his left eye only, and in that eye remained a fixed view of the huts. As he awkwardly made his way along a walled lane that led down towards Agios Stephanos beach, something suddenly changed. The entity in his left eye headed for the central hut. This additional motion was somehow very disconcerting, and Martin stumbled several times on the even road. An old man rushed out of his house to offer help while jabbering in Greek, but Martin, in English, politely waved him off. The stream of Greek continued as he shuffled away and around the next corner. He noticed a stout stick through his right eye and picked it up with his right hand to help steady himself and ease his unsteady gait.

When he was partway along the approach road to the Mediterranean, he was also inside his crude library on the island and he saw himself closing the two large volumes, gathering them up, leaving the hut, and then heading for the beach. *At least now we're both moving in the same direction,* thought Martin with a sigh.

Martin finally reached the basilica and the fissure in its base; and the book-bearer wound his way through the dunes towards the shore. Since his vision was so impaired, it was difficult to see if there were others near the basilica or along the Kefalos strand, and Martin decided to act as if there was no one there. *I probably won't be around tomorrow anyway, so what do I care?* he wondered. Despite his damaged left side, he attempted to go through most of the motions he'd used on the previous evening to try and return the staff, except for whacking his skull against the marble column, all to no avail. Exhausted and lost in his efforts to free himself of the staff, he now became aware that some time must have passed because it was somehow already nearing dusk.

The headache struck violently and was more painful than any he'd ever experienced, dropping him to his knees in tears. He could barely see out of his right eye with the dominance of the left-eye vision, most of his upper left side was useless, and now this mind-numbing headache was the last straw. In despair, Martin used the stick in his right hand to push himself upright again and then he began slowly doddering towards the sea and its welcoming solution to his agony. He tripped once, but the stick saved him from going down. He reached the firm part of the sand, just feet from the lapping waves when he was suddenly frozen. Try as he might, he couldn't move forward.

Then something happened in his left eye. There, bearing the books, he had reached the last dune above the shoreline and he carefully set the books down on the sand. The staff also emerged into his field of view, and as he had practiced up by the huts, he held it vertically before him and this time hundreds of points of light gathered at the top. They spiraled down the shaft at his command, entered the sand, and soon a deep pit had formed in the dunes. The fairy-lights then re-emerged and circled the pit.

Ah! thought Martin. *In* The Tempest, *Prospero snaps and buries his staff! If I could just somehow break the damn thing and bury it like I found it, maybe I'll finally be free of its spell!* He was anchored in place, clueless about how to make that happen, but trying to will it with all the strength he had left.

To his relief, on the island, he took his staff, gripped it with both hands horizontally and then raised it high above his head. His right knee came up and he brought the staff down hard across it, snapping the shaft in half. As he flung both pieces into the pit in this image, Martin felt as if something had also snapped within his skull and he nearly passed out from the additional pain.

There was no release for him after all. His head was throbbing unbearably, and the vision still persisted. *I wasn't watching my salvation,* Martin realized, *I was watching my death through my own nightmare.* Completely defeated, he accepted that he had no choice but to end it all. He strained to move toward the water but still felt utterly paralyzed. In his left eye, however, he reached down, gathered the books, and opened the top one bearing Greek lettering to the page depicting a landslide. He began waving his free hand above the pit and as he watched, the circling light specks shifted the sand, sliding it into the depths of the pit which was quickly refilled. Only smooth dunes remained when they were finished.

On the island, he closed the Greek volume and then turned with both books cradled in his arms, and headed toward the sea. Reaching the hard sand at the water's edge, he raised both books and myriad points of light were drawn to them. He appeared to give a command, and the specks took the books as he thrust them out before him. Bearing the two volumes, they floated over the water until well out from shore and when he clapped his hands, all plunged into the sea.

On the Agios Stephanos strand, Martin suddenly found he was free to move and, limping mostly on his right leg, aided by the stick, he hobbled across the damp sand. He waded out into the cold water, deeper and deeper, until he was almost to the point where he could float, when he felt a familiar warmth at his feet. He pushed off, tried an awkward swimming motion and then was underwater. He could swear that he saw the drifting books out before him, and they all went down together, him and the books, sinking to the warm layer waiting underneath. So welcoming—his desire to sleep here forever was soon to be realized. He was home. The books drifted away from him and slowly sank down to the seabed. He felt his shoulder touch the bottom and was conscious of little else other than the urge to breathe, and he knew he would be breathing water when he did. From somewhere, words that made absolutely no sense drifted into his mind.

A solemn air, and the best comforter
To an unsettled fancy, cure thy brains,
Now useless, boil'd within thy skull! There stand,
For you are spell-stopp'd.

His eyes snapped open, and he had a sudden change of heart. He needed air.

He broke the cold surface gasping for breath and immediately started to sink again. Much to his amazement, he was able to power back up with both arms and, coughing, took several deep breaths before swimming roughly for shore. He had use of his left side again. Weighted with wet, heavy clothes, he collapsed on the packed sand and then, after a moment, flipped heaving over onto his back. He lifted his hands, wiggling his fingers, joyously aware that he could see them out of both eyes. Letting his hands fall heavily onto his chest, he lay in the semi-dark, gazing in rapture at the stars that shown occasionally through the broken clouds racing by overhead. He closed his right eye, just to be sure, and then stared again at the wonderfully full sky that spread out from horizon to horizon. Eventually noticing the chill of the evening, he worked his way to standing and stretched up completely, reaching for the stars.

Martin almost skipped with his exuberance on his way back to the pension, and every motion seemed magical, everything he saw seemed alive. He felt like he was back in his element, back in the world and the land of the living. As soon as he was in his room, intent on calling Mandy and Leira and letting them know he was all right, he was overcome with such overwhelming fatigue that he barely had his clothes off before he was instantly asleep. It was a blissful, dreamless sleep.

Chapter 58.

Awakened by sunlight gratefully flashing on both eyes, Martin showered and then found that he was ravenous. He sought out an open café and ordered a spinach pie, fruit plate, pastries, and coffee. He ate it all. Sitting in the sun with another cup of Greek coffee, he suddenly remembered home and pulled out his cell phone intending to call the States. It was dead, having drowned in the Mediterranean the night before. Walking the short distance into town, he found a cell phone provider who was miraculously able to restore his contacts from his dead phone and transfer them to a new one.

It must be around midnight at home, he thought walking out of the shop, but he dialed Mandy's number anyway.

"Hello?" came a strained voice.

"Hi, Mandy, I..."

"Dad!" Mandy shouted immediately. "Thank god! I've been calling all day—where have you been?"

"I'm OK, honey. In fact, I'm better than OK. I think it's gone."

"Your left eye? The headaches?"

"Everything! I'm back to normal—I can see just fine with both eyes, and my head feels no pain. In fact, I feel great."

"Tell me! What happened?" asked Mandy.

"I'm not really sure. I tried to get rid of the staff the night before and nothing happened—oh, I called you about that. I woke up yesterday morning with what I thought was a stroke and couldn't use much of my left side, but managed to make it back to the basilica, where the crack was… then I don't remember much, but suddenly I was in the ocean swimming towards shore and everything was back to normal. Why I was swimming, I'm not really sure." As he thought about the previous day's events, they seemed to be fading in his memory, as a dream might. "Oh yeah, something about that staff…" and he recounted the bits he could piece together.

"Are you sure it's over?" asked Mandy when he was through. "Do you need to see a doctor?"

"No, I can tell that I'm absolutely fine now," said Martin.

"That's such a relief!" exclaimed Mandy. "When are you coming home?"

Martin thought about it. "You know, I've been so focused on what I thought were my last few days left to live, that I haven't really considered much else, especially what to do afterwards. My first impulse is to say that I'm coming home soon, but now it occurs to me that I'm already over here in Europe. I don't know. I think I'll stay in Kefalos a few days to decide. Maybe I'll continue my original trip."

"Wow, I just assumed you'd turn around and come right back home, but what you said makes sense."

"How are you doing, Mandy?" asked Martin. "Have you and Ferny found an apartment?"

"Yeah, we've found the cutest house to rent, and we've already started to fix it up. It's only four blocks from campus, has a yard and one of those sunrooms. It's perfect. I have ten more days till Christmas vacation starts, and we can spend that time really settling in. Oh! And Ferny gets to start her pre-med courses this January."

"That's great!" said Martin. "Make sure and say hi to Ferny for me."

"I will, Dad," said Mandy before hanging up. "Love you, and I'm so, so glad you are all right!"

"Thanks, Hon, I love you—both—too," said Martin.

"Dad? Call Leira. Right now. We've talked several times, and she's worried sick."

"Will do."

Martin thought of waiting to call Leira, but since it would be an hour earlier in Seattle than in Missoula, decided he'd better get in touch.

"Martin!" said Leira as soon as he rang. "I didn't recognize the number but guessed that it must either be you or bad news. I hope it's not both—are you all right?"

"Yes, I'm fine, Leira, and I'm sorry it took a while to call," he said.

"What happened?" she asked in a worried tone. Martin spent the next ten minutes describing the details he could recall of the previous day, finding in the process that most of them were unclear.

"What a couple of months you've had," said Leira, "and thank goodness you're OK. What are you doing now? When are you coming back home?"

"Mandy asked me the same thing," said Martin, "and I realized that I hadn't really thought too much about it."

"Don't you feel like you need to check in with Dr. Powell? You know, to make sure that this really is over?"

"No, I honestly can tell that I'm back to normal, Leira, and it is such a relief. As I told Mandy, my first inclination was to head back to the States, but then I realized that I could also make the most of already being over here. I'm not sure, but I could continue the trip I'd planned. Gather material for a new book."

"Oh, that reminds me!" said Leira, "I should call and postpone your meeting with Chatham-Grant, until you're back."

"Oh," said Martin, having momentarily forgotten about the meeting and about losing Leira as an agent. "Yes, could you do that for me?"

"Sure, Martin," she paused, "and please let me know about your plans as soon as you decide."

Martin thought about the kiss in the airport and was about to be frank and ask Leira about it. *Was it a spontaneous show of sympathy, or something more?* he wondered. "OK, talk to you soon," he said, and they hung up.

Chapter 59.

MARTIN AWOKE just before sunrise, pulled on a sweater, stepped outside into the slightly chilly air, and climbed the narrow white-washed steps to the roof of the pension. He sat on the lone white plastic chair situated next to a pile of old cigarette butts from other's visits and with a view of the bay to watch the Greek island greet the morning. He didn't want to stop looking and felt his eyes, especially his left, hungrily soak up the shapes and colors as they changed with the rising sun.

I feel like I did when I was twenty, Martin sighed content-edly. *I need to write like I did back then, too.* He hoped some fresh avenues would open up because he knew the old roads would never be the same. They'd been lucky forty-some years before, and all of the gates had been unlocked at the right time. One year after their trip, the princely state of Hunza was dissolved by Bhutto, with the Mir abdicating, and it then became a Northern Area of Pakistan. This didn't close the area off, but he wondered how it had impacted the valley. Five years after they'd travelled through Iran, the Iranian Revolution had occurred, and one year following that the Russians had invaded Afghanistan, additionally closing that country to travel. Within ten years there was no travel in northern Sri Lanka due to a civil war that lasted for another twenty-five years, and the northern section was an area of the island they'd especially loved. *Maybe I'll try the countries that were closed in the seventies, like Viet Nam, Laos, and Cambodia, that are open now,* he mused, lazing in the warmth of the morning sun.

He'd had a wonderful day, wandering up through Kefalos town and then along the beach, completely enjoying his full vision. *This must be what it feels like after having surgery for bad cataracts,* he thought. *I can see everything so clearly.* That afternoon, he'd also visited the basilica and searched in vain for the fissure, but there was none to be found. He verified that the column that had fallen during the earthquake was still there in its toppled condition and it was just as he'd remembered. *What a strange, strange experience,* he thought as he walked over to the *taverna* for dinner. *Maybe I should write about that,* and already started forming a storyline in his head.

Back in the pension, Martin was just dropping off to sleep when his phone rang.

"Hi, Leira, what's up?" he answered.

"Hi, Martin," said Leira sounding somewhat hesitant at first. "You can tell me if this is a terrible idea, or if it doesn't fit your plans... But I was thinking all last night after you called, and spent the morning talking to Mandy, too. Anyway, I haven't seen my folks for ages, and Mandy and Ferny were talking about wanting to visit Spain..." She paused and took a deep breath. "How about if you started your trip in Murcia? We could all have Christmas together, and you could meet my folks. Mandy and Ferny have winter break and are excited about the idea. My parents have tons of room and said we'd all be welcome... What do you think?"

"Well, I haven't really decided on my next move..." said Martin.

Leira rushed through on top of him, "I was also thinking that I really need some extended time away from my job. Maybe I could be a part of your next adventure?"

"Now that," said Martin with a rising feeling in his chest, "sounds absolutely fantastic."

A synopsis of the comedy (non-tragedy), The Tempest, by William Shakespeare

Prospero is the Duke of Milan but prefers his studies and library to the task of governance which he leaves increasingly in the hands of his brother, Antonio. Antonio aligns himself with Alonso, the King of Naples, and usurps the dukedom of Milan. He orchestrates that Prospero and his daughter Miranda be hidden onboard a ship and then transferred to a leaky dinghy, leaving them to their fate. The pair wash up on an island and survive with some supplies and books that a sympathetic councilor Gonzalo had secreted in their little boat.

The island is inhabited by Caliban, the son of the witch Sycorax who had been exiled there but died sometime after his birth. Before her passing, Sycorax imprisoned the spirit Ariel in a pine tree. Prospero frees Ariel with his magic and also commands the various sprites that inhabit the island. He tries to educate and befriend the feral Caliban but treats him as a slave because the boy is rebellious and sees Prospero as the usurper of his island.

Prospero commands the elements, especially through Ariel, but Ariel is unhappy under Prospero's control and begs for freedom. Agreeing to help Prospero on the promise of being set free at the end, s/he aids Prospero in a plan of revenge. They create a storm that wrecks a ship carrying Antonio, Alonso, Alonso's son Ferdinand and others. The ship is lost, and all passengers thrown into the sea. The seafarers emerge from the waves on separate parts of the island, all well and mysteriously dry with clothes in seemingly new condition after near drowning.

Thinking all others had perished, a solitary Ferdinand discovers Miranda, who had never met any man other than her father, and they fall in love. Trinculo and Stephano, a jester and a butler, find Caliban and together, drunken, they plot to kill Prospero. Antonio tries to convince Alonso's brother that, with Ferdinand seemingly drowned, he should kill his brother and take the crown of Naples for himself. Ariel thwarts both plots.

Prospero and Ariel orchestrate events so that, in the end, the ship is magically restored and sitting in the cove, intact, and awaiting their journey home, Prospero renounces his magic and staff and is restored as the Duke of Milan, Miranda is engaged to marry Ferdinand, Ariel is set free, and Caliban has his island back.

ACKNOWLEDGEMENTS

I want to thank Lynn Ate for her perseverance in editing, and Jessica Hatch of Hatch Editorial Services for her insightful editorial assessment. The beta readers at Entrada Publishing also provided most welcome comments about the first draft, and Kathy Haaga and Misao Kusuda helped shape the cover.

I also want to thank Raineka Ackley and Cody Strodtman for accompanying me to an outdoor steampunk version of *The Tempest* in Portland. They where there when the staff broke and inspiration struck.

ABOUT THE AUTHOR

David Ackley grew up in Fairbanks, Alaska and raised a family in Juneau. His professional career in Alaska included both fisheries biometrics and management positions with the state and federal governments. David is now retired and living in northern Idaho, where he began a small business in lutherie – building guitars, Irish bouzoukis, and ukuleles (www.dastringedinstruments.com). While his wife was conducting research during a recent stint in India, he devoted time to trying to improve his Tamil and writing fiction to escape the heat of mid-day. Finding himself unable to multi-task easily, the lutherie business has flagged somewhat while he gets some stories onto paper. Please visit the Rain and Breeze Books website, www.rainandbreeze.com, for more information about David and his books.

9 781950 631087